Fantasy

FANTASY

By
The Dark Angel

HELEN SLATER

TENTH STREET PRESS

THIS EDITION

Published by Tenth Street Press   2013

Cover image courtesy of Kataijudit
Design by Tenth Street Press

Edited by Ren McVittie for Tenth Street Press

ISBN-10: 0-9923034-8-6

ISBN-13: 978-0-9923034-8-8

PRINTED IN THE U.S.A.

TENTH STREET PRESS Ltd.
MELBOURNE LONDON
www.tenthstreetpress.com
Email: contact@tenthstreetpress.com

For Kelvin

CONTENTS

The Party

Jade had been invited to a party by her friend Louise. She was told there would be plenty of hot single men there. It was a fetish themed party. She decided to put on her latex mini dress, fishnet hold-ups, a PVC thong, black patent knee high boots and black latex elbow length gloves before phoning for a taxicab. The party was being held at a luxury hotel in the main function room. As she got out of the taxi and headed into the hotel, she noticed a tall mysterious tanned stranger. He was having a cigarette and dressed in skin-tight leather trousers, black shoes and a black fishnet top showing off his tanned muscular physique and his tattoos. His dark brown almost black eyes had a naughty look in them. Jade entered the function room and looked for Louise. She found her talking to the stranger she'd seen on her way in. She quickly took her to one side.

"Babes who is the hot bad boy?" said Jade.

"He's a fetish model. I've photographed him on many occasions. His name's Adam – and he's single", said Louise.

Jade smiled wickedly; a warm sensation flowing between her legs. She grabbed a glass of champagne from a table and sat close to him. He moved closer to her – smiling wickedly at his admirer.

"Hi you must be Jade. Your friend Louise had told me all about you", said Adam.

"Yes I am. All good things I hope", said Jade.

"Some wicked ones as well", said Adam running his hand up Jade's leg. Suddenly he pulled her towards him and kissed her passionately.

Jade was shocked and excited at the same time. She could feel the sexual energy between them. Adam pulled away, stood up and gestured for her to follow him. Jade followed him out of the function room and upstairs to a hotel room. He asked her to close her eyes. Jade held Adam's hand as he guided her into the room.

"You may open your eyes now", said Adam.

Jade opened her eyes and looked around the room. Her eyes fixed on the big four-poster bed. It was metal with black chiffon curtains with black PVC sheets. Attached to either end of the bed were leather restraints. Jade stood silently not knowing what to say. She became aware of Adam's lips on her neck.

"Do you have any unusual fantasies baby?" said Adam with a wicked glint in his eyes. He licked his lips suggestively, taking in every inch of Jade's body as he waited for her to respond to the question.

"I have fantasised about being a sex slave and being forced to submit to my master's kinky pleasures", said Jade unzipping her dress and taking it off along with her boots and gloves.

As she stood in front of Adam in her PVC thong and fishnet stockings, Jade was aware of the bulge in his tight leather trousers.

"On the bed now you filthy slut", said Adam In a stern voice. Jade did as she was told and laid on the bed.

"On all fours slut, you need to be punished for being a filthy slut", said Adam.

Jade got on all fours ready for her punishment. Suddenly she felt a hand on her ass. She turned her head to see Adam caressing her. He roughly pulled her thong down over her ass and down her legs. He moved each leg so that he could take it off. Jade wondered what he would do next. She didn't have to wait long to find out as she saw him get a leather paddle out of a holdall. He raised it in the air then brought it down hard across her bare ass. Jade flinched from the pain screaming.

"You will take your punishment you filthy little slut", said Adam reaching into the bag and producing a leather ball gag and a small leather whip.

Jade could feel the heat from her ass spreading to her pussy. She slid a hand between her legs and rubbed her aching clitoris then slid two fingers into her wet pussy, moaning softly. She felt her clitoris throbbing as the heat from her ass spread through her whole body. She rubbed it harder. Suddenly her hand was pulled away from her pussy. Adam put the ball gag in Jade's mouth and picked up the whip. He gave her ten of the best then turned her over, fastening the leather cuffs to her wrists then spread her legs wide open and fastened the second set of leather cuffs to her ankles. Jade was barely able to move. Her eyes lit up as she watched Adam take his fishnet top off and undo his leather trousers. She could feel the growing wetness in her pussy. Her nipples began to get hard as she watched him take the leather trousers off.

"You are my filthy sex slave. You will submit to my every need fulfil my pleasures", said Adam before grabbing the whip again.

He teased her nipples then trailed it down her stomach and over her pussy. Jade was powerless; she couldn't do anything. She wanted to rub her clitoris so badly. She was on the verge of climaxing. Suddenly Adam stopped what he was doing and knelt on the bed between her legs. She tried to push her pussy towards him but he held her legs down and teased her with the tip of his tongue. Then he abruptly stopped and rammed his big hard cock into her throbbing pussy. He took the gag out of her mouth and began fucking her softly at first then gradually harder. Jade screamed with pleasure. Adam fucked her even harder until she exploded into orgasm. She felt her juices running down her weak thighs. Adam pulled his cock out of Jade's soaking wet pussy and squirted his cum load over Jade's tits and face. Then he put his hand behind her head and made her suck his cock clean. He unfastened the leather cuffs. Jade rubbed the feeling back into her wrists and ankles.

"Wait here my little slut", said Adam getting off the bed and disappearing out of the hotel room returning a few minutes later with a leather collar.

It had a metal d-ring in the centre with a short chain which had leather cuffs attached by a chain linking the two parts together. Adam fastened the collar around Jade's neck then roughly pulled her wrists in front and into the leather cuffs. He helped her off the bed and sat her down on the floor.

"You will sleep on the floor my dirty little slut", he said.

"Yes master anything to please my master", said Jade, trying to get comfortable.

Adam helped her to lay down and covered her with a blanket before he got into the bed alone. The next morning Jade awoke to see Adam standing naked stroking his cock. His eyes wandered over her naked body. He took off her collar and cuffs.

"Bend over the bed for your master", said Adam.

Jade bent over the edge of the bed. Adam parted her legs. He spread her ass cheeks wide, wetting his finger and sliding it into her tight ass, fingering her gently before adding a second. Sliding them deep in her ass fast and hard. Jade moaned with pleasure. He abruptly removed his fingers and replaced them with his hardened cock, pushing it deep inside her ass. Grabbing her hair and fucking her harder and harder while rubbing her clitoris. Jade exploded into a violent orgasm as Adam pumped his cum into her ass, filling it so much that it spilled out running down her thighs. He pulled his cock out and got dressed. Jade felt satisfied and exhausted at the same time. She got dressed and they left the hotel, kissing passionately as they waited for a taxi.

"We must do this again sometime Jade", said Adam.

"Yes defiantly", said Jade.

A while later their taxi arrived. As it left the hotel car park Jade sat quietly a warm sensation between her legs as she thought about what had happened between her and Adam. She kissed him softly as the taxi pulled up outside her house and gave him her mobile number.

"Call me sometime and we can have a repeat performance", said Jade.

"I will babe", said Adam as the taxi pulled away and headed to his place.

Jade went into her house and had a hot shower, remembering every detail of what had happened between her and Adam and wondered when they would have a repeat performance. She hoped it would be soon – her whole body ached for him. She washed herself then got out of the shower and got dried. Heading into her bedroom and laying on her bed, she got a large real feel dildo out of her bedside cabinet and spread her legs wide. She teased herself with the tip, sliding it in her wet pussy. Then she began to fuck herself with it, moaning with pleasure. She closed her eyes while imagining the dildo was Adam's cock. Pushing it deeper inside her pussy. Fucking herself harder and deeper. Bringing herself to a shuddering climax. She pulled the dildo out of her wet pussy and sucked it clean. Suddenly her mobile phone started ringing. She smiled wondering if it was Adam. She was partially disappointed when she realised it was her friend Louise.

"Hi babes what happened with you and the gorgeous Adam last night? I want all the details. Come over to mine and we'll have a good chat about it", said Louise.

"Hi babes, it was amazing! He fulfilled a kinky fantasy of mine. I'll be over in an hour, see you soon", said Jade before hanging up.

She got of her bed and put on her red lace bra, matching thong, tight black vest top, skin-tight faded blue jeans and black Mary Jane shoes. She grabbed her bag and went downstairs and walked out of her house and into her car and headed over to Louise's house. Smiling to herself, she couldn't wait to tell her friend all about what happened between her and Adam. When she got to Louise's house she parked her car on the drive and got out. She rang the bell. A few minutes later Louise opened the door.

"Come in babes, I'm eager to hear the juicy details", said Louise holding the door open.

"I'll make us a coffee babes then you can tell me all about your kinky session with Adam. I had a feeling you two would hit it off. I know you have a kinky mind when it comes to sex and Adam's into some kinky stuff. I've seen his bedroom – it's full of whips and sex toys – he's really kinky! I've had fun with him before but it was a little too wild for my liking. We've remained good friends though", said Louise before heading into the kitchen and making them a cup of coffee.

She walked back into the living room and passed Jade her coffee and sat down beside her.

"So Jade babes tell me all the juicy details about last night with the gorgeous Adam", said Louise smiling.

"He made me his sex slave. Had me lay on a large four-poster bed and cuffed my wrists and ankles. He used a whip and a leather paddle on me before fucking me good and hard. I loved every minute of it and I'm hoping for a repeat performance. I gave him my number so I'm hoping he rings me soon. I've never met a man like him before. My past lovers seem vanilla compared to him. I've discovered a completely new side to myself. My fantasy became a reality last night but I want to explore it further", said Jade.

"Sounds like you had a great night. I've got a great idea babes. Adam's doing a photo shoot later today but the woman who was due to be doing the shoot with him has cancelled at the last minute on me. You've had some modelling experience, how about you take her place. It's a kinky photo shoot for 'Fetish Magazine'. You'll both enjoy it I'm sure. Then after you can go back to Adam's. As I said, he's got lots of toys and a variety of whips", said Louise smiling at Jade.

"That sounds like a fantastic idea. I can't wait to see him again. My whole body aches for him. He is like a drug to me. I need to get my fix I'm having withdrawal symptoms", said Jade.

"Don't worry babes, the shoots in an hour. I can help you pass the time. It's been so long since we've had any fun together", said Louise licking her lip suggestively as she ran her hand up and down Jade's thigh.

Jade quickly finished her coffee and put her cup on the table. Louise finished hers and got up off the settee taking Jade's hand and helping her up. She led her upstairs to the bedroom. They kissed passionately, hungrily undressing each other then Louise gently pushed Jade on to the bed, getting her on all fours and parting her legs. She got a strap-on out of her bedside cabinet and put it on before getting on the bed and kneeling behind Jade. She pushed the dildo into Jade's soaking wet pussy and began to fuck her softly and slowly at first. Reaching round and squeezing her breasts as she plunged the dildo in and out of her pussy, slowly increasing the speed. Jade moaned with pleasure grinding her pussy against the dildo.

"Oh god fuck me harder babes. Treat me like your dirty bitch. You know I love it when you're dirty", said Jade breathlessly. Louise grabbed Jade's hips and fucked her harder and faster.

"Yeah take that dildo my dirty bitch. Cum for me", said Louise moaning as the other end of the dildo rubbed against her clitoris.

She fucked Jade harder and faster. Jade moaned louder with pleasure, her legs shaking as she reached a shuddering climax. Her juices squirting out all over the dildo. Louise gently pulled the dildo out of her pussy and turned Jade to face her.

"Suck it clean bitch", said Louise pushing the dildo towards Jade's mouth.

Jade took the dildo in her mouth sucking it clean before letting Louise remove the dildo. She took it off then they got into the sixty-nine position – Jade on top. They licked each other's pussies clean before kissing passionately, sharing each other's cum between their hungry mouths.

"Oh god I want you to fuck my tight ass Jade, babes. I'll get my fat dildo for you. I love the way it stretches my tight hole", said Louise gently pulling away from Jade and getting of the bed.

She got her large fat dildo replacing the dildo on her strap-on with the fat one. Then she took her strap-on off and handed it to Jade along with a bottle of anal lube. Jade got Louise on all fours and knelt behind her. She poured a little of the lube into Louise's tight ass then she slowly pushed the dildo into her tight hole. Grabbing Louise's hips and fucking her slowly at first teasing her.

"Fuck me good and hard babes", said Louise breathlessly.

Jade fucked Louise harder and deeper. She screamed with pleasure pushing her ass back against the dildo, taking every last inch of it in her tight hole. Screaming with pleasure as it filled her tight hole – stretching it. Jade fucked Louise harder and faster. Moaning with pleasure as the other end of the dildo rubbed against her swollen clitoris. Her legs shaking as she reached a shuddering climax. She reached between Louise's legs and finger fucked her wet pussy quickly bringing her to a shuddering climax then she gently pulled out of her tight ass, taking the strap-on off and laying next to Louise on the bed; pulling her close. They kissed passionately before gently pulling away from each other and getting dressed.

"That was amazing as usual babes. We better get going. The outfits are provided by a friend of mine so we just need to get to the studio and get set up ready for the shoot", said Louise as her and Jade made their way downstairs.

"Yes it was babes, always is with you. It's a shame we can't have a threesome with Adam. Would be so horny", said Jade licking her full lips suggestively at Louise as she spoke to her.

"I'll think about it babes lets go", said Louise unlocking her front door.

They walked out and got in Jade's car. She started the car and headed to the studio. She'd been there before several times with Louise so she knew her way. When they got to the studio Jade parked up and they headed inside. They smiled as they saw that Adam was already there. Jade walked over to him.

"Hi Adam its lovely to see you again. I'm going to be doing the shoot with you as the other model has cancelled at the last minute", said Jade.

"That's so hot babes, you will look amazing in the latex catsuit and thigh high boots", said Adam licking his lips.

"Thank you Adam gorgeous", said Jade.

"Right you two go and get changed while I set up the camera", said Louise smiling.

Jade and Adam got their outfits from the rail and went to the changing area. Jade's consisted of a shiny black skin-tight latex catsuit and shiny black thigh boots while Adam's consisted of shiny black latex trousers and black ankle boots.

"You look hot babes, you just need a collar now as you're my slave for this shoot. It will be so hot. I'm going to ask for a print to be enlarged and get it framed", said Adam.

"Thank you Adam – or should I say master! That sounds a great idea", said Jade.

Adam put a leather collar around Jade's neck and attached a lead to it then he led Jade out of the changing area. He walked her over to the latex covered throne type chair that Louise had put out for the photo shoot.

"Sit down Adam. Jade, you kneel at his feet. Lick his boots. Hold her lead Adam", said Louise smiling at them both.

Adam sat on the chair looking every inch the master while Jade knelt at his feet running her tongue over his boots. He held her lead not letting her go.

"Good keep that pose", said Louise taking several photos then she walked over to Jade and unzipped her catsuit a little showing off her cleavage and took the lead off her collar.

"Sit on Adam's lap and look provocative. Adam run your hands over Jade's body", said Louise licking her lips as she looked at Adam and Jade enjoying the way the latex clung to their hot bodies. Jade sat on Adam's lap looking provocative as Adam ran his hands over every inch of Jade's body licking his lips.

"Mmmmm, keep going, this is hot. I'm going to need a cold shower after this session", said Louise licking her lips. Her free hand wandering between her legs rubbing her aching pussy as she took photos of Adam and Jade.

"Okay that's it for today guys. Let's go back to mine, I'm so horny", said Louise putting her camera and other equipment away.

"Good idea Louise babes. That's if Adam is willing to share his sex slave with you", said Jade licking her lips suggestively at Louise and Adam.

"Of course! Can my sex slave can we keep these clothes please?" said Adam.

"I can't see why not Adam. I want to change into my latex. when we get to mine", said Louise smiling.

The three of them left the studio and got into Jade's car. She set off towards Louise's house feeling so horny. Her whole body ached for Adam. She was addicted to him. She had to get a fix. The photo shoot they had done together had been so hot but she needed more. She wanted a repeat performance of what they had done at the party. She'd been unable to stop thinking about him. No other man had this effect on her. She understood now why people became addicted to drugs and alcohol – except that she was addicted to kinky sex with Adam. He was her own personal brand of cocaine. When they got to Louise's house Jade parked up and the three of them got out. They walked up to the front door and Louise quickly unlocked the door. They walked in and headed straight upstairs to the bedroom – all extremely horny. They walked into Louise's bedroom sharing a passionate three-way kiss. As they began to undress each other they gently pulled away and walked over to Louise's bed and its latex sheets. They laid down together and caressed each other. Adam cuffed Louise's wrists and ankles to the bed using the leather cuffs attached to the bed by metal chains. Then he got another set of leather cuffs from the bedside cabinet. He got Jade into a spread eagle position cuffing her wrists and ankles before getting a leather whip. He teased Jade and Louise's breasts with the whip before raising the whip in the air, giving them ten of the best on their breasts. They moaned as the pain turned to exquisite pleasure. Their nipples becoming erect.

"Good slaves. Time for a little treat. I think Louise should get master's cock first. Jade you can use a vibe for now. Get that cunt nice and wet for me", said Adam licking his lips suggestively as he leaned over the bed and got a large dildo.

He unfastened Jade's wrists and ankles before passing her the dildo. Then he unfastened Louise's ankles and got on top of her, pushing his hard cock deep in her wet pussy. Putting her legs over his shoulder and fucking her hard and deep. She moaned with pleasure. Grinding her pussy against Adam's hard cock. He fucked her harder and deeper. Jade fucked herself with the dildo as she watched Adam fucking Louise. It turned her on so much. She fucked herself harder and faster. Her juices gushing out of her pussy. Licking her lips as she watched Adam pounding Louise's wet pussy. Her legs shaking as Adam brought her to a shuddering climax. She squirted her juices all over his hard cock. He pulled out and moved across the bed to Jade. He knelt next to her face, pushing his cock towards her mouth. She eagerly opened her mouth and let him slide his cock in. She sucked it clean, enjoying the taste of Louise's juices on his cock before allowing him to slowly remove himself. He moved down the bed removing the dildo from Jade's wet pussy, passing it to Louise.

"Suck it clean baby", said Adam before getting on top of Jade.

He pushed his cock deep in her wet pussy and began fucking her hard and deep. She moaned with pleasure, grinding her pussy against his cock. Adam leaned over and took each nipple in turn between his teeth, gently pulling on them. As he fucked Jade harder and deeper, she screamed with pleasure. Her legs shaking violently as Adam brought her to a shuddering climax with her juices squirting out over Adam's cock.

He gently pulled out and moved across the bed to Louise, removing the dildo from her mouth and replacing it with his cock. She eagerly sucked his cock clean, enjoying the taste of Jade's juices. Adam slowly removed his cock from Louise's mouth and lay down on the bed.

"Right ladies, let me watch you two play together. Be really dirty for me. I want you to make me shoot my load everywhere", said Adam licking his lips suggestively at Jade and Louise.

They smiled knowing that it would be a turn on for them as much as it would be for Adam. They loved to pleasure each other as often as they could. Having someone as hot as Adam watching them made it all the more exciting knowing that watching them both would turn him on immensely. Louise got off the bed and opened her bedside cabinet. She took out a large double-ended dildo and rolled Jade on to her back and spread her legs wide. Then she pushed one end of the dildo into her wet pussy. She straddled her, pushing the other end into her pussy. She leaned over and kissed Jade passionately, pressing her breasts against Jade's. She responded to Louise's kiss. Grinding her pussy against the dildo, making it go deeper into Louise's pussy. They moaned against each other's lips. Their juices running down there thighs. Adam stroked his hard cock as he watched the two women – Pre-cum oozing from the tip.

"Mmmmm yes fuck each other harder girls. You've got me so horny. My balls are getting full with spunk. I want to explode", said Adam groaning as he wanked his cock harder.

Louise and Jade fucked each other harder and deeper. Screaming with pleasure. As the dildo rubbed against their G-spots. Their legs shaking violently. As they brought each other to a shuddering climax – their juices squirting everywhere.

"Oh yes girls now lick each other clean. I want to see you give each other a golden shower. While you're at it, I'm almost there", said Adam licking his lips suggestively.

Louise gently removed the dildo from her and Jade's pussies. Then they got into the 69 position and began to lick each other clean while simultaneously finger fucking each other's pee holes until they started to piss over each other's faces. They licked each other piss soaked pussies while Adam wanked his cock, harder and faster. Groaning as he reached climax, his cum squirting everywhere.

"Good girls now come here and lick your master's cock clean", said Adam licking his lips.

Jade and Louise knelt either side of Adam. They licked and sucked his cock clean. Before running their tongues over his stomach. Getting every last drop of his cum. Kissing each other passionately. Sucking each other's tongues, sharing Adam's cum before gently pulling away and laying down either side of Adam.

"That was amazing master. I hope we will get to do this often. Louise knows how much I love sharing her with a man. Especially one as hot as you. I'm so glad I met you at the party. I've enjoyed indulging my submissive fantasies", said Jade smiling at Adam and Louise.

"Yes it was Jade my sexy slave. This is only the beginning of your submissive adventure. I plan to make you both my personal slaves. You're both so hot and very willing to submit to me", said Adam.

"We would love that wouldn't we Louise babes?" said Jade licking her lips suggestively.

"Hell yes Jade babes. I think we should all chill for a while now. Get our energy back for some more fun later", said Louise wrapping her arm around Jade and Adam.

They all held each other tight as they fell into a blissful sleep for the rest of the afternoon. Jade knew that from now on her life would never be the same again. Adam had made sure of that. She was addicted to his kinky sex games. It was like a drug to her. Sex with him would never be dull. He knew exactly what she needed. Knew how to pleasure her in every way. This was the beginning of a submissive adventure for her and for Louise. She couldn't wait to have more kinky fun with her and Adam. He was her ideal master sexy as hell and dominant but not too much so. She had fantasied about finding a guy like Adam for so long. She never thought she would meet him until the night she did. She planned to enjoy every second they spent together. He was perfect. All her other boyfriend paled in comparison.

The idea of being dominant – telling her what to wear. She needed a man like Adam. Now she'd found him she didn't want him to get away. She would willingly submit to his every desire. No matter how kinky or perverse it was. She lived to please her master. It was a fantasy come true for her. Nothing compared to it.

From now on she was Adam's slave and lover. She loved sharing him with Louise. It made the experience so much more pleasurable. Having two people to pleasure her. They both turned her on so much. She'd never had so many orgasms as she'd had with Adam and Louise. They were amazing.

A Random Encounter

I was in London for the week staying with a friend. Unfortunately, the night I got there she had to go to work. She gave me some money and told me to go and explore London. I found a trendy wine bar and went in. As I ordered a drink I noticed a tall dark haired mysterious looking stranger standing near the bar. His shirt was partly open to reveal his tanned chest. He looked older and more experienced but still hot. He smiled at me and I politely smiled back. Then got my drink and sat down. He walked over to me.

"Is this seat taken?" He said in a posh but sexy voice.

"No help yourself", I said. He sat beside me moving rather close I could smell his expensive aftershave.

"You are beautiful baby", he said eyes wandering over my body hand running up my thigh.

Then without warning he kissed me with such passion I felt my legs go to jelly. I put my arms around him responding to his kiss our tongues caressing. We kissed for what seemed like hours. When we stopped kissing he whispered in my ear that he would love to spend a night with me treating me like a slut and then a princess. I was shocked but excited at the thought of it. I explained that I was staying with a friend. He told me to call her and tell her that something had come up. I did as he asked. Then we left the bar and headed to his place. When we got to his flat he took my hand and led me into the bedroom. I told him I needed the toilet first. I went to the toilet sitting with my legs wide open as I had a piss. Suddenly he walked in knelt on the bathroom floor and started licking my pussy. I was so excited I came in his face. He licked it all up tasting my piss and my cum. Then he told me to bend over the toilet and part my ass cheeks. I did as he asked. He sniffed my ass then pushed his tongue deep inside, making me moan with pleasure. He lubricated my ass with my pussy juices. Then slid his cock up my ass. Fucking me hard and deep. I moaned louder and louder. Pushing back against his cock as he fucked me deeper and harder until we both came. He pumped his hot cum in my ass filling it with his hot sticky cum until it dripped down my legs.

"From now on your every trip to the toilet will be for my pleasure, my filthy little slut", he said.

"Yes", I said as we went into the bedroom. He undressed me and pushed me onto the bed. Then stripped naked and joined me. He told me to squat over his face and chest. I did as I was told wanting to please him so bad.

"I want you to piss on my face and chest my dirty little slut", he said.

I squatted over him so he could watch as my piss came out over his face and chest. Afterwards he spent ages licking my pussy clean. Then we lay on the bed together, kissing passionately. I sucked his tongue tasting my piss, then he climbed on top of and started fucking my pussy deep and hard. Then he pulled out and turned me over. Getting me on all fours, he slid his cock deep in my pussy, fucking me harder and deeper until my legs started to shake. As I climaxed violently he pulled his cock out and came over my face and tits. I used my fingers to scoop it up and licking them clean. Afterwards we went downstairs and relaxed on the sofa together kissing and cuddling. Later he bent me over the settee and fucked my ass hard and deep until I came to a shuddering climax and collapsed on the settee. He picked me up and carried me to bed. The following morning I awoke to see him stroking my hair. He kissed the top of my head and told me how beautiful I was. Suddenly my mobile rang. It was my friend. I told her I would see her soon and got dressed. We kissed passionately then I left until the next time. I hoped I would see the handsome stranger again. I had enjoyed my random encounter with him and I hoped it wouldn't be just a one off.

That night as I slept I dreamed about him using me like a slut. He invited his friends round. They took turns to fuck my pussy and ass and then my mouth. Filling all three holes with their spunk until I had it dripped down my body an into a messy pool on the floor.

He watched as they fucked me then he joined them on the bed and all six of them knelt over me, pissing over my face and tits. I sucked their cocks clean one by one. I felt myself getting wet; my clitoris throbbed. I reached down between my legs and rubbed my clitoris slowly at first. Then gradually faster and harder. Quickly bringing myself to climax. Squirting my juices everywhere. The next morning I woke up to find an envelope on my pillow. Inside was some money and a note.

"Gone to work babes, see you later. There's £20000 for you to treat yourself. buy yourself something nice and have a nice day in London love Amber xxxxx".

I got out of bed and went into the en suite bathroom and switched the shower on. Then I took of my nightie and got in. The warmth of the shower felt so good against my bare skin. I grabbed a bottle of shower gel and poured a little on to a soft cloth and began to wash myself. As I made my way down to my pussy. It started to tingle aching for attention. I closed my eyes as I slid my hand down to my pussy imagining it was his hand caressing me. I teased myself gently rubbing my aching pussy before sliding my fingers inside. Fingering myself hard and deep, all the time pretending it was him as I brought myself to a shuddering climax. I needed to see him again. I washed the soap suds off me then got out and dried myself before going into the bedroom and putting on a bra and thong along with my favourite skinny jeans, a tight black vest top, thigh high boots, and a denim jacket. Then I put the money in my purse and put my purse into my handbag before leaving my friends studio flat and heading to the bus stop.

A while later the bus arrived. I got on smiling to myself as I thought about the night before. When I got to my stop I got off and headed towards the shopping centre. Eager to find a hot outfit and some sexy underwear. As I walked through the shopping centre. I sensed someone watching me. I turned round and smiled as I saw a familiar face. He was sat at a café having a coffee. He looked even sexier than he had last night.

"Hello baby come join me. I was hoping to see you again", he said beckoning me over.

I walked over and sat next to him. His hand wandered up

my thigh. Moving higher towards my pussy. He grabbed my hand and placed it over his crotch – he was rock hard. I licked my lips – God I wanted him.

"I'll get you a coffee baby. then we can have a nice chat before we go back to mine. You will need to ring your friend as I want you to stay with me for a week or two. I can't stop thinking about you, there's so much more I want to do with you", he said smiling at me before gently removing my hand from his crotch.

He removed his hand from my thigh and went to get me a coffee. I could feel my pussy throbbing beneath my jeans. I couldn't wait to spend more time with him. He was the best lover I'd had in a long time. The sex was amazing and so much more exciting than it had been with past lovers. A few minutes later he returned with my coffee. He put it down in front of me then sat down moving his chair closer to mine. He leaned over and kissed me passionately. I wrapped my arms around him responding to his kiss. Our tongues rubbing against each other as we kissed for what seemed like an eternity – I couldn't get enough of his kisses. When we eventually pulled away my coffee had gone slightly cool but I drank it anyway. Then he paid the bill before taking my hand and leading me towards the car park. As we walk over to his black BMW he smiled at me. His hand caressing my ass through my tight jeans.

"You better ring your friend and let her know. You're going to be staying with me for a week or so", he said smiling.

I rang my friend and explain the situation to her. She tells me to ring her when I can so she knows I'm okay. I reassure her that I will before saying bye to her. He unlocks the car door, a wicked grin on his face as he opens the passenger door for me. I get in and he closes the door behind me before getting into the driver's seat. He leans over and kisses me passionately, his hand wandering up my thigh, moving further over towards my pussy. He slowly unzips my jeans and unbuttons them before sliding his hand down my thong. Licking his lips as he realizes I'm soaking wet for him. He rubs my aching pussy while continuing to kiss me. I respond to his kiss, reaching over and unzipping his jeans. Sliding my hand inside and gently stroke his cock. He moans softly against my lips while he slides his fingers deep in my wet pussy. Finger fucking me. He quickly brings me to a shuddering climax. My juices covering his fingers. He takes them out of my pussy and pulls away from me and slides his wet fingers in my mouth. I eagerly suck and lick them clean.

"Good girl. We had better get to mine. I'm so horny. I want to watch you pee and get really dirty with you baby", he said as he gently removed my hand from his cock and zips himself up.

I zip my jeans up and fasten the button before putting my seat belt on. He starts the car, driving out of the car park and towards his studio flat. When we get there he parks up and gets out of the car, walking around and opening the passenger door for me, taking my hand and leading me into the flat. He takes me straight into the bathroom and hungrily undresses me then strips naked. I lick my lips as I look as his hot naked body and his hard cock.

"Squat over the toilet for me baby let me watch you pee",

he says licking his lips at me.

I do as he asks squatting over the toilet and spreading my pussy lips wide. I finger my pee hole until I start to pee. I'm unable to stop. He strokes his cock as he watches me pissing. Then he knelt on the floor and began to lick my wet pussy while I continue to pee he starts to tongue fuck me and slides two fingers up inside me. I start to cum in his face. He licks my pussy clean tasting my cum and piss then he stands up and kisses me. I suck his tongue enjoying the exquisite cocktail of piss and cum. He gently pulls away from me and leads me into the bedroom.

He bends me over the bed and spreads my legs wide before ramming his cock in my wet pussy so hard that I scream. He starts to fuck me hard and deep. I moan with pleasure, pushing my pussy against his cock, taking every last inch of it in my pussy. He pulls my hair roughly as he fucks me harder and deeper bringing me to climax over and over again. My legs shake violently as he fucks me harder still. I squirt everywhere. He continues to fuck me until he fills my pussy with his hot cum. He gently pulls out and picks me up in his arms and lays me on the bed. He joins me laying beside me and stroking my hair as his other hand wanders over my body. I gently stroke his chest, enjoying the feel of it against my fingers. Suddenly the doorbell went.

"Wait here my dirty little slut. I've invited a few friends of mine over. I'm sure you will get on well with them. Let me blindfold you quickly", he said while getting a black satin blindfold from his bedside cabinet. He got off the bed and went downstairs to answer the door.

I heard several voices – some male and some female. I could feel my pussy aching in anticipation of what would inevitably happen. After what seemed like an eternity I heard footsteps coming up the stairs. He walked into the bedroom followed by two men and three women. I wished I could see them.

"Please take my blindfold off. I want to see your friends", I say to him.

he walked over to me and took the blindfold off. I looked at his friends – they were all hot.

"I hope you're ready for this my dirty slut. You will have cum dripping out of every hole and be covered in cum and piss. My female friends here will want to piss in your mouth and over your tits and pussy and you will have three cocks to suck", he said smiling at me.

"I'm ready for it lets get started. I want to be your dirty little cum hungry slut", I said licking my lips.

"Good girl. Let's begin the fun. Liam come over here and give my dirty little slut a good hard fuck in her pussy. Jay you fuck her ass", he said to his two male friends.

They followed him over to the bed after stripping naked and joined me. They got me into position then Liam pushed his cock in my wet pussy while Jay pushed his cock in my ass. They began to fuck me while he pushed his cock in my mouth inch by inch. I sucked him hard and deep while his two friends fucked my holes harder and deeper. Bringing me to climax over and over again. They swapped over every so often so that they both got to fuck my pussy and my ass until they filled me with their hot cum while I deep throated him. He groaned as he reached climax filling my mouth with his hot cum until it dripped down my chin. I swallowed every last drop, scooping the remainder off my chin, licking and sucking my fingers clean then I sucked his cock clean before letting him remove it from my mouth. He got me to lay on my back and beckoned Nadine over, the youngest of the three women. She walked over to the bed and sat beside me.

"Squat over her and give her a golden shower while I fuck her lovely wet pussy and ass. If she's good I might even give her a little treat. I bet you would love my pee in your pussy and ass wouldn't you my dirty little slut?" he said smiling at me.

"Yes I would, oh god fuck me please", I said.

Liam and Jay sat and watched. He slid his cock in my pussy first while Nadine squatted over me and gave me a golden shower. It felt so warm as it covered my tits and my face. I pushed my tongue deep in her wet pussy, tongue fucking her as she continued to piss on me while he fucked me deeper and harder. Suddenly I felt a warm sensation. I realized he was pissing up my wet pussy while he fucked me. I moaned with pleasure. Grinding my pussy against his cock. Making him fuck me harder and deeper. My legs shook violently as I reached my climax. He continued fucking me bringing me to climax over and over again until he climaxed filling my wet pussy with his hot cum. Then he slid out of my pussy and pushed his cock in my tight ass. I continued to tongue fuck Nadine until she climaxed then she moved down and began to lick my piss and cum soaked pussy while he pounded away at my tight ass. I screamed with pleasure. Pushing my ass against his cock taking every inch of it in my tight hot ass. He fucked me harder than ever. Filling my tight hole with piss and cum before pulling out. He got off the bed and was soon replaced by Jay who pushed his big cock in my tight hole. Fucking me hard and deep while Liam knelt at the side of me and pushed his cock in my mouth. He began to fuck my mouth almost gagging me as the tip of his cock hit the back of my throat. I managed to stop myself. His cock swelled in my mouth as he got close to his climax. He fucked my mouth harder and faster. Groaning as he climaxed. Filling my mouth with cum until it spilled out down my chin. I swallowed every drop of it. Sucking him dry before scooping up the remainder with my fingers and sucking them clean while Jay fucked my ass harder and deeper. Groaning as he reached climax. Pumping my ass full of cum until it ran down my thighs. Then he pulled out, knelt beside me and wanked over my face and tits. Covering me with his hot thick man cum.

"Open your mouth baby. time for you to taste my piss", said Jay.

I opened my mouth wide for him and he started to piss in my mouth. I swallowed it down as best I could. It felt warm in my mouth. After wards he made me suck his cock clean then Liam did the same. Then Nadine, Leah, and finally Joanne. Then the three men wanked over me covering my whole body with their cock juice.

"You're a good little slut. I'll run you a bath so we can get you nice and clean. You guys can go home now, my little slut is all mine now. Thank you once again for coming", he said.

Jay, Liam, Nadine, Leah and Joanne got dressed and left the flat while he ran me a bath. I laid on the bed while I waited for him to tell me the bath was ready. A few minutes later he walked back in.

"Your bath's ready baby", he said scooping me up in his arms and carrying me into the bathroom and gently putting me down into the bath.

"I feel like you're still a stranger – which is nice. But at the same time I want to get to know you if we're going to spend so much time together. For instance, what's your name?" I said smiling at him.

"My name's Paul. I'm 43 years old single and I love dirty kinky sex. that's all you need to know for now. I like to keep a little mystery", said Paul as he began to wash me with a soft flannel. Washing the cum of my face and body. His touch was so gentle and yet at the same time very sensual. I moaned softly at his touch.

"Nice to meet you Paul. I'm Helen I'm 34 years old and I also love dirty kinky sex. It's been an amazing experience. I'm so glad it's become more than just a random encounter. My body's been aching for your touch since I left yours. I was hoping to see you again before I had to go back home. My friend's letting me stay with her a little longer as we haven't see each other much since she moved down here", I said smiling at Paul.

"Why don't you live down here with me? you can see your friend whenever you want. then we can have fun together. your amazing baby, I can't get enough of you. I want to explore all your fantasies – especially the dirty ones", said Paul stroking his cock as he spoke, then he slowly got into the bath with me moving close to me and kissing me passionately.

My legs went to jelly I held on to his shoulders as I kissed him back sliding my hand down to his cock and stroking it softly as we kissed for what seemed like an eternity. When we eventually pulled away he finished washing the last bit of cum off my body then he let me wash his body before helping me out of the bath. We dried each other then went back into the bedroom and laid on the bed together. He kissed every inch of my body, working his way down to my wet pussy. He teased me with the tip of his tongue before gently parting my pussy lips and pushing his tongue deep inside, tongue fucking me. I moaned with pleasure, grinding my pussy against his tongue making it go deeper. He licked me deeper and harder. My legs shook as he brought me to climax. My juices squirting into his mouth. He licked me clean then moved up the bed getting on top of me and gently sliding his cock into my wet pussy while he kissed me passionately. I sucked his tongue tasting myself on it. As he began to slide his cock in and out of my pussy softly and slowly, he gently pulled away from me and bent his head, sucking my nipples hard. I moaned with pleasure.

"Fuck me please Paul. Treat me like a dirty slut", I said.

Paul put my legs over his shoulders and began to fuck me hard and deep while sucking and biting my nipples. I screamed with pleasure, grinding my pussy against his cock. Making it go deeper inside me, until the tip was nudging against my G-spot as he fucked me harder making me squirt. He started to pound my pussy. I screamed louder with pleasure. My legs shaking violently as he brought me to climax over and over again. My juices soaking the sheet. He slid out and turned me over moving me down the bed so that my face was near the damp patch. He pushed my face down so that my ass was high in the air and parted my ass cheeks – ramming his cock down my tight hole.

"Lick it up slut while I pound that sexy ass of yours", said Paul spanking my ass as he fucked me hard and deep.

I obediently licked up every last drop of my cum from the bed sheet, pushing my ass back against his cock. Taking every inch of it in my ass. I could feel my tight hole stretching to accommodate his big cock as he fucked me harder and faster, groaning. I screamed with pleasure. He fucked me faster and harder. Groaning as he reached climax. Pumping my ass full of cum until it dripped down my thighs. Then he gently pulled out and lay down on the bed. Pulling me close and wrapping his arms around me.

"Have you thought about what I said baby?" said Paul smiling at me as he ran his hands through my hair gently.

"Yes I have and I'd love to. It's the perfect solution. I need to get some rest now. I'll ring my friend in the morning and tell her the good news", I said resting my head on Paul's chest. We both fell into a blissful sleep.

I had enjoyed being with Paul again and I couldn't wait to be spending more time with him. Moving in with him felt so right; it was perfect. I would see more of Amber and get to have lots more dirty fun with Paul as I slept that night I wondered what else he had in store for me. What other dirty fantasies he wanted to explore with me. He was the best lover I'd had in a long time. The sex was never boring and I never knew what would happen next. It was so exciting the way he would treat me like a slut one minute and a princess the next. The combination made him all the more irresistible. I couldn't get enough of him. He was like a drug to me. I had to get my fix of him on a regular basis. He'd had an effect on me from the moment we'd met. We would explore our fantasies together. I knew that it would be amazing whatever he had in mind for us to do. The next morning I woke up to find him laid on his side just watching me. I smiled at him.

"Morning sexy, I can't wait to explore more dirty fantasies with you but first I want your mouth and tongue on me. while I use mine on your cock. I can't get enough of it Paul. It's so big and fat, feels so good in my pussy and my ass", I said licking my lips as I noticed how hard his cock was I reached over and gently stroked it he moaned softly.

"You're a good girl. Get that sexy ass of yours in my face baby. I want to taste both holes while you suck my big cock deep and hard", said Paul smiling at me.

I sit on his face and lean forward. Taking his cock in my mouth and sucking it deep and hard while he runs his tongue down the crack of my ass to my tight hole. He gently parts my ass cheeks, grabbing them as he pushes his tongue in my tight anus. Using his tongue like a mini cock – tongue fucking me. I moan against his cock, taking more of it in my mouth until the tip touches the back of my throat. His cock starts to swell in my mouth. I deep throat him sensing his impending climax. I start to wank him into my mouth. He licks down my ass towards my pussy. Running his tongue along my wet slit. My pussy lips part easily for him and he gently pushes his tongue inside. Licking me slowly and softly at first then gradually harder and deeper. He begins to tongue fuck me. I moan with pleasure. Wanking him harder until he explodes in my mouth. I suck him dry as he tongue fucks me to climax. My juices squirt into his mouth. He licks me dry. Then I get off him and lay at the side of him. He pulls me close and we kiss passionately sharing our cum.

Then he rolls me on to my stomach and gets me on all fours, parting my legs before ramming his cock in my warm wet pussy. He pulls my hair roughly as he fucks me hard and deep. I moan with pleasure, grinding my pussy against his cock. Taking every last inch of it in my pussy until the tip nudges against my G-spot. As he fucks me harder still, I squirt everywhere, my legs shaking violently. He fucks me harder and deeper than ever before bringing me to a violent climax. My juices gushing out of my pussy, soaking the sheets. He slides out and pulls me further down the bed so that my head is just below the wet patch my juices have made. He pushes my head down so that my ass is high in the air. Then he parts my ass cheeks. Kneeling behind me and licking my tight hole making it open up. He replaces his tongue with his big cock. Ramming it in my tight hole. I scream with pleasure as he pounds my ass. His balls slapping against my pussy. He forces my head down making me lick the wet patch as he fucks me harder and deeper reaching round and pulling my nipples, I scream louder with pleasure. He groaned as he reached climax emptying his balls in my tight hole. He gently pulls out and moves up the bed. Rolling me on to my back, he pushes his cock into my mouth. I suck his cock clean tasting my ass on his cock for the first time as I lick and suck his cock. He gently pulls out of my mouth and lays down beside me running his fingers through my hair. His hands wander over every inch of my body. I moan softly as his hand wanders down to my pussy. He gently rubs it teasing me as his fingers move further down towards my wet hole. His fingers slide inside me. He starts to finger me deep and hard. Sliding more fingers inside until he has four fingers deep inside me. He takes his fingers out of my pussy and makes a fist. before pushing it deep in my pussy – fisting me! I scream with pleasure as his fist stretches my pussy lips.

He fists me harder and deeper making me squirt over and over again. Then he slides his fist out of my pussy and forces it in my mouth. I lick and suck his fingers clean before pulling him close and kissing him passionately. He rolls on to his back and pulls me on top of him. I slide down on to his cock. He pushes his cock deep in my wet pussy. I start to bounce up and down on his cock. He grabs my hips and bounces me up and down harder and faster, sitting up slightly and sucking my nipples hard making them stick out like sore thumbs. They were so sensitive after he'd used his lips and tongue over them. The slightest touch had me trembling. He ran his thumb across them making my whole body tremble. My juices gushing out of my pussy.

He fucks me harder and faster. His balls slapping against my ass. He reaches over the bed and grabs a large fat dildo and a bottle of lube. He lubes up the dildo then makes me lean forward. He parts my ass cheeks making my tight hole open for him. He slowly slides the dildo into my tight hole. I scream at it stretches my tight hole.

"Take the pain baby, the pleasure will soon follow. I want you filled in both holes. Need that tight hole stretching", said Paul as he pushes the dildo deeper inside my tight hole the pain soon turns to pleasure.

"Oh god fuck my ass, treat me like a dirty little slut. I want you to fill every hole with spunk and piss. Want you to piss over my face and tits and my wet cunt and then cover me in spunk. I want to be a dirty little slut for you. I need to treated like a slut makes me feel so horny and wet", I said.

Paul starts to fuck my ass with the dildo. While pounding my pussy so hard that I cum everywhere. He continues to fuck me harder and harder until he fills my wet pussy with spunk and piss. He slides the dildo out of my ass and replaces it with his cock, ramming it in my ass so hard that I scream. He fucks my ass hard and deep. I scream with pleasure taking every inch of his cock in my ass. Loving the way it filled my tight hole. He spanks me hard as he fucks me.

"You're a good little slut. So dirty and horny", said Paul pounding my ass harder and deeper groaning as he reached a second climax. Pumping my ass full of his cum until it dripped out down my thighs.

He scooped it up and made me suck them clean. I eagerly licked and sucked them clean then he gently pulled out of my ass and lifted me off him.

"Let's have a shower and get dressed. I'll take you shopping you need some sluttish outfits to wear for me baby. I want to dress you up as sluttish schoolgirl later on. I'll be the headmaster you are in detention for playing with yourself in class. I punish you for being a slut making you bend over my knee, panties round your ankles and skirt up over your ass with the hem tucked into the waistband. I'll spank you good and hard leaving red marks on your ass cheeks. It turns you on being spanked and you start to play with your tight wet young cunt and trying to get at my cock.

I make you beg me for it, getting you on your knees at my feet. Begging me to fuck you like the horny little slut that you are. You beg me to fuck you over and over again. Showing me your cunt and your tight ass. You grab a ruler off my desk and use it fuck yourself, moaning for me as you bring yourself to climax over and over again. I wank my cock as I watch you. I walk over to you standing over you and covering you in my spunk before helping you up off the floor and roughly bending you over the desk ramming my cock in your tight little wet cunt and fucking you good and fucking hard. You scream with pleasure, grinding your cunt against my cock wanting more. I oblige fucking you like the whore that you are", said Paul smiling as he notices that I'm rubbing my wet pussy.

"Mmmmm, that sounds so horny", I said breathlessly.

He gently removes my hand from my pussy and helps me off the bed. We walk into the bathroom and he turns on the shower. We get in and wash each other's naked bodies kissing passionately. I press myself against him. His role-play idea had got me so horny that I needed a quick fuck to satisfy my aching pussy.

"Later baby. I need you hungry for it. I want you to be aching for me so bad that you will be begging for my cock for real. I know you love my big hard man sized cock but I want you to make you wait for it. The pleasure will be so much more intense I assure you", said Paul getting out of the shower and getting dried.

I followed him switching off the shower before getting myself dry then we went back into the bedroom and got dressed before leaving his flat and getting into his car. He drove into town and parked up in a multi story car park. We got out and headed out of the car park and towards the shops. We headed into a shop called 'Naughty Pleasures' that had several outfits in the window.

We headed inside and looked around at the various outfits. Paul picked out a naughty schoolgirl outfit consisting of a white shirt, short red and green pleated skirt blue striped tie, and white knee high socks. We take it to the counter and he pays for it then we leave the shop and head into a lingerie shop. He picks out a tiny white thong for me along with several pairs of barely there thongs in red and several pairs of hold-up stockings.

"These are perfect baby lets pay for them then all we need is some sluttish skirts, dresses, tops and some boots for you", said Paul smiling at me as we walk over to the counter.

He pays for the thongs and stockings then we have a look around. We find several short skirts, low cut tops and short dresses. He gets me to try them on licking his lips.

"Mmmm, you look like a sexy little slut, baby", said Paul as he looks at me in the short denim skirt and low cut top. He holds the top and skirt for me then picks out several other skirts, dresses, and tops. We go into a shoe shop. He buys me a pair of knee-high boots then we make our way back to the car. When we get in he smiles at me with a wicked glint in his eyes.

"Get in the back and take off those jeans along with your bra and thong. Put the denim skirt on for me and the boots. I want you dressed as a slutty cunt on show for me at all times", he said.

I get in the back of the car and take off my jeans, bra, thong and boots before putting the skirt and tight vest top on. My nipples sticking out through the front of the top then I put the boots on. I get back into the front of the car and sit with my legs wide open, showing Paul my wet pussy. He licks his lips. Reaching over and rubbing my wet slit with his fingers.

"You are a horny little slut aren't you?" said Paul as he continued to rub my sensitive cunt.

I moan softly. Grinding my pussy against his fingers. Wanting them inside me. He moves his hand away and fastens my seat belt up then his own before starting up the car and driving back to his flat leaving me frustrated. When we get there he parks up and we hurry inside he takes me into the bedroom and helps me get changed into my schoolgirl outfit. I put my hair in pigtails for him.

"Mmmmm, you look like a dirty sluttish schoolgirl now

baby. Right, let's go into my study which for today is a classroom. You sit down on one of the chairs with your legs wide open and play with that wet cunt for me", said Paul taking my hand leading me out of the bedroom and into his study.

I sit down on a chair at the opposite side of his desk my legs wide open. I start to finger my wet pussy. Moaning softly while Paul sits behind his desk pretending to mark some homework. He looks up for a moment and watches me.

"You dirty little slut! You can stay behind for detention young lady", said Paul.

"Please sir I can't help myself I'm so horny I need cock", I said.

"Come here and bend over my knee. Panties round your ankles! skirt tucked up so I can spank that ass of yours for being such a dirty little slut!" said Paul.

I get up and walk over to him. Pulling my thong down to my ankles. Then I bend over his knee. He tucks the hem of my skirt into the waistband then he starts to spank me hard.

I moan with pleasure as the pain turns to pleasure. He leaves red marks on my ass but I don't care. He'd got me so horny I rub my wet pussy as I try to unzip his trousers wanting that amazing cock. He moves my hand away.

"On your knees and beg me for my cock", said Paul. I get on my knees in front of him.

"Please fuck me sir. I'm so horny I need a big cock", I said opening my legs wide and showing him my wet pussy.

Then I turn around and show him my tight ass before crawling over to his desk and grabbing a ruler. I push it deep in my wet pussy and fuck myself with it, making sure he's watching me. He walks round and sits on the edge of his desk so he can watch me. He unzips his trousers and takes out his cock, wanking his big hard cock as I fuck myself harder and deeper. Moaning with pleasure as I bring myself to climax, covering the ruler in my cum. He walks over and stands over me, wanking harder until he covers me with his spunk then he helps me up and takes me over to the desk, roughly bending me over it and ramming his cock in my wet pussy. He pulls on my pigtails roughly as he fucks me so hard that I cum over his cock while he fills my hungry cunt with cum. He continues fucking me harder and faster. Spanking me as he fucks me.

"Yeah that's it slut, take sirs big cock in that tight wet little cunt", said Paul as he pushes his cock deeper inside me till the tip nudges against my G-spot as he pounds my pussy his cock stretching my pussy lip as it swells. I grind my pussy against his cock.

"Oh god yes sir, fuck me harder. I want every last drop of your spunk. I'm a dirty little spunk loving whore", I said breathlessly.

Paul grabs my hips and fucks me harder than ever before. His balls slapping against my ass. I cum over and over again. My juices gushing out of my pussy. He reaches round and fingers my pee hole hard and deep, making me pee for him. It covers his cock as he continues to fuck me.

Groaning as he reaches climax. Filling my wet pussy with his spunk until it drips out of my wet pussy and down my thighs. He pulls out spreads my ass cheeks and rams his cock in my tight ass, pounding my tight hole. I take every inch of his cock as he fucks me hard and deep grabbing a large fat dildo from his desk drawer and pushing it in my cum soaked pussy. Fucking me with it while his cock plunges in and out of my ass. I scream with pleasure. My legs shaking as he brings me to a shuddering climax. I hold on to the desk as my legs go to jelly. He fucks my ass harder still, removing the dildo from my pussy and forces it in my mouth. I eagerly lick and suck it clean while he pumps my ass full of spunk. He pulls out wiping the remainder of his spunk on my ass, rubbing it into the sore areas, soothing the pain away. He removes the dildo from my mouth then he takes my hand and leads me into the bedroom, undressing me and then stripping himself naked. He picks me up and lays me on the bed joining me. He lays next to me and runs his fingers through my hair and gently kisses me. I kiss him back running my fingers through his hair.

"That was so good Paul. my legs have gone to jelly now. I need to rest a while", I said smiling at Paul.

"I'll run you a nice hot bath you can have a relaxing soak while I go and prepare us some lunch baby. You should ring your friend as well. Explain that you are going to be living with me from now on", said Paul getting off the bed and walking into the bathroom.

He ran me a hot bath then came back into the bedroom and scooped me up. Carrying me into the bathroom and gently putting me into the bath.

"Have a nice long soak baby. Come and find me when you're ready", said Paul walking out of the bathroom

I laid back in the bath and relaxed. As I lazily washed my body, the water felt so nice against my skin. I had enjoyed my role-play session with Paul but right now I needed to relax. My legs slowly began to feel normal again. The climax he'd given me had made them go so weak. I felt as though I would collapse. I washed my body clean then relaxed for a while before getting out and drying myself then went into the bedroom and rang my friend letting her know that I was going to be living in London with Paul. She was happy for me. After I'd finished I got dressed, putting the short denim skirt on with a low cut halter neck top and the knee high boots before going to find Paul. I soon found him in the kitchen. He beckoned me over to him. I walked over to him and he pulled me close, grabbing my ass so I was pressed against him. I smiled as I felt his hard cock pressed against me. I reached down and stroked his cock.

"Suck it baby let me fill that mouth of yours with my spunk", said Paul.

I get on my knees in front of him and take his cock in my mouth. Sucking it deep and hard. He moans softly. Putting his hands on the back of my head. Pushing me further down on to his cock. I breathed through my nose so that I didn't gag as I deep-throated his cock. He began to fuck my mouth. His cock swelling until it filled my mouth. I sucked harder and began to wank him into my mouth sensing he was close. He fucked my mouth harder and deeper. Groaning as he climaxed – coming deep down my throat. I swallow every last drop of his sweet cum – sucking him clean. He slowly removes his cock from my mouth and helps me up. Taking my hand and leading me over to the kitchen sink. He bends me over it, roughly pushing my skirt up over my ass then he unfastens my top letting it fall down over my breasts. He squeezes them as he rams his cock in my warm wet pussy making me scream with pleasure as he fucks me hard and deep. His cock nudging against my G-spot. My juices squirting over his cock as he pounds my pussy harder than ever before. I grip the edge of the sink my legs shaking violently as Paul brings me to another shuddering climax. My juices gushing out of my pussy and down my thighs making a pool on the kitchen floor. He continues to fuck me pulling my hair and spanking my bare ass.

"You love it when I'm rough with you don't you baby? I'm going to fill that pussy of yours with my hot sticky cum you horny little slut. Bounce on my big hard cock", said Paul. I bounce on his cock as he fucks me hard and fast.

"Oh god yes I love it when you fuck me like this. love it rough gets me so wet. I want filling with your spunk", I said breathlessly as he brings me to climax again and again until finally he explodes in my pussy. Filling me with his hot sticky cum until it drips down my thighs. He pulls out of my pussy and spreads my ass cheeks.

"Time to fuck that tight ass of yours", said Paul ramming his huge cock up my tight asshole one again.

I scream with pleasure as he fucks my tight hole hard and deep. His balls slapping against my pussy as he pounds my tight ass reaching round and pulling on my nipples. Making me scream louder. He makes a fist with his hand and rams it up my cum soaked pussy. Fist fucking me hard and deep. I squirt everywhere while he continues to fuck my tight ass harder and faster. Groaning as he reaches climax. Filling my tight hole with his cum until it drips down my quivering thighs. He pulls out and turns me round to face him. Kissing me so passionately. I have to hold on to his shoulders to stop myself from collapsing. My legs turn to jelly. He picks me up in his strong arms and carries me into the living room, laying me down on the sofa. He sits down leaning over running his hands through my hair.

"You're so beautiful baby I'm so glad you decided to move in with me. I can't get enough of you. I want to fuck you all day and night. my cock gets hard every time I look at you and your such a dirty slut exactly the kind of woman I like", said Paul smiling at me.

"I can't get enough of you either. You're like a drug to me. I need a constant fix. You drive me wild and the sex is amazing. No other man has made me cum like you. I can't get enough of your cock I love to suck it and have it inside me", I said licking my lips suggestively as I look at Paul taking in every inch of him. He smiles at me running his hand over my body gently working his way down to my pussy he runs his fingers over my pussy lips then he rubs my clitoris gently, making me moan softly.

"I want to watch you piss. Then I want you to piss over my cock while I fill your pussy with piss and spunk. I know you want it dirty baby. I know you get off on dirty sex – I can tell. This is why were so in tune with each other. Your other lovers didn't know what you want and need like I do. No other man will ever give you as much satisfaction as I can. I know what you need, I can give you everything you want and need for as long as I'm capable of doing it. You will never be bored in bed again", said Paul getting of the settee.

"Mmmmm, I love dirty sex so much. god you know just how to turn me on Paul", I said following him out of the living room and upstairs to the bathroom.

I get undressed and squat over the toilet spreading my pussy lips. He kneels on the floor and watches as I start to pee. Unable to stop he moves closer and begins to lick my pussy clean. Pushing his tongue deep inside tongue fucking me till I cum. Then he removes his tongue helps me up and turns me round, putting the toilet seat down before bending me over. He rams his cock in my piss soaked pussy. Fucking me so hard that we both cum and piss at the same time. I moan with pleasure. The warm sensation driving me wild. He continues to fuck me harder and deeper. Making me scream with pleasure. He pulls out for a minute, pushing his cock in my tight hole. He begins to piss in my tight hole then he pushes his cock back in my wet pussy and fucks me harder and faster than before I scream with pleasure as he brings me to climax over and over again until I collapse in his arms. He holds me round the waist steadying me as he pumps me full of his hot sticky cum once again before gently pulling out.

"Oh god that was so good babe. Let's go rest a while", he said taking my hand and leading me into the bedroom.

We lay on the bed and kiss passionately. Getting our energy back after another steamy session. My legs feel almost numb but I know that it's worth it to get such a good seeing to by such a strong hot man. I'm so glad to have met him. I thought back to when I almost cancelled my trip to London. If I had I'd never have met Paul and I'd still be spending a fortune on sex toys and DVD's while trying desperately to find a man to fulfil my wildest fantasies – like Paul had done since the first time we fucked.

He knew how to fuck me and what I needed in bed. It was almost as if he could read my mind. He seemed to know all of my fantasies – even the dirtiest ones. He fulfilled every last one of them. No other man had dared to even try them yet Paul wanted to do them all. He loved dirty rough sex as much as I did which is why we were so sexually compatible. We both dozed off for a while as we laid on the bed together. Both satisfied – for now at least. I knew we would continue later though. I was addicted to sex with Paul. Being without it would drive me mad which is why I had agreed to live with him. I knew that I couldn't go even a day without his cock. He was like my own personal brand of cocaine. I had to get my daily fix of him or I would go insane. I would have spent a small fortune going back and forth to London so living with him was the best option for me, both financially as well as physically. It was the best decision I'd ever made in my life. I was so much happier with Paul than I'd been in a long time. He satisfied my every need and our love life was never and would never be boring which was a good thing for me. Later that day we woke up from our nap. I smiled as I looked at Paul he smiled back. Leaning over and kissing me passionately. I respond to his kiss pulling him close. He got on top of me. Putting my legs over his shoulders and pushing his cock in my wet pussy. He fucks me hard and deep. I moan with pleasure grinding my pussy against his cock. He fucks me harder and deeper making me scream with pleasure my legs shaking as I reach a shuddering climax. He fucks me harder still bringing me to climax over and over again. My juices squirting everywhere. He continues to fuck me until he reaches his own climax. He pulls out and turns me over on to my stomach getting me on all fours and spreading my ass cheeks.

He rams his cock in my tight ass fucking me hard and deep. I scream with pleasure. He spanks my bare ass as he pounds my tight ass harder and faster. Groaning as he reaches climax. Pumping my tight hole full of hot sticky cum. He pulls out and lays beside me pulling me close and kissing me passionately running his hands through my hair. I kiss him back running my hands over his chest. His gently touch feels so nice. So different from the rough treatment but still nice. He moves up the bed and pushes his cock towards my mouth. I take it in my mouth, sucking it hard and deep tasting my ass. He fucks my mouth hard and deep until he fills my throat with hot sticky cum. I swallow every last drop sucking his cock clean.

He pulls out and moves down the bed kneeling between my legs. He gently parts my pussy lips and begins to lick my wet pussy slowly and softly at first then gradually harder and faster, making me moan with pleasure. He starts to tongue fuck me hard and deep bringing me to a shuddering climax. My juices filling his mouth. He licks me clean then he moves back up the bed and kisses me. I respond to his kiss, sucking his tongue tasting myself. He pulls away from me and squats over me, wanking his cock hard and fast until he covers my breasts with his cum. He does the same to my pussy before pushing his cock in my mouth. I suck it clean.

"Good girl you look such a slut laid there covered in my cum. how about I invite a few of my friends round later. We'll take turns fucking you then we will all cover you in spunk. It will be on your tits and pussy and in your hair. Come on let's have a nice hot shower then I'll make us something to eat. You will need your energy for tonight", said Paul.

"That's sounds so horny I can't wait. It's one of my ultimate fantasies, god you're amazing", I said following Paul into the bathroom.

He turns on the shower and we get in. Washing each other's naked bodies clean while kissing each other passionately. Running our hands over each other's bodies. Then we get out and dry each other off before putting on our dressing gowns and going downstairs. Paul makes spaghetti bolognaise. We sit at the dining table to eat it. He pours us both a glass of red wine which goes down nicely with the meal we eat in silence. He takes out plates in the kitchen and washes them while I relax on the settee. He joins me a while later, wrapping his arms around me and holding me tight.

Later that night five of Paul's friends come over. We go into the bedroom and they take turns to fuck me in both holes bringing me to climax over and over again. Then the six of them wank over my naked body. Their cum covering my tits and pussy. Some of it lands in my hair making it sticky. I suck their cocks clean enjoying the taste. We spend all of that night fucking. I love the different cocks in my holes and their hands on my body. It makes me so horny. I cannot get enough of them. My pussy and ass get stretched to the limit as they fuck me two at a time over and over again all through the night and again the next morning. I can't get enough of their cum. They fill my mouth, pussy and ass with it. As well as covering my body with it.

Suddenly I wake up in my own bed my pussy throbbing. It had all been a dirty dream – yet had felt so real. I could almost taste the spunk. I grabbed my dildo from the bedside cabinet and fuck myself with it, bringing myself to climax over and over again. Closing my eyes imaging the dildo was a real cock. I moan with pleasure while bringing myself to a shuddering climax. My juices squirting everywhere. I let the dildo slide out of my pussy itself. Then I get out of bed and take a shower before getting dressed. I make myself a coffee and take it up to my study.

I get out my notebook and write about my explicit dream with my pussy still throbbing. I decide to go into town and find myself a man. I finish off my coffee and walk downstairs and out of my house. Heading down the street to the bus stop just in time to catch the bus. I get on paying my fare and sit down. A while later the bus gets to my stop. I get off and head into a trendy wine bar. A tall dark haired stranger smiles at me as I walk in. I have to take a second look. The stranger is the spitting image of Paul. I get myself a drink and walk over to him. He pats the chair beside him. I sit down smiling.

"Hi baby my name's Paul. What brings you here?" he said.

"I err need some male company", I say smiling nervously. He puts my drink on the table and kisses me passionately my legs go to jelly.

"Let's go back to mine baby", said Paul.

I quickly finish my drink then follow Paul out of the wine bar and down the road to his penthouse apartment. My pussy wet with anticipation of what was to come. When we get to his apartment I have to go to the toilet. He follows me in, watching me as I pee then he licks me so hard that I cum in his face. He licks me clean then helps me up, taking my hand and walking me into the bedroom. He strips me naked then undresses himself before bending me over the bed and ramming his cock in my wet pussy. Fucking me hard and deep. I moan with pleasure. He fucked me harder still, my legs going to jelly with the force of my climax.

I had found my dream man and this time it was real – or was it???

Pussy Worship

Joey looked over at his latest conquest licking his lips as he saw her smooth pussy. He'd always loved pussy, ever since he'd first seen one when he was 15. Now aged 21 it had become a fetish for him. He couldn't get enough of it. He moved down the bed between her legs. Gently spreading her pussy lips and pushing his tongue inside licking her hard and deep and making her moan with pleasure, grinding her pussy against his tongue. He pushed his tongue deeper inside her wet pussy, licking her harder and deeper. Her legs shook as she reached a shuddering climax filling his mouth with her juices. He licked her clean spending ages running his tongue over every inch of her pussy, enjoying the taste of her pussy unable to stop himself.

"Oh baby your pussy tastes so damn good. I can't get enough of it", said Joe.

"Mm mm, I can tell gorgeous. Now get your cock in my wet pussy. I want a good hard fuck", said Chevaughn licking her full lips suggestively at Joe.

He reluctantly removed his tongue from her pussy and replaced it with his cock. Putting her legs over his shoulders and fucking her hard and deep. She moaned with pleasure, grinding her pussy against his cock. He fucked her harder, deeper, faster pushing the full length of his cock in her wet pussy. His balls slapping against her ass as he pounded her wet pussy making her scream with pleasure. Her legs shaking as she reached a shuddering climax, her juices squirting everywhere. He continued fucking her harder still until he reached his own climax. Pumping her full of hot sticky cum. He pulled out and moved up the bed. Kneeling next to her head and pushing his cock towards her lips. She eagerly sucked and licked his cock clean.

"Oh baby, that was amazing. I must go though gorgeous. I need to get to work before I get the sack. I've been late twice this week already. I'll call you sometime", said Chevaughn getting of the bed and hurriedly getting dressed.

"Bye sexy don't keep me waiting for that call. I need pussy. Yours is just so juicy and it tastes divine", said Joe.

"You really have got it bad for pussy. I err, think you need help. You're a good fuck but a little obsessive when it comes to pussy. I just wanted a one night stand to be honest. Anyway I'm off", said Chevaughn walking out of the bedroom and downstairs. She opened the front door and left his flat.

'Damn I need to find a willing female who will let me worship her pussy. I'll try the fetish club in town. There's bound to be some hot female in there who will be willing to let me worship there pussies', thought Joe. His cock getting harder as he closed his eyes imagining a hot naked female letting him worship her pussy over and over again. Then another took over. A long queue of females formed. Each of them letting him worship there pussies. His mouth overflowing with their juice. They each took turns to sit on his face almost suffocating him with their pussies – he was in heaven. Pre-cum oozed from his cock as he thought about the potential for a fetish fantasy come true.

Joe laid on his bed slowly stroking his hard fat cock as he reminisced about the first time he'd seen pussy. He was 15 years old and the female was 18 years old. She was a friend of his older sisters. Her name was Cynthia Watson. She'd seen him watching through the doorway as she undressed and invited him into her bedroom. She couldn't believe her luck as she laid on the bed in just a tiny pink thong. He began to slowly take it off revealing her smooth pussy. Not a single hair on it. He had stood near the bed just staring at her pussy. His cock getting hard beneath his jeans as he watched her fingers sliding down her stomach to her pussy. She brazenly pleasured herself knowing it was turning him on. He stroked his cock harder as he remembered Cynthia opening her pink pussy lips for him.

She was nice and wet from pleasuring herself. She'd beckoned him over to her. He'd eagerly joined her on the bed and she'd sat over his face rubbing her wet pussy across his lips. He could smell her juices loving her aroma. She'd begged him to worship her pussy with his tongue. He'd done as she'd asked. She'd taught him how to lick her pussy that night. As well as taking his virginity. They secretly met up for several months after that until her dad got a job in London. He'd been devastated but he'd had plenty of pussy since but no one other woman had let him worship her pussy like Cynthia had. He stroked his cock harder still squirting his load over his stomach as he thought about seeing her pussy. He'd fantasied about her since she'd left. The last he heard she'd set up a dominatrix company with a few friends. What he'd give to have her sat on his face again or be knelt in front of her, worshiping her pussy over and over again. Joe went into his bathroom and switching on the shower. He got in and washed himself clean before getting out and drying himself. He wrapped the towel around his waist and went back into his bedroom, opening his wardrobe and taking out a clean shirt, black leather trousers, and black shoes. He got dressed and spiked his short black hair and spraying on a little aftershave.

He got his mobile from the bedside cabinet and rang for a taxi before going downstairs and grabbing his lighter & cigarettes, leather jacket and keys. He walked out locking the door behind him, getting a cigarette out of the pack and lighting it, blowing smoke rings as he waited for the taxi to arrive.

The taxi sets off towards *'House Of Fetish'* a fetish club in the town centre. A while later the taxi pulled up, Joe paid his fare and got out and heading towards the entrance to the club. A small queue was forming outside. He joined the queue smiling as he noticed several hot females. He would be in heaven if he could worship their pussies. His cock grew hard as he thought about the possibility of worshiping a pussy or two. He eventually got to the entrance and paid the entrance fee before heading into the main area of the club and walking over to the bar. He ordered a bourbon and coke looking around the club he was in heaven he paid for his drink and walked over to a table where he had the best view. As he sat down he noticed a tall dominant looking brunette looking at him.

He smiled at her his brown eyes fixated between her legs. He could see the outline of her pussy lips through her shiny black skin-tight latex trousers. She smiled back and beckoned him over. He grabbed his drink and walked over to her smiling. His eyes unable to stop looking between her legs. She was one hot woman but all he could think of was the possibility of being allowed to worship her pussy over and over again. His cock was rock hard beneath his leather trousers at the thought of it. He would do anything for the chance to worship the pussy of such a smoking hot sexy woman like her.

"Put your drink and get on your knees at once. I'm Mistress Vandora. but you will refer to me as Mistress", said Mistress Vandora.

"Yes Mistress", said Joe obediently putting his drink down and kneeling in front of Mistress Vandora. She spread her legs wide unzipping her latex trousers between her legs revealing a smooth pussy.

"Oh Mistress may I worship your pussy", said Joe unable to stop himself from staring at Mistress Vandora's pussy. It glistened with her juices.

"You will worship my pussy slave but first strip naked for me then kneel before me once again. Arms behind your back. I will restrain you. I do not allow slave to touch me unless I give them permission to do so", said Mistress Vandora.

Joe got up off the floor and stripped naked before kneeling in front of Mistress Vandora arms behind his back. She got a pair of leather cuffs from her bag. Then she got up and walked over to Joe kneeling behind him and cuffing his wrists together before sitting down in front of him once again putting her hands on the back of his head pushing his face against her pussy.

"Worship my pussy slave. Show your mistress how much you appreciate her. If you're good I might let you be my permanent slave. You will worship my pussy 24/7 as well as worshiping my right hand woman Cynthia. She's into pussy worship like myself", said Mistress Vandora.

His eyes lit up at the thought of worshiping pussy 24/7 as well as hearing Cynthia's name although he didn't know for sure if it was even the Cynthia he'd lost his virginity to. He began to lick Mistress Vandora's pussy running his tongue over every inch of her pussy. She put her legs over his shoulders and pulling him closer, his nose almost touching her pussy. He inhaled deeply enjoying the sweet scent of her juices.

As he continued licking her pussy. She moaned with pleasure and began grinding her pussy against his tongue. He pushed it deeper inside her wet hole, licking her hard and deep sensing her impending climax. She moaned with pleasure, her juices gushing out of her pussy running into his mouth and dripping down her latex covered thighs.

"Oh yes slave don't stop. make your mistress cum over and over again", said Mistress Vandora breathlessly.

Joe continued to lick Mistress Vandora's pussy, tongue fucking her harder and deeper till she filled his mouth with cum. He licked her clean while she parted her pussy lips for him. He pushed his tongue deeper inside her pussy, the tip brushing against her g-spot. He licked her slowly and softly at first. Then gradually faster and harder, making her cum over and over again. He used his tongue on her g-spot. Making her squirt everywhere. He licked up every drop of it from her pussy, sucking her clitoris and pussy lips until she gently pushed him away. He licked his lips tasting her cum savoring the taste.

"You are amazing slave. Let me unfasten these cuffs then I will give you a treat. We will go back to mine first though", said Mistress Vandora smiling as she stood up and walked around to the back of Joe.

She knelt on the floor unfastening his cuffs then helped him to his feet smiling.

"Get dressed and we'll go back to mine. I'm not done with you yet. You're the perfect slave. You know just how to worship my pussy. You love pussy don't you?", said Mistress Vandora.

"Yes Mistress I do, it's become a fetish for me. I was hoping to find a woman who would let me worship her pussy. I can't get enough of it, said Joe getting dressed hurriedly while Mistress Vandora zipped up her trousers.

Joe downed his bourbon and coke before following Mistress Vandora out of the club and over to a long black limousine. She opened the door and he got in and joined him shutting the door behind her. The limousine driver set off towards Mistress Vandora's mansion where she lived and worked as a professional Fem-Dom along with Cynthia the woman who had taken his virginity, as well as letting him worship her pussy to a certain extent. Although Joe didn't know this yet but he would soon be fulfilling his fetish fantasies with both Mistress Vandora and Cynthia. A while later the limousine pulled up outside Mistress Vandora's mansion. The limousine parked up on the long driveway. Mistress Vandora got out and Joe followed her shutting the door behind him. They walked up the steps to her front door. She opened it and they walked in shutting the door behind them. Mistress Vandora locked the door then took his hand and led him upstairs to her master bedroom. firmly His eyes lit up as they walked into the bedroom and laid on the bed naked except for her black lace-top stockings. She smiled as she saw him, a look of recognition on her face. Joe couldn't stop himself from staring at her smooth hairless pussy. The sight of it making his cock grow harder still.

"Hi gorgeous long time no see. come here and lay on the bed so I can sit on your face and let you worship my pussy. You will need to strip naked though as I'm sure you will have pleased Mistress Vandora so she will be giving you a little treat", said Cynthia licking her lips suggestively.

"Hi Cynthia, yes I have pleased Mistress Vandora and I will please you. I've been wanting to worship your pussy again for so long", said Joe hurriedly undressing before laying on the bed next to Cynthia smiling at her.

She sat on his face and he began to lick her pussy running his tongue over every inch of it and sucking her swollen clitoris. She moaned softly grinding her pussy against his expert tongue. He licked her harder and deeper making her moan with pleasure while Mistress Vandora undressed and joined them on the bed, straddling Joe and guiding his hard cock into her wet pussy. She began to ride him while he continued to Cynthia's her pussy, making her moan with pleasure. Her juices filling his mouth. She rubbed her clitoris fast and hard, riding his tongue as if it was a miniature cock. Taking it deeper inside her pussy till it brushed against her g-spot. She squirted over his face and in his mouth. He continued licking her harder and deeper. She pushed his face against her pussy, screaming with pleasure as he continued licking her pussy.

"OH GOD TONGUE FUCK ME SLAVE. I'M GOING TO CUM", said Cynthia breathlessly.

Joe obliged tongue fucking her hard and deep. Her legs shook. As she reached a shuddering climax, filling his mouth with her juices. He licked her clean, lapping up every last drop from her pussy. She got off him, a big smile on her face, her juices gushing from her pussy and running down her thighs. Joe licked his lips. Tasting the remainder of her juices. Enjoying the taste of them.

"Fuck that was good slave. Let me clean your face up a little then you may kiss me. I want to taste my cum", said Cynthia getting a tissue and wiping his face. Then she put the tissue in the bin and leaned over, kissing Joe passionately and sucking his tongue.

He responded to her kiss while Mistress Vandora bounced on his cock, moaning with pleasure. He felt his balls swelling as they filled with cum. He was going to explode, his fetish fantasies were coming true and it turned him on immensely. He couldn't get enough. He never wanted the fun to end.

"Grab my hips slave and pound my pussy. Cynthia leave me with our new slave awhile please", said Mistress Vandora.

Cynthia gently pulled away from Joe and walked out of the bedroom. Joe grabbed Mistress Vandora's hips, holding her still while he pounded her pussy. Making her scream with pleasure. Her legs shaking as she reached a shuddering climax covering his cock and balls with her juices. He continued fucking her, groaning as he reached his own climax. Pumping her full of hot sticky cum and emptying his balls. His cum dripping from her pussy and running down the inside of her thighs. She got off and knelt in front of him, sucking and licking his cock clean. Enjoying the combined tastes of his cum and her pussy juices. She milked him dry before removing her mouth from his cock and sitting on the bed next to him, licking her full lips suggestively at him.

"Oh god slave, you are amazing. I need a cigarette and a stiff drink. Wait here and I'll get us both a drink. You will be mine and Cynthia's live in slave and learn the delights of pussy worship. I need to test you further but for now we will rest", said Mistress Vandora getting off the bed and putting on a red satin dressing gown leaving it partly open, giving Joe a glimpse of her puss and her pert breasts.

Not that he was interested in them. Although he had to admit they looked nice. He was more interested in her smooth pussy. His friends at school had all ogled Cynthia's DDS's on many occasions He would pretend to look, just so he didn't feel left out. Mistress Vandora's were slightly smaller. He guessed she was about a 36C or there about. If his friends could see him now! They'd be so jealous of him! Getting to not only see her pussy, but get to taste it – fuck it. Having two lots of pussy would make them really jealous. Especially his friend Kirk who had tried and failed to get in Cynthia's knickers as well as her sister Paris's knickers. Both had turned him down flat. He'd boasted that he'd had two women in one night. Both of who had apparently took turns to sit on his face while the other one bounced on his cock. It turned out that the two women in question, Katie and Marie had been propositioned by Kirk but they had turned him down on account of the fact that they preferred pussy. They'd told Joe one night he'd laughed at the time. Kirk later admitted he'd only said it because the other lads had been bragging about their conquests. Joe smiled as he thought about what kind of test Mistress Vandora had in mind. He knew it would involve pussy worship which he loved, he couldn't get enough.

A while later Mistress Vandora walked back into the bedroom with two glasses of bourbon and sat next to Joe and passed him his glass before taking a pack of cigarettes and a lighter out of her dressing gown pocket. She took two out passing one to Joe. He put it between his lips, he lit Mistress Vandora's cigarette then his own. She got a small glass ashtray from her bedside cabinet and put it on the bed between them, smiling at Joe as she took a drag and blew smoke rings over him. He smiled back at her before taking a drag of his cigarette.

"So slave how do you and Cynthia know each other?", said

Mistress Vandora taking a long drag of her cigarette and blowing smoke rings.

"I met her through my older sister when I was sixteen Mistress. Her pussy was the first one I saw and she took my virginity. She allowed me to worship her pussy for eight months before she moved to London until I met you. I've been unable to find another woman who's willing to let me worship her like you and Cynthia. I had a one night stand with a girl named Chevaugn. She let me lick her pussy and fuck her several times but she said I was too obsessed with pussy", said Joe smiling in-between taking drags of his cigarette.

"That's nonsense slave. You just appreciate pussy. You love the taste of it and the smell of it. I think I know Chevaugn. Is she by any chance a waitress?", said Mistress Vandora.

"Yes Mistress. She is. I met her at a club near where she works. May I ask how you know her?" said Joe more than a little curious about how Mistress Vandora would know Chevaugn. As far as he knew she didn't go to fetish clubs.

"Let's just say she used to be pretty good at letting men worship her pussy for a while. Then she started to complain so I kicked her out", said Mistress Vandora.

"I see Mistress well I've got two women who love having their pussies worshiped. I'm willing to worship pussy 24/7. I can't get enough of it. As I've said before, it's become a fetish for me. My fetish fantasies are coming true with you and Cynthia. It's going to be a wonderful adventure for me being a live in slave", said Joe finishing off his cigarette and putting it out before sipping his bourbon.

"Yes it will be slave, let's get some sleep. We will continue in the morning", said Mistress Vandora downing her bourbon and laying down next to Joe.

He quickly downed the rest of his bourbon, putting his glass on the bedside cabinet next to Mistress Vandora. He laid down turning off the light, slowly drifting off into a blissful sleep and dreaming of pussy worship and being a live-in slave for Mistress Vandora and Cynthia.

The next morning Joe woke to find himself alone in the bed. He got out and went to look for Mistress Vandora and Cynthia. He stopped outside the bathroom hearing voices, recognizing them as Mistress Vandora and Cynthia. He opened the bathroom door. His eyes lit up as he saw them both naked. His cock rock hard as he looked at their smooth pussies. Eager to be allowed to worship them over and over again.

"Come here slave", said Cynthia licking her full lips suggestively as he fingers trailed down her stomach to her pussy. Joe walked over to Cynthia.

"Kneel on the floor and worship my pussy. In fact I've got a better idea. Let us test how good a slave you are. I need my morning piss. Your tongue will serve to clean me up as well as licking me till I cum", said Cynthia a wicked glint in her eyes.

Joe knelt on the floor and let Cynthia squat over his face. She spread her pussy lips wide as she began to piss. The warm golden liquid covering his face. He closed his eyes and waited to be allowed to lick her pussy clean and make her cum in his mouth. Cynthia pushed his face against her pussy licking her full lips suggestively as she looked down at Joe knelt on the floor.

"Lick me clean slave. Worship my pussy with that expert tongue of yours", said Cynthia.

Joe began to lick Cynthia's pussy running his tongue over every inch of it before gently parting her pussy lips and pushing his tongue inside. Licking her hard and deep and sucking on her clitoris. She moaned with pleasure, grinding her pussy against his tongue. He pushed it deeper inside her pussy and began tongue fucking her, hard and deep. She screamed with pleasure. Her legs shaking as she reached a shuddering climax. Her juices filling his mouth. He licked her clean, lapping up every last drop of her cum. Savoring the taste of it. He couldn't get enough of it. If this was his last meal he would be gorging himself on it. If it his last drink he'd be sipping it and making it last. Nothing compared to the taste and smell of pussy.

"Oh god don't stop, make me cum again slave. Show your mistress how much you worship and adore her", said Cynthia breathlessly.

Joe continued licking Cynthia's pussy harder, faster, deeper, making her cum everywhere, her juices filling his mouth and covering his face. He lapped at her pussy getting every last drop of her cum before she pushed him away and knelt beside him running her tongue over his face getting the remainder of her cum off it before pulling him close and kissing him passionately. He responded to her kiss sharing her cum with her before she gently pulled away and stood up. She smiled at Joe then at Mistress Vandora, licking her lips suggestively at them both.

His cock was rock hard. Pre-cum dripped from the tip of it – being allowed to worship pussy – making him hard and horny – he couldn't get enough – it was becoming an addiction.

"My turn now slave", said Mistress Vandora squatting over his face.

He closed his eyes and mouth once more as he felt the warm sensation of piss running down his face. In a seemingly endless stream until finally she finished. He began to lick her clean running his tongue over every inch of her pussy. She quivered a little, her juices trickling into his mouth. He began to lick her hard and deep. She moaned with pleasure pushing his face against her pussy. He pushed his tongue deeper inside, tongue fucking her hard and deep. Quickly bringing her to climax.

He lapped at her pussy getting every last drop of her cum. She rubbed her pussy against his tongue, making it go deeper inside her pussy until the tip nudged against her g-spot. He ran his tongue over her g-spot hard and fast till she squirted in his mouth. Then he ran his tongue over every inch of her pussy till it was clean once more. She gently pushed him away, smiling down at him as he knelt on the bathroom floor.

"Well done slave, you have past your first test. There will be more but for now I will let you and Cynthia get

reacquainted as a treat for being such a good little slave",
said Mistress Vandora smiling.

"Thank you Mistress", said Joe watching as Mistress
Vandora walked out of the bathroom leaving Joe and
Cynthia alone in the bathroom.

"Come with me Joe to my bedroom so we can get
reacquainted", said Cynthia taking his hand and helping
him up.

He smiled at Cynthia's use of his name as opposed to just
calling him slave. They walked out of the bathroom and
into her bedroom, next to Mistress Vandora's master
bedroom. The room was dominated by a black wrought
iron four poster bed with red satin curtains and sheets. She
walked over to the bed with him and let go of his hand
before laying on the bed. He joined her and pulled him
close kissing him passionately before pulling away and
straddling his face. He began to lick her pussy and suck on
her swollen clitoris. She moaned with pleasure, moving
back and forth on his tongue making sure it touched every
part of her pussy as he continued to lick her pussy. Her
pussy juices trickling into his mouth.

"Mm mm, yes don't stop. I want it deeper inside my pussy.
Let me open my pussy for you", said Cynthia reaching
down and spreading her pussy lips for Joe.

He pushed his tongue deep inside her pussy, lapping at her
g-spot while she rubbed her swollen clitoris, moaning with
pleasure.

"Oh god tongue fuck me Joe. I'm going to cum", said

FANTASY

Cynthia breathlessly her head thrown back in ecstasy.

He began to tongue fuck her pussy hard and deep. She held on to his shoulders. Her legs shaking as she reached a shuddering climax filling his mouth with her juices. He ran his tongue over every inch of her pussy, lapping up every drop of her cum, making her cum even more. She lifted herself up and slid down his body. Sitting on his hard cock. It slid inside her easily. She began to bounce on his cock, leaning over and kissing him passionately. Tasting her juices on his tongue as she bounced up and down on his cock faster and harder.

"Oh god, grab my hips and hold me still while you pound my pussy. I need a good hard fuck. This is your treat for worshiping mine and Mistress Vandora's pussies so expertly", she said.

He grabbed her hips holding her still while he pounded her pussy, smiling as he saw Mistress Vandora stood in the doorway rubbing her wet pussy. He continued fucking Cynthia harder, faster, deeper, her legs shaking as she reached a shuddering climax while at the same time he pumped her pussy full of hot sticky cum. His way of thanking Cynthia for allowing him to worship her beautiful wet pussy. He pulled out and let her get off him. She knelt between his cock clean while Mistress Vandora removed her fingers from her wet pussy, licking and sucking them clean as she watched Cynthia sucking his cock clean, licking her lips suggestively at him. Cynthia removed her lips from Joey's cock and got off the bed. Walking over to Mistress Vandora she pulled her close and kissed her passionately. She responded to her kiss sucking her tongue tasting Joey's cum and Cynthia's pussy juices before gently pulling away smiling at Joey as she walked over to the bed joining him. She straddled him, guiding his cock into her wet pussy. She began to ride him, moving back and forth on his cock. Moaning softly and rubbing her clitoris. Joey grabbed Mistress Vandora's hips bouncing her up and down on his cock. She moaned with pleasure, leaning forward and pushing her breasts in his face. He eagerly licked and sucked her nipples while she used her pelvic muscles to squeeze his cock milking him dry. His cum dripping down her thighs. She continued riding him, bouncing up and down on his cock harder and faster. Her legs shaking as she reached a shuddering climax. Her juices squirting everywhere.

She gently got off Joe and laid on the bed next to him, beckoning Cynthia over. She joined Mistress Vandora and Joe on the bed. Kneeling between Mistress Vandora's legs and licking her cum filled pussy. Running her tongue over every inch of it and getting every last drop of his cum, enjoying the combined taste of cum and vagina juice.

"Lick my pussy Joe while I lick Mistress Vandora's. I'm wet and juicy for you. I want to fill your mouth with my cum till it drips down your chin", said Cynthia turning her head and licking her lips suggestively at Joe.

Joe knelt behind Cynthia and began to run his tongue over her wet pussy. She moaned softly pushing her pussy against his tongue. He gently parted her pussy lips pushing his tongue deep inside her pussy. He began to tongue fuck her pussy and rub her swollen clitoris. She moaned with pleasure, her juices trickling into his mouth and running down her thighs. Soaking the sheets.

"Oh god yes harder! I'm going to cum don't stop", said Cynthia breathlessly.

Joe tongue fucked Cynthia's wet pussy harder and faster. She screamed with pleasure. Her legs shaking as he brought her to a shuddering climax, filling his mouth with her cum. He kept going making her cum over and over again until she begged him to stop. He licked her clean while she licked Mistress Vandora's pussy clean then she kissed Joe passionately, sharing her cum with him before gently pulling away and kissing Mistress Vandora passionately.

The three of them laid on the bed together getting their energy back. Later that day Joe worshiped both Cynthia and Mistress Vandora's pussies once again before they took a shower together enjoying a passionate three way kiss before Cynthia got out of the shower and got herself dried.

"I have some business I need to take care of. I will be back later slave. Mistress Vandora will take care of you while I'm gone and I think Charlotte will be calling round later. She's into pussy worship too. Her clitoris is pierced as well, and her pussy lips so she's very sensitive down there. You'll have her climaxing over and over again", said Cynthia before going back into the bedroom and getting dressed, leaving Joe in the capable hands of Mistress Vandora.

"Well slave, I have you to myself – for a while at least.

Let's get dried then we can go back into my bedroom and have some fun. I need my pussy worshiped and fucked as well as my ass and mouth. You're such a good slave you deserve a treat. I know Charlotte will be in heaven with you later", said Mistress Vandora smiling at Joe as they got out of the shower and got dried before walking back into Mistress Vandora's master bedroom.

"Thank you Mistress. I live to worship yours and Cynthia's pussies as well as any other pussy. I love to worship pussy", said Joe following Mistress Vandora over to the bed.

Mistress Vandora laid on the bed legs wide open. Joe joined her on the bed, kneeling between her legs and running his tongue over every inch of her pussy. She put her hands on the back of his head pushing his face against her pussy. He gently parted her pussy lips, pushing his tongue inside and licking her hard and deep and sucking her clitoris. She moaned with pleasure.

"Oh god yes slave, tongue fuck me. Make me cum with your tongue before you fuck me", said Mistress Vandora rubbing her pussy against his tongue. Making it go deeper inside her pussy.

He began to tongue fuck her hard and deep. She screamed with pleasure, her legs shaking as he brought her to a shuddering climax. Her cum filling his mouth. He licked her clean getting every last drop of her cum. Taking his time. Savoring the taste of her cum like a wine expert savors a fine wine. Letting the taste fill his mouth and slide over his taste buds. loving the flavor.

"Fuck me now slave. I need a good hard fuck", said Mistress Vandora gently pushing his face away from her pussy and getting on all fours.

He knelt behind her sliding his cock in her wet pussy. He began to fuck her hard and deep. She moaned with pleasure, pushing back against his cock, taking every inch of his cock in her pussy. He grabbed her hips fucking her harder and deeper. His balls slapping against her ass as he pounded her pussy making her scream with pleasure. Her juices squirting everywhere.

He continued fucking her harder still. Groaning as he climaxed. Pumping her pussy full of hot sticky cum. He gently pulled out. Mistress Vandora turned to face him, kneeling in front of him and sucking his cock clean. He held her head in place and fucked her mouth with hot sticky cum. She swallowed every last drop, sucking his cock clean once again before gently removing her mouth from his cock and getting on all fours once again and spreading her ass cheeks for him. He knelt behind her and slid his cock in her tight asshole. Grabbing her hips and fucking her hard and deep. She screamed with pleasure. Pushing her ass back against his cock. Making it go deeper up inside her. He fucked her harder, deeper, faster. His balls slapping against her cum filled pussy as he pounded her tight little hole. She screamed with pleasure.

"OH GOD YES FILL MY TIGHT HOLE WITH SPUNK", said Mistress Vandora breathlessly.

Joe fucked Mistress Vandora's tight fuck hole harder still. Groaning as he climaxed. Filling her with hot sticky cum till it dripped out down her thighs. He pulled out and lay on the bed next to Mistress Vandora, smiling at her.

"Thank you for that Mistress", said Joe.

"You're welcome slave. We better get cleaned up. Charlotte will be here soon", said Mistress Vandora getting off the bed and walking into the bathroom.

Joe followed her and they had a shower together cleaning themselves up before getting dried and walking back into the bedroom. Mistress Vandora opened her wardrobe and took out a pair of black leather trousers, a black leather corset style top, black thigh high boots with stiletto heels, a pair of black leather trousers and a black dog collar. She put them on the bed and got herself dressed while Joe put his leather trousers on along with his shoes. Then she put his dog collar on before sitting on the edge of the bed and putting her boots on and zipping them up. She stood up and walked towards the bedroom door, smiling at Joe and licking her full lips suggestively at him. He smiled back a large bulge in his leather trousers in anticipation of what was to come.

"Let's go downstairs and wait for Charlotte to arrive. I need a cigarette and a glass of bourbon after that session slave. You're my best one yet", said Mistress Vandora walking out of the bedroom.

Joe followed her and they went downstairs into the living room. Mistress Vandora walked over to her drinks cabinet and got a bottle of bourbon and two whiskey glasses. She poured them both a glass of bourbon before getting her cigarettes, lighter and a glass ashtray from a drawer. She walked over to the large leather sofa and sat down, patting the space next to her. Joe sat next to Mistress Vandora and she passed him a glass of bourbon while offering him a cigarette. He took one putting it between his lips and lighting Mistress Vandora's cigarette then his own. She smiled, licking her lips suggestively. Joe smiled back unable to stop staring between her legs. Thinking of their session. He loved worshiping her pussy so much.

"Thank you again Mistress for allowing me to worship your beautiful pussy. I look forward to worshiping Charlotte's pussy. I love worshiping pussy so much", said Joe before taking a long drag of his cigarette blowing smoke rings. A while later the doorbell rang.

"This will be her, now wait here. I'll go and let her in", said Mistress Vandora putting her drink on the table and getting up of the settee and walking out of the living room and towards the front door. Smiling as she saw Charlotte stood on the doorstep dressed in a black halter-neck PVC catsuit which showed off her ample cleavage. Her long brown hair was slicked back in a high ponytail. Her sea blue eyes outlined with black eye-liner. She had her trademark black thigh high stiletto boots on.

"Hi Vandora, it's lovely to see you again. I hear you've got a new slave. I'm in need of someone to worship my pussy", said Charlotte licking her full lips suggestively.

"Hi Charlotte yes I have. Come in, he's in the living room. His name's Joe and he is amazing at worshiping pussy", said Mistress Vandora holding the door open for Charlotte.

She walked in closing the door behind her following Mistress Vandora into the living room, sitting down on the settee next to Joe, spreading her legs wide and unzipping her catsuit between her legs revealing her smooth pussy with its pierced clitoris and pierced pussy lips. Joe was unable to stop himself from staring at her pussy. Wanting to worship it over and over again.

"Worship my pussy slave", said Charlotte licking her full lips suggestively at Joe.

He got up off the settee and knelt between Charlotte's legs. Running his tongue over every inch of her pussy and sucking her clitoris. She moaned with pleasure, her juices filling his mouth. He gently parted her pussy lips and pushed his tongue inside licking her hard and deep. She reached down pushing his face against her pussy. He began to tongue fuck her hard and deep. Her legs shook as she reached a shuddering climax filling his mouth with her cum. He continued licking her pussy bringing her to climax over and over again until she begged him to stop. He was a little reluctant having enjoyed the taste of her pussy but he wanted to please Charlotte so he did as she asked hoping that she would allow him to worship her pussy again later.

"Fuck me slave", said Charlotte gently pushing his face away from her pussy and laying back on the settee.

Joe got undressed and got on top of Charlotte sliding his cock in her wet pussy, putting her legs over his shoulders and fucking her hard and deep. She moaned with pleasure rubbing her pussy against his cock. He fucked her harder, faster, deeper, bringing her to climax over and over again. For the rest of that day Joe worshiped Charlotte, Mistress Vandora and Cynthia's pussies. He loved every minute of it. A week later Joe moved in with Mistress Vandora and Cynthia. He spent his days and nights worshiping their pussies – as well as several other females.

His fetish fantasies had come true. He loved every minute of being allowed to worship pussy 24/7 365 days a year. Nothing compared to the feeling he got.

The Voyeur

Daniel had been a voyeur for as long as he could remember. It had all started when he was 16. The girl across the street from his parents house would deliberately leave the curtains open at night when she was undressing and even when her many male lovers came round. She was two years older than him and at the time he hadn't realized that Shauna was an exhibitionist. He just thought she liked to have the curtains open. He would wait until his parents went to bed then he would get his binoculars out that he'd bought out of his pocket money and kept hidden. He'd get them out of his secret hiding place and stand at his bedroom window watch Shauna as she got undressed. So slowly, he could swear she was putting on a show just for him. He'd stroke his cock slowly while he watched as each item came off. Teasing himself – wanting the pleasure to last.

One night she had two guys around. He'd watched as she'd let both of them fuck her at the same time. He'd cum loads that night. The sight of her being fucked had turned him on immensely. Since then he'd watched females as much as he could. Even watching his wife as she'd had sex with her many lovers – both male and female. That was until she left him for her rich older lover and his girlfriend. She moved out and went to London to live with them. That was almost two years ago now. She had filed for divorce which had recently been finalized, a few months after his now ex-wife Tamara had left him. A hot female moved in across the street. He'd begun watching her secretly while masturbating as he watched her stripping naked and pleasuring herself. He'd done this for two whole weeks without her knowing. Then one night he noticed a car pulling up outside her house and a tall muscular shaven headed man getting out. Zara had greeted him at the door in a red and black micro mini skirt, black fishnet top no bra underneath and black thigh high boots. It was obvious to Daniel that he was her lover as she'd pulled him inside and kissed him passionately before closing the door.

A while later Daniel observed them in the living room. The shaven headed male obviously didn't mind people watching as he fucked Zara right in front of the window. Daniel had masturbated several times that night. He hadn't realized it but Zara had seen him watching her. The next day she came over to see him making the excuse that she needed some milk. She was dressed in a short denim skirt that barely covered her ass, a red low cut vest top that showed off her ample cleavage and black thigh high boots. Her long black curly hair cascading down her back. Her large brown eyes emphasized by black eye-liner and her full lips showed off by her glossy red lipstick.

She had a wicked glint in her eye as she asked for the milk. He'd asked her to come in as it was a little chilly outside. She'd walked into the living room and sat on the sofa crossing her legs. He could see she wasn't wearing any panties.

"You like to watch don't you Daniel?" she'd said.

"Y… yes I do" Daniel had said back to her nervously

stuttering as he looked at Zara.

She'd uncrossed her legs and spread them wide laying back a little and sliding her fingers in her pussy. Fingering herself deep and hard. Daniels cock had gone instantly hard as she continued to finger herself. Licking her full lips suggestively noticing his bulge.

"Mm mm, you really do like to watch don't you big boy? Now how about I get a camera put in each room in my house and you get a monitor so that you can watch me get fucked by my many lovers? You see I love being watched. It turns me on knowing people are getting off on me being fucked, sucking cock, licking pussy... god I'm getting horny just thinking about it. I wish you'd do more than watch me Daniel. You're so damn hot and it's a shame to let such a big hard cock go to waste", Zara had said removing her fingers from her pussy and getting up off the sofa before getting on her hands and knees and crawling over to Daniel. Kneeling in front of him, her hand sliding towards his crotch and unzipping his jeans.

"Wait let me set up my camcorder so I can watch us later", Daniel had said before getting his digital camcorder from a box beneath the TV unit. He'd set it up then walked back over to Zara.

"You can continue now sexy. I must admit I find you attractive" Daniel had said before taking his shirt off revealing his tanned muscular physique and his many tattoos.

Zara had hungrily pulled down his jeans and boxer shorts

and took his cock in her mouth — expertly sucking him hard and deep. She took the full length of his cock in her mouth, her tongue running over the tip as she deep-throated him. He groaned — his body arched as she brought him to climax. He'd pumped her throat full of hot sticky cum. She'd swallowed every last drop, sucking him clean before laying down on the floor and letting him return the favor which he'd done eagerly. He'd expertly brought her to climax with his tongue then they'd stripped each other naked. He'd got her on all fours and fucked her pussy and ass hard and deep. Filling both holes with cum. Then she'd gently pushed him on to his back and straddled him. Riding his cock and pushing her tits in his face. He'd sucked her nipples like a hungry baby and bounced her up and down. She'd screamed with pleasure. Squirting everywhere while he pumped her full of cum till it dripped down her thighs. Then she got off him and had him wank over her tits and pussy. Then they'd switched off the camera and gone upstairs to the bathroom and had a shower together, washing each other clean before getting out and drying each other off. Then they went back downstairs and Zara got dressed and left as if nothing had happened.

He'd watched the video of them over and over again. Masturbating several times. That had been two weeks ago. Since then Zara had got cameras fitted in each room in discreet places so only her and Daniel knew they were there. Daniel had got a monitor so he could watch Zara. She had not disappointed him. Putting on a hot show for him as she sucked cock, licked pussy and got fucked in every possible position. Getting Daniel's cock rock hard constantly. He'd lost track of the number of times he'd cum over watching Zara. Today was no exception. Hhe'd looked out of the living room window and seen a red Porshe pulling up outside Zara's house. A tall dark haired male and a busty blonde, both dressed in shiny black skin-tight latex had stepped out of the car. The female had a catsuit on that clung to every curve and thigh high boots with a stiletto heel while the man had latex trousers and a matching latex vest on along with black ankle boots. He watched as they walked up the steps to the front door. Zara opened the door dressed in a shiny red skin-tight latex catsuit and matching shiny red thigh boots. Her full lips emphasized by glossy red lipstick. She'd shared a passionate three way kiss with them before the three of them had walked into her house and into the living room.

Daniel sat at his desk in the lounge unzipping his jeans and taking out his hard cock. Stroking it slowly as he watched Zara and the other female. Taking turns to suck the male's cock. Then the male had unzipped Zara's catsuit between her legs and laid her on the sofa – legs wide open. He licked her pussy while the female unzipped the top of Zara's catsuit revealing her breasts. She leaned over sucking and licking her nipples while unzipping her own catsuit between her legs and rubbing her wet pussy. The two women moaned with pleasure. The male removed his tongue from Zara's pussy and pulled her down towards him, ramming his hard cock in her wet pussy and fucking her hard and deep while the female squatted over her face rubbing her pussy against her lips. Zara licked her pussy while the male fucked her harder and deeper. Daniel could feel his balls swelling as they filled with cum. He was ready to explode. He slowed his pace down wanting the pleasure to last – although it was almost impossible as he watched

Zara being fucked. The male put Zara's legs over his shoulders, pushing the full length of his cock in her wet pussy, his balls slapping against her ass. He pounded her pussy while the female's legs shook as Zara brought her to a shuddering climax. Her juices filling her mouth. She licked her clean then the female got off Zara's face and sat next to her, kissing her passionately and sucking her tongue before pulling away and getting a very large dildo from a cupboard in the corner of the living room.

She walked over to the settee with it and sat with her knees bent, legs wide open. She grabbed the dildo with both hands and fucked herself with it – moaning in unison with Zara who was on the brink of climax as was Daniel.

He couldn't hold back any longer. He stroked his cock harder and faster. His cum squirting everywhere while at the same time on the screen. He saw Zara's legs shaking as she climaxed. Her juices squirting everywhere. The male pulled out off her pussy and got up of the floor. He looked over at the blonde and beckoning her over to him. She removed the dildo from her pussy and walked over. He bent her over the settee in front of Zara, ramming his cock in her wet pussy, fucking her hard and deep while she licked Zara's wet pussy – moaning with pleasure as they climaxed over and over again. The male pounded the blonde's pussy harder and faster. From the look on his face he was ready to explode. He pulled out of her pussy and got Zara and the blonde to kneel in front of him while he masturbated over their open mouths, sharing his cum between them. They swallowed every drop, taking turns to suck him clean before they kissed passionately sharing thick cum. Then the three of them went upstairs.

Daniel watched in anticipation as he waited to see what would happen. He didn't have to wait long as a few minutes later they walked into the bathroom, hungrily undressing each other before getting in the shower and washing each other's naked bodies clean. Then they got out and dried off before going into the bedroom. Daniels eyes took in every detail as he watched the male gently pushing Zara and the blonde on to the bed. He joined them and cuffed their hands above their heads. Then he took turns fucking them in all three holes. Filling them with his hot sticky cum. Then he unfastened their cuffs and got a large strap-on dildo out of Zara's bedside cabinet. He passed it to Zara and she swiftly put it on while the blonde straddled him, taking his cock in her wet pussy – leaning forward and spreading her ass cheeks. Zara knelt behind her grabbing a bottle of lube from the top of the bedside cabinet and pouring a little on to the dildo lubing it up before pushing it into the blonde's tight hole grabbing her hips and fucking her tight hole while the male simultaneously fucked her pussy.

Zara and the blonde moaned in unison. She reached round and squeezed the blonde's breasts pinching her nipples while she pounded her tight hole – making her scream with pleasure. She bounced on the male's cock. Daniel stroked his cock as he watched the three of them. He could tell Zara and the blonde were getting close to climax. He wanted to cum with them. He gradually built up his speed as Zara and the male fucked the blonde harder still. She screamed with pleasure. Her legs shaking at the same as the blonde. Their juices squirting everywhere while Daniel squirted his cum all over his stomach. He grabbed a wet wipe and cleaned himself up while he watched as Zara pulled the dildo out of the blonde's tight hole wiping it clean before taking it off. Then she swapped places with her, passing her the strap-on while she straddled the male. Pushing his cock in her wet pussy and leaning forward – spreading her ass cheeks. The blonde put on the strap-on and knelt behind Zara pushing the full length of the dildo in her tight hole. Grabbing her hips and fucking her hard and deep while she bounced on the males cock. The two women moaned in unison. Daniel couldn't help himself from stroking his cock again. Zara turned him on so much putting on a real hardcore show for him. He could feel his balls filling with cum once again as he watched Zara being fucked in both holes. Her legs shaking violently as they brought her to another shuddering climax while at the same time the blonde reached climax – their juices squirting everywhere. Zara got off the male while the blonde removed the dildo from Zara's tight hole. They laid on the bed next to each other. This time the male masturbated over their tits and pussies covering them with his cum. Daniel stroked his cock hard and fast. Squirting his cum everywhere as he watched Zara and the blonde suck the males cock clean then lick the cum off each other's tits and pussies.

Then the male and the blonde left Zara on the bed and went downstairs, getting dressed and walking out the front door. Zara laid on the bed getting her breathe back before having a shower and getting dried. Then she went downstairs grabbing her catsuit and putting it back on along with her boots before walking out of her front door. Daniel suddenly realized she was coming over to his as he saw her walking across the road. He wiped his cock and his hands clean and put his cock away just as she knocked on the door he opened it and smiled.

"Come in sexy I loved the show so much", said Daniel quickly closing the door behind Zara.

"Good I'm glad Cain and Becky are so hot. They love rough kinky sex which is just what I needed today. I have many lovers that cater to my every mood and need", said Zara slowly unzipping her catsuit.

"Mm mm I could tell you were loving every minute of it. Come here you sexy exhibitionist" said Daniel pulling Zara against him and kissing her passionately. She rubbed herself against his cock through his jeans. Pressing her tits against his bare chest.

"Oh god I want you right now", said Zara pulling away from Daniel and walking into the living room.

He followed her in unzipping her catsuit between her legs and bending her over the settee roughly, hurriedly unzipping his jeans and pulling his cock out. Ramming it in her wet pussy. Grabbing her hips and fucking her hard and deep. She moaned with pleasure, grinding her pussy against his cock. He pushed the full length of his cock in her wet pussy, pounding her harder, deeper, faster. His balls slapping against her ass. She screamed with pleasure. Her hands grabbing the edge of the settee to steady herself as she reached a shuddering climax. Her juices squirting everywhere. He continued fucking her harder still. Groaning as he reached climax. Pumping her full of his hot sticky cum until it dripped down her thighs. He gently pulled out and turned her to face him. She sank to her knees eagerly sucking his cock clean.

"Oh god Daniel that was so good. I want more lets go into the kitchen next. I'm so horny. I can't get enough of you and I know you're horny too", said Zara removing her lips from Daniels cock and taking off her boots before stepping out of her catsuit.

"Oh Zara you make me so horny. I didn't even need to film us this time. Watching you got me so horny. I came loads I could fuck you all night. I'm so horny", said Daniel following Zara into the kitchen and hurriedly undressing himself.

She laid down on the floor, her legs wide open, licking her lips suggestively. He got on top of her, sliding his cock in her tight hole and putting her legs over his shoulders. She screamed with pleasure as he fucked her tight hole hard and deep. He leaned over licking, sucking, and gently biting her nipples while he pounded her tight hole.

"OH GOD YES FILL MY ASS WITH SPUNK", said Zara.

Daniel fucked Zara harder still, groaning as he reached climax. Filling her tight hole with his hot sticky cum. He gently pulled out and helped her up taking her hand and leading her out of the kitchen and through the lounge. They walked towards the stairs and headed up to the bathroom. He switched the shower on. They got in washing each other's naked bodies paying extra special attention to each other's intimate areas. Then Daniel gently pushed Zara against the shower screen and kissed her passionately. Wrapping her legs around his waist and sliding his cock in her wet pussy. She bounced on his cock moaning with pleasure. Her juices running out over his cock and balls. He fucked her harder and deeper, his balls slapping against her ass. She screamed with pleasure holding on to his shoulders as she reached another shuddering climax. He carefully got out of the shower – his cock still in her pussy and grabbed a large towel, taking her into the bedroom and laying the towel on the bed.

He laid down removing her legs from around his waist and putting them over his shoulders. Fucking her harder than ever. Making her scream with pleasure as he brought her to climax over and over again until she couldn't take any more. He pulled out of her pussy and laid on the bed letting her sit on his face and lean forward – taking his cock in her mouth. She deep-throated him while he licked her pussy clean. Her expert mouth making his cock swell. He fucked her throat hard and fast till he shot his load. Filling her mouth with cum until it dripped down her chin. She swallowed every last drop – sucking him clean before scooping the rest up off her chin with her fingers. Sucking them clean.

"Oh Daniel that was amazing I need a drink and a cigarette after that", said Zara breathlessly.

"I'll get us a glass of bourbon and my cigarettes from downstairs. Wait here and get your breathe back. You know how to wear a man out. Mind you I know later I'll be wanting to fuck you some more, you're irresistible. I wish my ex-wife had been more like you", said Daniel putting on a black satin dressing gown.

He went downstairs and into the lounge, opening his mini bar and getting a bottle of bourbon and two glasses. He poured them both a glass of bourbon then put the lid on and put the bottle back before grabbing his cigarettes. He picked up the two glasses of bourbon and taking them upstairs, he smiled as he looked at Zara laid on the bed lazily running her hands over her body. She sat up and got the small glass ashtray off the bedside cabinet, placing it on the bed next to her, smiling at Daniel.

He placed the glasses of bourbon on the bedside cabinet and sat next to Zara. He took two cigarettes out of the pack and passed one to Zara. She put it between her lips and he lit it before lighting his own.

"This is the beginning of a new adventure for me Zara. The idea of watching you get fucked and having horny fun with men and women then coming over and fucking me is hot. If my wife had paid this much attention to me, well let's just say things would be very different. Anyway lets raise a toast to a new adventure and lots more horny fun", said Daniel passing Zara her glass of bourbon and raising his glass.

"To new adventures and lots more horny fun cheers", said Zara.

"Cheers", said Daniel clinking his glass against Zara's.

"There will be plenty more horny fun. I better go soon. Jaiden the tall skinhead will be coming over later. He's my bit of rough. He loves to fuck me roughly, pull my hair, spank my ass, pull on my nipples…", said Zara.

"I've noticed that. I've also noticed how much you love it. Let's drink up and smoke these cigarettes. All this dirty chat is making me horny", said Daniel, downing his bourbon and putting his glass down before finishing off his cigarette and putting it out.

He watched Zara down hers and finish her cigarette before stubbing it out. He took her empty glass off her and the ashtray and put them on his bedside cabinet.

"Come ride me Zara I want to fuck you again. before you go", said Daniel his eyes wandering up and down her naked body. she straddled him taking his hard cock in her wet pussy.

"Cum in my mouth this time. Jaiden doesn't like me to have another man's spunk in my pussy or ass" said Zara.

"I'll fill that mouth of yours with my spunk then" said Daniel.

Zara bounced up and down on Daniels cock hard and fast, moaning with pleasure. He sat up a little sucking, licking, and gently biting her nipples while she bounced on his cock faster and harder, screaming with pleasure. Daniel grabbed Zara ass bouncing her up and down on his cock harder and faster. She screamed with pleasure. Her legs shaking as she reached a shuddering climax. Her juices squirting everywhere.

"Suck me Zara I'm close to exploding", said Daniel.

Zara got off Daniels cock and knelt in front of him taking his cock in her mouth and deep-throating him. His body arched as she expertly brought him to climax. Shooting his load in her mouth till it dripped down her chin. She swallowed every drop, sucking him clean before scooping the remainder off her chin. Sucking and licking her fingers clean.

"I better get dressed and get home. I need to shower and get changed before Jaiden arrives. He likes me dressed in sluttish outfits. You can watch of course. Enjoy the show", said Zara getting off the bed and going downstairs.

Daniel followed her watching as she put her catsuit and boots back on. Then he let her out before going into the kitchen and making himself a coffee. Then he quickly ran upstairs and got his cigarettes and lighter. Before coming down and sitting at his desk. He took a cigarette out of the pack and lit it, taking a long drag before blowing out the smoke as he watched the screen.

A while later Zara appeared on the screen on front of him. She was in her bedroom putting on a short denim skirt that barely covered her ass and a red low cut halter neck top that showed off her ample cleavage. She left her hair loose and put black knee high boots with stiletto heels on. Daniel watched the screen as Zara walked into the lounge and sat on the settee and lit a cigarette, her legs crossed. He saw glimpses of her pussy beneath her skirt his cock getting hard. A while later she walked out of the living room. Daniel looked out of his living room window and saw Jaiden walking up the steps to Zara's front door. She opened it pulling him inside and kissing him passionately before shutting the door behind him. Jaiden roughly pushed Zara on to the settee and positioned her so that she was near the edge then he hurriedly unzipped his jeans and pulled them down his cock rock hard. He rammed it in her wet pussy making her scream with pleasure, grabbing her hips and fucking her hard and deep. She moaned with pleasure, pushing her top up over her tits. He leaned over licking, sucking, and biting her nipples as he pounded her pussy. She screamed with pleasure. Daniel unfastened his dressing gown giving himself better access to his cock and began to wank slowly, not wanting to cum too soon. He wanted the pleasure to last as long as possible.

As he continued to watch the screen Jaiden slid the full length of his cock in Zara's pussy, his balls slapping against her ass as he fucked her harder still. Her legs shaking as she reached a shuddering climax. Her juices squirting everywhere. Daniel couldn't take any more his cock swelled in his hand. He was ready to explode once again. He masturbated harder and faster. Shooting his load everywhere. He continued till he'd got every last drop then he cleaned himself up, watching as Jaiden continued fucking Zara. His body arched as he climaxed filling her pussy with his hot sticky cum till it dripped down her thighs. He pulled out and got her to kneel in front of him. She eagerly sucked his cock clean then he got her to kneel on all fours and spread her ass cheeks ramming his cock in her tight hole. Fucking her hard and deep and pulling her hair roughly. She screamed with pleasure. He began to spank her ass hard with his other hand making her scream louder with pleasure. Pushing her ass back against his cock. Taking every last inch of his cock in her tight hole. His balls slapping against her pussy as he fucked her tight hole harder still until he pumped her full of hot sticky cum till it dripped out of her tight hole and down to her pussy – mixing with her juices. He slid four fingers in her cum soaked pussy getting them wet and sticky before pushing them in her mouth. She eagerly sucked and licked them clean.

Suddenly Jaiden slid his cock out of Zara's tight hole and left the room leaving Zara alone. He returned a short time later with a tall red haired female in a red and black tartan mini skirt, black fishnet top, and black thigh high boots. She was younger than Zara about 18 years old Daniel guessed. He noticed that the red head had pierced nipples which made her nipples stick out. She looked at Zara and licked her lips. He realized her tongue was pierced too. Then she lifted her skirt and showed her pierced clitoris. He couldn't take his eyes off her.

"Zara this is Candy. She's a horny slut too. She loves cock and pussy. She wants a three-sum with us. I know how much you love licking pussy and using toys so before I fuck you both I want you to put on a little show for me. Let me get your box of tricks while you too get to know each other", said Jaiden a wicked glint in his eyes.

Daniel couldn't believe his luck. Two hot women getting it on. Candy walked over to Zara and sat next to her. Turning her to face her and kissing her passionately. She responded to her kiss sliding her hand beneath Candy's short skirt and rubbing her pussy. Candy pulled away from Zara. Removing her hand from her pussy and helping her undress before undressing herself. Then she straddled Zara grinding her pussy against Zara's pussy as they kissed passionately. Their hands wandering over each other's bodies. Zara bent her head and began to lick and suck Candy's pierced nipples. making her moan with pleasure. She smiled as she saw Jaiden stood in the door way fully naked now. A large black box in his hands. He walked into the living room and put it down.

"Now my sexy sluts, time to put on a show for me", said Jaiden sitting on the sofa.

Candy got off Zara and walked over the box getting a large strap-on dildo. She passed it to Zara and helped her put it on. Daniel slowly stroked his cock. He was so horny. He hoped Zara would be over later. He needed a good session. If she brought Candy with her that would be even better. He could feel his balls filling with cum again as he watched Zara getting Candy on all fours and sliding the dildo in her pussy. Grabbing her hips and fucking her hard and deep. The two women moaned with pleasure. Jaiden stroked his cock as he watched them as did Daniel. He'd be needing a cold shower tonight that was for sure.

"Mm mm, fuck her harder Zara spank her ass she loves that", said Jaiden.

Zara fucked Candy harder and deeper. Spanking her ass hard. She screamed with pleasure. Her legs shaking as she reached a shuddering climax. Her juices squirting everywhere. She pulled out and turned Candy to face her. She eagerly licked and sucked the dildo clean before kissing Zara passionately. She kissed her back sucking her tongue.

"Mm mm you horny sluts. my cock needs a good suck.

come here and suck it for me both of you", said Jaiden licking his lips suggestively.

Daniel couldn't believe his luck. Watching two hot women sucking cock. He began to wank his cock again. In his mind's eye he saw Zara and Candy. Sucking his cock milking him dry. Swallowing every last drop of his cum. He stroked his cock harder as he watched Zara and Candy taking turns to suck Jaiden's cock. Taking every inch of it in their mouths – deep-throating him.

"Candy kneel behind Zara and use that pierced tongue on her juicy wet cum filled cunt while I fuck her mouth", said Jaiden.

Candy knelt behind Zara spreading her legs and gently parting her pussy lips while Jaiden put his hand on the back of Zara's head. Holding her in place as he fucked her mouth hard and deep while Candy licked her pussy – flicking her pierced tongue over her clitoris. Daniel masturbated harder. Pre-cum dripping from the tip of his cock while on the on the screen Jaiden filled Zara's mouth with cum. till it dripped down her chin. She swallowed every last drop sucking him clean while Candy licked the cum from her pussy then began to tongue fuck her hard and deep, quickly bringing her to climax. Her juices filling her mouth. She licked her clean then turned Zara to face her and kissed her passionately. Sharing cum with her before gently pulling away then Jaiden stood up and helped Candy and Zara up. Taking their hands and leading them out of the living room. Daniel stopped stroking his cock a moment while he waited for the three of them to go upstairs. A few minutes later they walked into Zara's bedroom. Jaiden got on the bed and beckoned Zara and Candy to join him. They laid either side of him.

"Sit on my cock Candy. Zara get that nice big dildo for me. The one you keep in the bottom of the wardrobe and some baby oil. I want you to open up Candy's tight hole for me. She's not had my cock fully inside her as yet. even though she wants it badly", said Jaiden.

Candy straddled Jaiden sliding his cock in her wet pussy while Zara got off the bed and got a large flesh colored real feel dildo and a bottle of baby oil from the bottom of the wardrobe. She got back on the bed pouring a little oil on the dildo, lubing it up before spreading Candy's ass cheeks and slowly sliding it inch by inch in Candy's tight hole. It soon opened up allowing Zara to push the dildo further inside. Spreading her hole wider to accommodate its width and length. She screamed with pleasure as Zara fucked her tight hole and Jaiden simultaneously fucked her wet pussy. Her legs shaking as she reached a shuddering climax and squirting everywhere. It was too much for Daniel. He shot his load all over his hands and stomach. He cleaned himself up once again and for the rest of that afternoon Jaiden took turns with both women. He went downstairs and got dressed and left Zara's house. A while later Daniels doorbell rang. He quickly fastened his dressing gown and opened the door smiling as he saw Zara and Candy.

"Come in ladies I enjoyed the show you got me so horny", said Daniel.

"Mm mm, I can tell we've come round to help you out",

said Zara looking at Daniels cock poking through the front of his dressing gown as she walked into his house followed by Candy. Daniel shut the door behind them. Then the three of them walked into the living room. He unfastened his dressing gown taking it off before sitting on the settee.

"Come and suck my cock ladies. I've been wanting your lips round it since I watched you both sucking Jaiden's cock", said Daniel licking his lips suggestively at Zara and Candy.

They knelt in front of him. Taking turns to suck his cock. Deep-throating him and running their tongues over his shaft as well as the tip. Suddenly the doorbell went. Zara and Candy reluctantly stopped what they were doing and Daniel quickly put his dressing gown back on, fastening it before walking out of the living room and opening the door. A look of shock on his face as he took in the tall dark haired woman stood on the steps. He recognized his ex-wife. Despite her hair being slightly longer and her being dressed in a very sluttish outfit which she had never worn all the years they were married.

"Tamara what are you doing here? I hope you're not going to be long as I've got company", said Daniel. Tamara smiled a wicked grin in her eyes.

"Let me in Daniel I'm sorry I left you for Richard. He's thrown me out and I have a little confession to make", said Tamara licking her full lips suggestively. He let her in reluctantly, unable to stop himself from taking in every inch of her body – she was looking good. He quickly shut the door behind her.

"What's this confession? Be quick as I said I've got company. I don't want to keep them waiting," said Daniel. Tamara smiled.

"I know what you've been up to with Zara and Candy etc. the idea of watching you with another woman or two gets me so horny and wet. I've missed you gorgeous let's try again", said Tamara.

"Come watch us then if you must. I will think about it. you always did know how to turn me on. I loved watching you. but you never let me fuck you or join in afterward", said Daniel walking into the room where Zara and Candy were busy undressing each other.

"This is my ex wife Tamara. She wants to watch me with you both. I hope that's okay my sexy exhibitionists?" said Daniel sitting back down on the settee.

"Mm mm of course it its Daniel", said Zara kneeling back in front of Daniel and taking his cock in her mouth while Candy knelt next to her. They took it turns sucking his cock while Tamara sat next to Daniel pushing her skirt up over her ass and spreading her legs wide and rubbing her wet pussy while she watched the two women sucking Daniels cock.

"Oh god I'm going explode. Open your mouths ladies ready for my spunk", said Daniel.

Zara and Candy opened there mouths wide while Daniel masturbated over their mouths hard and fast. His body arched as he climaxed sharing his cum between their mouths. They swallowed every last drop, sucking him clean before kissing passionately. Tamara finger fucked herself hard and deep as she watched the two women.

"Oh Daniel I'm horny I need your cock so badly watching you isn't enough for me", said Tamara.

"Get on all fours on the floor then Tamara. I'll fuck you first while Zara and Candy pleasure each other", said Daniel.

Tamara hurriedly stripped naked and knelt on all fours on the floor for Daniel. He knelt behind her ramming his cock in her wet pussy. Grabbing her hips and fucking her hard and deep. She moaned with pleasure. Zara got dressed and smiled at Daniel.

"I'm going to go and get a couple of strap-on from mine gorgeous. I won't be long", said Zara walking out of the living room and out of Daniels and across the road to her house.

Daniel fucked Tamara harder and faster. She screamed with pleasure. Her legs shaking as he expertly brought her to a shuddering climax, her juices squirting everywhere. Candy laid in front of Tamara pushing her head towards her wet pussy. She licked her wet pussy hard and deep while Daniel pounded her wet pussy harder, deeper, faster, groaning as he reached his own climax. Filling her pussy with his hot sticky cum till it dripped down her thighs just as Zara walked into the living room carrying two strap-on dildos.

She stripped naked once again and sat next to Candy

kissing her passionately while Daniel pulled out of Tamara's pussy turning her round to face him. She eagerly sucked his cock clean. She took one of the strap-on dildos from Zara and put it on. Zara gently pulled away from Candy and gently pushed Daniel on to his back and straddled him Tamara knelt behind her pushing the dildo in her wet pussy, lubing it up before pushing her forward a little and spreading her ass cheeks, pushing the dildo in her tight hole. Grabbing her hips and fucking her hard and deep while she bounced on Daniels cock and Candy knelt behind her – pushing her strap-on dildo into Tamara's tight hole. Fucking her hard and deep. The three women moaning in unison.

Daniel was in heaven. Despite his ex wife turning up. He realized that from now on things would be better. For the rest of that night. He fucked the three women in every hole. Filling them with hot sticky cum. Not wanting the fun to end. Although he didn't think it would any time soon. They were having far too much fun and were all very satisfied plus the variety kept things interesting. They all like different kinds of sex which Daniel found very exciting. It would be dull if they all liked the same thing. The excitement kept him interested for years to come.

Medical Fantasies

Nick had been in hospital for three weeks now after a car accident. He'd flirted with the nurse who looked after him on several occasions. Enjoying it when she gave him his bed bath. She paid extra special attention to his cock. He had fantasied over her so many times. She loved to tease, leaning over him so that he could see down her nurses dress and she would accidentally on purpose drop something on the floor so she had to bend over, giving him a good view of her tiny thong and her pert ass. If his legs and arms hadn't been in cast he'd have walked over to her and pulled her thong to one side before pushing his cock in her pussy and fucking her hard and deep. That night Nurse Amy came to give Nick his expected bed bath. She was wearing stockings for him. His cock became instantly hard.

"Hi Amy you sexy little tease. How about you come here and nurse my cock better. It needs some TLC", said Nick.

"You are naughty Nick", said Nurse Amy closing the curtains then she began to slowly unzip her nurses dress.

"Oh Amy I can't help it, you tease me so much. You get me all hard and horny", said Nick licking his lips as he looked at Amy taking off her nurses dress revealing black fishnet hold-ups; her breasts and pussy bare.

"Oh Nick, I shouldn't be doing this but I've been wanting to ride that big hard cock. since I first saw it. I can't control myself any longer. I have to have it inside me", said Nurse Amy getting on the hospital bed and straddling Nick.

She pushed his cock in her wet pussy then began to ride him, moaning with pleasure. She leaned over and kissed Nick passionately. He kissed her back, wishing he could caress her breasts and finger fuck her pussy.

"Oh god Amy harder baby bounce on my cock", said Nick breathlessly.

Amy bounced up and down on Nick's cock harder and faster – screaming with pleasure. Her legs shaking as she reached a shuddering climax. Her juices squirting out over Nick's cock and balls and down her thighs. Nick groaned as he reached his own climax filling Amy's pussy with his hot sticky cum. She gently got off him and washed him clean. Before getting dressed.

"I'll come back for more in the morning. Your pots come off tomorrow so you can get those hands on me", said Amy as she walked out of Nick's cubicle.

"Bye sexy, I can't wait to get my hands on you. Every sexy inch of you", said Nick.

As Nick slept that night he dreamt about fucking Amy in every position possible. She begged him for more and he obliged. He hoped that one day his dream would come true. She was his ultimate fantasy come true. A hot nurse who loved cock what more could he ask for. The next morning Dr Phillips came to see Nick.

"Good morning Nick. It's time for those casts to come

off. We'll get you down to the other ward and get them off then I can see how well your healing", said Dr Phillips helping Nick into a wheelchair and wheeling him down to another ward. He helped Nick onto a bed and got a metal tool which he used to cut off the casts.

"You're healing well Nick", said Dr Phillips smiling.

"I'm so happy doctor. When will I be able to go home?" asked Nick.

"You will need some physio but I think a couple more weeks and you should be fully healed and ready to", said Dr Phillips as he cleaned Nicks legs and arms.

Then he helped him into the wheelchair again and wheeled him back to his ward. Nick got on to his bed and made himself comfortable.

"You rest Nick. Stacy will be round to see you later today. she will assess you and decide what exercises will suit you best", said Dr Phillips.

"I'm so glad you chose a female physio", said Nick.

"I know you will like her. She's hot with long legs, blonde hair, pert ass, full lips and a nice pair of tits", said Dr Phillips.

"I can't wait to meet her", said Nick.

Dr Phillips left Nick to rest while he went on his rounds. Later that day Stacy the physiotherapist came to see Nick. He couldn't help but notice the tight outfit she was wearing. It showed off her curvaceous figure a treat.

"Hi Nick, I'm Stacy. I'll be doing your physio for the next two weeks", said Stacy sitting on the edge of the bed, her thigh brushing against Nick's. She gently moved his left foot from side to side.

"Hi Stacy I look forward to working with you", said Nick.

"Tell me if this hurts at all", said Stacy as she gently moved Nick's foot back and forth.

"A little Stacy but you're so gentle and gorgeous. I do have a lot of pain further up. I'm so stiff I need you to help me relax", said Nick.

"With pleasure Nick", said Stacy getting off the bed and shutting the curtains.

She helped Nick out of his pyjamas before undressing herself then she joined Nick on his hospital bed kneeling between his legs and taking his hard cock in her mouth, sucking it hard and deep, moving her mouth up and down.

"Oh Stacy, don't stop. That feels so good", said Nick groaning with pleasure.

Stacy took Nick's cock deeper into her mouth. Sucking him harder then she stopped and moved further up the bed, turning round and sitting over Nick's mouth leaning forward and taking his cock in her mouth once again. Nick began to lick Stacy's pussy hard and deep while she deep throated his cock. He licked her harder and deeper until they both climaxed. Stacy swallowed every last drop of Nick's hot sticky cum while he licked her pussy clean, then she sucked him dry before getting off him and sliding down his body. Straddling him, she gently took hold of his hands and placed them on her breasts. She slid down on to his cock and began to bounce up and down, moaning with pleasure. Nick caressed Stacy's soft breasts, carefully sitting up and taking each nipple in his mouth. Sucking, licking, and gently biting them. Making Stacy scream with pleasure. She bounced up and down harder and faster. Her legs shaking as she reached a shuddering climax. Her juices squirting everywhere. She lifted up and leaned forward spreading her ass cheeks before sliding Nick's cock in her tight ass. Suddenly Nick heard footsteps coming towards his cubicle, then the curtain opened. He smiled as he saw Amy.

"Mmmmm, I see you've met Stacy. I hope you will share with me babes", said Nurse Amy closing the curtain behind her.

"Of course babes but first I want to try this big cock in my tight hole. lick my pussy while he fucks my ass", said Stacy breathlessly.

Amy knelt behind Stacy and licked her wet pussy. Stacy helped Nick to grab her ass and bounce her up and down. He fucked her ass hard and deep. While Amy tongue fucked Stacy's pussy, bringing her to climax. Amy squatted over Nick's face. He licked her wet pussy, while he fucked Stacy harder and deeper, making her scream with pleasure until he filled her tight hole with his hot sticky cum. Stacy got off Nick's cock and Amy got off his face. She moved down the bed and knelt on all fours for Nick.

"Fuck my tight ass now Nick", said Nurse Amy turning her head and licking her lips at Nick as she spread her ass cheeks for him.

He pushed his cock in her tight ass and began to fuck her hard and deep. Stacy fingered her wet pussy as she watched Nick fucking Nurse Amy hard and deep, making her scream with pleasure. He fucked her harder, deeper, faster. Groaning as he reached climax. Filling her tight hole with his hot sticky cum. He gently pulled out.

"Oh ladies that was amazing. Amy you had better give me my bed bath. Then get back to work or you will be in trouble", said Nick.

"It's okay Nick I'm finished for today. We better let you rest but first lets kiss", said Amy gently pulling Nick and Stacy towards her. They shared a three way kiss then Amy and Stacy cleaned Nick up and helped him back into his pyjamas before getting themselves dressed.

"We will have more fun tomorrow. You rest Nick – bye for now", said Amy and Stacy.

"Bye ladies and thank you, I needed that", said Nick as he watched the two women leave his cubicle shutting the curtain behind them.

Nick laid down and closed his eyes gradually falling into a blissful sleep dreaming about Amy and Stacy. His medical fantasies were coming true, he never thought that being in a hospital could be so much fun. All he needed now was a hot female doctor.

The next morning Nick was woken up by footsteps coming from outside his cubicle and two voices. One male which he recognised as Dr Philips voice and the other an unfamiliar female voice. The curtains opened and Dr Philips walked in with a very attractive female doctor with long straight red hair, legs up to her breasts, and from what he could see of them a nice pair of tits.

"Good morning Nick this is Dr Amanda Richards. She's recently started working here. I've got a family emergency so I have booked a couple of weeks off. Amanda will be looking after you. I'm sure she will be gently with you. she's single so you can flirt happily with her. Although I'm sure you will be doing more than that. she's very popular with the male patients and a few select female patients as well as the male staff and a couple of our female staff, namely Stacy and Amy. I will leave you in her very capable hands. I wish you a speedy recovery", said Dr Phillips smiling as he left Nick's cubicle.

"Now Nick, let's get you undressed so I can examine you properly", said Amanda licking her lips suggestively and taking off her white coat.

Nick's eyes popped out as he saw that she was wearing a red lace Basque underneath and stockings. Her smooth shaven pussy on show. She helped Nick out of his pyjamas then she began to run her hands over his body. Starting at his chest and working her way down his stomach. Nick's cock was rock hard.

"Oh doctor my cock needs attention so bad. I want those lips round it", said Nick looking Amanda up and down.

She closed the curtain then she got on the bed moving up to Nick's face. She turned round so her ass was facing him.

Leaning forward and taking the full length of his cock in her mouth. Sucking it hard and deep. Moving her mouth up and down and running her tongue over his shaft. Nick pushed his tongue deep in Amanda's pussy licking her hard and deep. She moaned against his cock making it throb. He managed to lift his hips and fuck her mouth hard and deep, groaning as he climaxed. Coming deep in her throat. She swallowed every drop. Sucking him dry while Nick tongue fucked her pussy hard and deep bringing her to a shuddering climax and her juices running into his mouth. He licked her clean then Amanda got off his face removing her mouth from his cock and moved down his body, straddling Nick and pushing his cock in her wet pussy. She took off her Basque. Helping him sit up and pushing his face against her breasts. He hungrily sucked, licked, and gently bit her nipples while she teased him moving back and forth. Grinding her clitoris against Nick's cock. Moaning with pleasure. She began to ride him faster and harder.

"Oh god Nick I'm going to cum", said Amanda breathlessly. Nick removed his mouth from Amanda's nipples and kissed her passionately she kissed him back for a moment then she pulled away.

"Oh god Nick play with my ass get it ready for your big hard cock. Fuck you're an amazing lover. Amy and Stacy were so right when they told me how big and fat it was and how good it was with you. I hope we can all have fun properly when you recover. Stacy's going to continue your physio in her own special way. She can't get enough of you", said Amanda breathlessly as she helped Nick move his hand down to her ass.

She leaned forward parting her ass cheeks for him. He managed to slide two fingers into her tight hole. Finger fucking her hard and deep while she bounced on his cock harder and faster.

"OH GOD I'M COMING", screamed Amanda her legs shaking as she reached a shuddering climax.

Her juices squirting everywhere. She lifted herself up and let Nick's cock slide out of her pussy then she reached back and gently removed Nick's fingers from her tight ass replacing them with Nick's cock. Taking it all in her tight hole. Nick smiled as he heard Stacy and Amy outside his cubicle.

"Come in ladies the more the merrier", said Nick.

Amy and Stacy opened the curtain and walked in both naked. Except for their red fishnet hold-ups. Stacy had a strap-on dildo on.

"Time for a hot foursome Nick. We all love your cock and want to share it. Let's get you in a better position Amanda so you can be filled in both holes while Amy gets her pussy and ass licked", said Stacy helping Amanda to get on all fours.

She knelt behind her on the bed and pushed the dildo into her wet pussy, grabbing her hips and fucking her while Nick pounded her tight ass. Amy squatted over Nick's face spreading her pussy lips for him. He began to lick her pussy, running his tongue along her wet slit and down to her tight hole. He parted her ass cheeks and slid his tongue in, licking her hard and deep before moving back to her pussy. He went back and forth bringing her to climax over and over again while he fucked Amanda's ass. She screamed with pleasure – her legs shaking as she climaxed, squirting everywhere. He fucked her tight hole harder and deeper while tongue fucking Amy's wet pussy. The three women moaned in unison as they climaxed again and again. Nick groaned as he reached his own climax filling Amanda's tight hole with cum until it dripped down her thighs. He gently pulled out. Laying back and licking Amy's pussy clean. She got off his face and waited while Stacy removed the dildo from Amanda's pussy. She got Amanda to suck it clean then she took off the strap-on and passed it to Amy. Then she straddled Nick taking his cock in her wet pussy while Amy slid the dildo in her tight hole. Amanda took Amy's place over Nick's face. The three women took turns with Nick for the rest of the night until they had worn him out then they let him rest.

That night Nick dreamt of all the fun he'd be having with Amy, Stacy, and Amanda. When he was fully healed he'd be giving them all a good fucking in every position possible and letting them suck his cock. It would be so horny. A few weeks later after several sessions of Physio Nick was allowed to go home. He gave Amy, Stacy and Amanda his mobile number and address inviting them to come over as often as they could. A couple of days after he'd gone home his mobile rang.

"Hello gorgeous. Are you coming over?" said Nick smiling as Stacy's name and photo came up on his phone's screen. "Hello sexy, of course I am. I fancy a one-on-one session with you. I want it dirty and rough. I'm horny as fuck for you. I'm parked in my car not far from yours in a secluded lane with my hand down my wet thong. I'm soaking wet and I need cock", said Stacy.

"Oh god get over here before I cum in my boxers", said Nick. The phone went silent, he realised she'd gone.

A while later Stacy arrived at Nick's house. He let her in closing the door and pushed her against it, ripping off her thong and hurriedly unzipping his jeans. Pulling them down along with his boxers. Then he rammed his cock in her wet pussy, wrapping her legs around his waist. He pushed her top up and sucked on her nipples like a hungry baby, as he fucked her hard and deep. She moaned with pleasure. He held her around the waist and carried her into the dining room. His cock still inside her. He sat her on the table gently laying her down, putting her legs over his shoulders and fucking her harder and deeper. She screamed with pleasure as Nick brought her to climax over and over again. He slid out and helped her down. Turning her around and bending her over. Spreading her ass cheeks and ramming his cock in her tight ass. He fucked her hard and deep. Pounding her tight hole. Making her scream with pleasure. He groaned as he reached his own climax. Pumping her tight hole with his hot sticky cum. He pulled out and turned Stacy round to face him. Kissing her passionately.

She kissed him back pressing herself against him. Nick had one on one sessions with all three women over the next few months. Then on the day of his 30th birthday the three women came over dressed as naughty nurses and took turns taking Nick's cock in all three holes. They spent the night with him, continuing their fun in the morning before they had to go to work. Nick's medical fantasies had all come true. Over the next few months the three women came over to Nicks on a regular basis, sharing his cock their threesomes would get dirtier each time. They made several home-made porn videos. A few months later the three women packed in their jobs and decided to make money making amateur porn videos together – enjoying every minute of their kinky sessions. Stacy continued her physio sessions in her own special way. Her and Nick had several one on one sessions together. She eventually moved in with him followed by the other two women. They would share Nick despite them being a couple although sometimes they would have a one-on-one while Stacy and Amy had their own fun. They had become a couple themselves. They loved to put on a show for Nick, using their toys on each other. Teasing Nick until he had to join in. Fucking each one of them in turn. Filling their pussies and asses with his cum before wanking over their mouths. Afterwards the three women shared a passionate three way kiss, sharing Nick's cum between them.

One day Nick got a letter from the hospital asking him to go in for a check-up. He got dressed and left the three women to have fun while he headed to the hospital. He checked in at the reception and took a seat. A while later a rather hot brunette came over to him.

"Hello Nick I'm Doctor Jodie Mitchell. I'll be doing your check up today. Follow me please I promise to be gentle", said Dr Jodie smiling at Nick he got up and followed her into a small room.

"Take off your clothes and lay on the bed for me please",

said Dr Jodie shutting the room door and locking it.

Nick hurriedly undressed and laid on the bed. His cock rock hard despite having an early morning session with Stacy, Amy and Amanda. Dr Jodie walked over to the bed taking off her coat revealing a red lace Basque and black fishnet stockings. Her smooth pussy on show. She got on the bed and straddled Nick, teasing him as the tip of his cock rubbed against her wet slit. She took off her Basque and leaned over, pushing her breasts in Nick's face. He eagerly sucked, licked, and gently bit her nipples.

"Oh god push my cock in that wet pussy baby. Ride me. I want to fill you with spunk you sexy little tease. I'm going to fuck you like the sluttish doctor that you are", said Nick licking his lips at Dr Jodie.

She lifted up and pushed the full length of his cock in her pussy. She began to ride him, grinding her clitoris against Nick's cock, moaning with pleasure as she bounced up and down on Nick's cock. He grabbed her ass, bouncing her up and down harder and faster. Pushing his cock deeper into her wet pussy. She screamed with pleasure. Her legs shaking as she reached a shuddering climax. Her juices squirting everywhere. Nick held Jodie's hips while he fucked her hard and deep. Pounding her pussy. His balls slapping against her ass. She screamed with pleasure.

"Oh god Nick play with my ass. while you fuck my wet juicy cunt baby", said Jodie breathlessly.

Nick wet his fingers then he slid two of them in Jodie's tight ass. Finger fucking her while he fucked her pussy harder and deeper. Bringing her to another shuddering climax, groaning as he reached his own climax. Pumping her full of hot sticky cum. He gently pulled out and removed his fingers from her tight ass. She got off him and knelt between his legs and took his cock in her mouth, sucking it deep and hard. He groaned with pleasure sitting up on the bed.

"Deep-throat me baby. I want to fill your throat with spunk", said Nick.

Jodie deep throated Nick's cock, wanking him into her mouth until he filled her throat with hot sticky cum. She swallowed every last drop sucking him clean then she got off the bed, standing in front of it and bending over it and spreading her white ass cheeks.

"Fuck my ass baby. Spank me and pull my hair. I want it rough", said Jodie licking her lips suggestively at Nick.

He got off the bed and stood behind Jodie. Ramming his cock in her tight hole. Spanking her ass and pulling her hair roughly as he fucked her hard and deep, making her scream with pleasure. She pushed her ass back against his cock, taking every inch of it in her tight hole. He fucked her harder and deeper, his balls slapping against her pussy – sticking to it. Suddenly there was a knock at the door. Nick stopped for a moment.

"Keep fucking me baby, they will go away", said Jodie. Nick obliged as the knocks got louder.

"Who is it I'm busy", said Jodie.

"It's me Mitzee. I'm here for my training. I'm sorry I'm

late", said Mitzee, the student doctor.

"Just a minute Mitzee. Nick let me get the door. She's a sluttish student doctor. I caught her on her first day sucking one of the doctor's cocks in the staffroom while another fucked her from behind. I gave her a good spanking and licked her juicy wet cunt while she gave mine a good licking. She loved it especially as she got to suck a big cock at the same time", said Jodie.

Nick removed his cock from Jodie's ass and she opened the door for Mitzee, licking her lips as she looked at her, dressed in her usual short skirt and tight vest top no bra. Her hard nipples straining against the material.

"Lock the door you sexy sluttish student doctor. I hope you've remembered my rule", said Jodie.

"Yes Jodie I have", said Mitzee lifting her short skirt up and showing Jodie her smooth shaven pussy. She slid a hand between her legs and rubbed her wet slit as she looked at Nick and Jodie.

"Mmmmm, come here and bend over the bed you dirty little whore of a student doctor. I'm going to fuck that tight ass while Jodie licks your juicy wet cunt", said Nick stroking his hard cock as he looked at Mitzee.

She walked over to the bed and bent over it spreading her ass cheeks for him. He stood behind her and rammed his cock in her tight hole. Fucking her hard and deep while Jodie knelt on the floor and began to lick Mitzee's wet pussy and suck on her clitoris. She moaned with pleasure as Nick and Jodie fucked and licked her harder and deeper., bringing her to a shuddering climax over and over again. Her juices gushing out filling Jodie's mouth and running down her thighs. Jodie licked her clean while Nick pounded her tight ass harder and deeper. Groaning as he reached climax. Filling her tight hole with hot sticky cum till it dripped down her thighs. He pulled out and sat on the bed watching as Jodie and Mitzee tongue fucked each other, bringing each other to climax before they shared a passionate three way kiss with Nick – sharing their cum with him.

"Oh ladies that was so good. what time do you both finish work?" said Nick smiling.

"We're finished Nick. I asked Mitzee to come in as I knew you would love a session. Shall we come back to yours? I think Stacy, Amy and Amanda would love to share us with you. I know Mitzee is eager to have some more fun with the three of them", said Jodie.

"Let's go then ladies. God that was a hot set up", said Nick getting himself dressed.

He waited for Jodie and Mitzee to get ready then the three of them left the hospital and got in Jodie's car. She drove them to Nick's house. When they got to Nick's house Jodie parked up and they got out. Jodie locked the car up then the three of them walked up the drive to the front door. Nick opened the door and they walked in. He shut the door behind them and locked it then he walked upstairs followed by Jodie and Mitzee. They headed into the bedroom where Stacy, Amy, and Amanda were laid naked on the bed, kissing each other and using toys on each other.

"Hello ladies, we've got company. This is going to be one horny session – five hot ladies in one night. It's a good job I've got plenty of stamina!" said Nick stripping naked and laying on the bed next to Stacy.

He watched as Jodie and Mitzee got undressed before joining him on the bed. Mitzee straddled Nick and pushed his cock in her wet pussy, leaning forward and spreading her ass cheeks. Stacy put a strap-on on. She knelt behind Mitzee and pushed the dildo in her tight ass, fucking her hard and deep while she bounced up and down on Nick's cock. Amy sat over Nick's face while Jodie put a strap-on on and fucked Stacy's pussy while Amanda fucked hers. The five women took turns fucking each other and letting Nick fuck all three hot holes as well as licking their wet pussies. He was in heaven. They spent the next few days having dirty fun together. Nick filmed their sessions loving every minute of it, as did the five women. He couldn't have had it better. He had a hot nurse, physiotherapist, two hot doctors and a hot student doctor. All his medical fantasies were coming true. He was in heaven.

As time went on he got Jodie and Mitzee to make some amateur porn videos with him helped by a friend of his who was in the porn industry. They enjoyed it so much that they packed in work and decided to get a bigger house and moved in together. They had a bed specially designed so that the six of them could sleep together at night. Nick couldn't believe his luck. He had five hot women who loved cock. Never in a million years did he imagine that going into hospital could be so good.

He'd always had a thing about uniforms, especially nurses.

The women would put on uniforms for him. They would be a lot shorter than their normal ones but he loved them. It got him so horny seeing them dressed as sluttish nurses and naughty horny little doctors. He would sometimes get Mitzee, who at 18 was the youngest to be a patient. He'd give her a thorough examination then she'd swap roles with him. The fun never stopped. Nick couldn't get enough.

All his medical fantasies were being fulfilled and then some. He was in seventh heaven with his hot ladies. They satisfied him completely.

The Sex Doctor

Sasha laid on her bed, her fingers frantically rubbing her throbbing clitoris For the past three months her pussy had been constantly throbbing. She'd had to masturbate daily but no matter what she did the throbbing wouldn't go away. She never felt fully satisfied. Her ex boyfriend John hadn't been good in bed. She'd had several one night stands since but none of them had satisfied her. She decided to ring her friend Yvonne and ask her advice. She stopped rubbing her clitoris and got her mobile off the bedside cabinet, dialling Yvonne's number. A few minutes later Yvonne answered.

"Hi Sasha babes long time no chat how's the love life?" said Yvonne sounding a little breathless.

"It's none existent. I need your advice with a sexual problem. I'm hoping you can advise me on what to do. I'm having to masturbate on a daily basis but I'm left unsatisfied, no matter what I do my pussy still throbs", said Sasha.

"Oh dear babes you need Dr Andre Patterson A.K.A the sex doctor. He specialises in sexual problems. He helped me out no end. I'll ring him and make an appointment for later today. I'll ring you back in a bit", said Yvonne.

"Thank you Yvonne chat soon", said Sasha.

Later that day Sasha's mobile rang. She smiled as she saw Yvonne's name and picture.

"Hello again Yvonne did you manage to get me an appointment with the sex doctor?" said Sasha.

"Hello Sasha he wants to see you to go and see him right away. I'm on my way over. I'd wear something sexy, he's gorgeous and amazing in bed – plus he'll show you how to pleasure yourself too", said Yvonne.

"I will do babes see you soon", said Sasha before hanging up.

She got her red halter neck mini dress and red thigh high boots out of her wardrobe. She decided to go commando. Her thongs always got soaked through anyway. The low cut neckline of her dress showed off her cleavage a treat. She put her boots on zipping them up then she grabbed her handbag walking downstairs, just in time to get the door. She smiled as she saw her friend Yvonne.

"You look hot babes lets go", said Yvonne.

"So do you Yvonne", said Sasha walking out of the front door. she locked it then followed Yvonne to her car.

She got in the passenger side, shutting the door behind her. Yvonne got in the driver's seat and set off towards the sex clinic where Dr Andre Patterson worked.

"I will drop you off babes. then I'll have to get to work", said Yvonne smiling at Sasha.

"Okay babes I'm a big girl. I'm sure I can handle him", said Sasha smiling back at Yvonne.

A while later they arrived at the sex clinic. Yvonne parked

up and Sasha got out.

"I'll ring you later babes and let you know how I got on", said Sasha giving Yvonne a friendly peck on the cheek before heading towards the clinic.

"Okay babes have fun", said Yvonne before driving away. Sasha walked into the clinic and headed to the reception.

"Hi can I help you?" said Chantelle the receptionist.

"Hi I've got an appointment with Dr Andre Patterson", said Sasha.

"You must be Sasha come with me. He's been waiting for you", said Chantelle walking round to the front of the reception desk and along the corridor. Sasha followed her to a room at the end of the corridor. Chantelle knocked on the door.

"Come in", said Dr Andre Patterson.

Chantelle opened the door and let Sasha walk in. She couldn't help but notice that Dr Andre was incredibly hot.

"Hi you must be Sasha. Strip for me and lay on the bed, legs wide open. I need to examine you intimately so I can find out what's wrong with you", said Dr Andre smiling.

Sasha stripped naked and took off her boots before laying on the bed her legs wide open. Her pussy throbbed intensely. She noticed a large bulge in Dr Andre's tight trousers, she hoped she would get to experience his cock. It had been a while since she'd had a good hard fucking. Dr Andre walked over to Sasha and sat down on a chair next to the bed. He slid a hand between Sasha's legs rubbing it over her smooth pussy. She moaned softly as his fingers moved down to her wet slit. Sliding his fingers inside her. He began to finger her softly.

"Oh doctor that feels so good. I do this every day but my pussy still throbs none stop", said Sasha breathlessly. Dr Andre began to finger Sasha harder and deeper.

"You just need to know how to do it properly Sasha. May I ask when was the last time you climaxed without penetration?" asked Dr Andre.

"That would be about six months ago doctor. I used my fingers and my trusty vibe. It was amazing but when I try that now, it's not as good. Oh god I want to cum", said Sasha.

"You will Sasha you'll be coming over and over. Move up a little for me", said Dr Andre smiling.

Sasha moved up the bed a little. Dr Andre slid his fingers out of Sophie's pussy, sucking them clean before getting up of the chair and kneeling on the edge of the bed. He began to run his tongue over Sasha's pussy. Licking every inch of it and flicking his tongue over her clitoris. Sasha moaned with pleasure, grinding her pussy against Dr Andre's tongue.

"Oh god yes, yes – yes doctor. Fist fuck me while you lick and suck my clitoris. I'm going to cum", said Sasha.

Dr Andre made a fist and began to fist fuck Sasha while licking and sucking her clit. She screamed with pleasure.

Her legs shaking violently. Her juices squirting everywhere. Dr Andre removed his fist, parting Sasha's pussy lips and pushing his tongue and fingers inside, tongue and finger fucking her. Making her cum over and over again. He stripped naked and knelt in front of Sasha, pushing his cock in her wet pussy and putting her legs over his shoulders. He began to fuck her softly and slowly at first, leaning over licking, sucking, and gently biting her nipples. Kissing her passionately. She responded to his kiss, moaning against his lips. He began to fuck her harder and faster. Making her scream with pleasure. As he brought her climax over and over again. Sasha couldn't get enough.

"Oh doctor you're so good, fuck me harder, pound my pussy then my ass. It's been so long. I need a good seeing too", whispered Sasha breathlessly.

Dr Andre obliged grabbing Sasha's hips and pounding her pussy, making her scream with pleasure. Her legs shaking as he brought her to another shuddering climax. He groaned as he reached his own climax, pumping her pussy full of his hot sticky cum. He pulled out and moved up the bed, pushing his cock towards Sasha's mouth. She eagerly took his cock in her mouth, licking and sucking it clean before allowing him to remove his cock from her mouth. He turned her over getting her on all fours parting her ass cheeks. He got a bottle of anal lube pouring it directly into her tight hole using his fingers to rub it in before replacing them with his cock.

He grabbed her hips fucking her hard and deep, making her scream with pleasure. He reached round and roughly squeezed her breasts as he fucked her harder and deeper, groaning as he reached climax pumping her tight hole full of his hot sticky cum. He gently pulled out and turned Sasha round to face him.

"You just needed a good seeing to Sasha, by someone who knows what he's doing. As for your self-pleasure, let me show you the art of self-pleasure", said Dr Andre spreading Sasha's legs wide.

He took her hand guiding it towards her pussy placing his hand on top. He gently moved her fingers over her swollen clitoris. She moaned softly, beginning to rub it frantically wanting to make herself cum.

"Slow down a little, tease yourself. The pleasure will be worth waiting for I promise you", said Dr Andre removing his hand and sitting beside Sasha, watching her as she slowly rubbed her clitoris, sliding her fingers over it and down to the opening of her pussy.

"Not yet Sasha. Part your pussy lips and rub your clitoris a little harder now, but be gentle. You want this to be a pleasurable experience not a painful one", said Dr Andre. Sasha parted her pussy lips and began to rub her clitoris harder moaning with pleasure her legs shaking.

"Oh god can I slide them in now. I need to cum I always rub my G-spot with one hand while rubbing my clitoris with the other until I cum everywhere. My boyfriend loved it", said Sasha licking her lips as she noticed that Dr Andre was wanking as he watched her.

"'Mmmmm, do that for me Sasha, let me see you squirt. You're learning well. Make me squirt my spunk over your pussy", he said breathlessly as he wanked his cock harder.

Sasha slid two fingers into her wet pussy, rubbing her G-spot softly and slowly at first. Then gradually faster and harder while she rubbed her clitoris with her other hand, moaning with pleasure. Her whole body shaking violently as she reached a shuddering climax squirting everywhere.

Dr Andre leaned over her wanking faster and harder until he covered her pussy with his cum. Sasha reached down and scooped it up with her fingers, licking and sucking them clean before kneeling in front of Dr Andre, taking his cock in her mouth sucking and licking that cock clean.

"Oh god doctor your amazing. I hope we can continue this. I haven't had sex like this for a long, long time".

"We will Sasha, you're my last patient. Let's go to mine. I want to give you so much pleasure, your beautiful. I love to watch a women when she climaxes", said Dr Andre pulling Sasha close and kissing her passionately.

She kissed him back holding him against her for a moment before allowing him to gently pull away. They got dressed and walked out of Dr Andre's room, smiling as they walked through the reception area and towards the door.

"I see Dr Andre has pleased another patient", said Chantelle walking to the front of the reception desk.

"As I always do Chantelle lock up for me. I'm taking Sasha to mine. She deserves a lot more pleasure. I will see you in the morning", said Dr Andre passing Chantelle a set of keys.

"See you in the morning Dr Andre. You're so lucky Sasha, he's amazing in bed. I was once a patient of his. I still think of him when I masturbate when I'm single of course", said Chantelle licking her full lips suggestively.

"He's the best I've had in a long time Chantelle. I can't wait to have more of him. God I'm wet just thinking about it. We better go before I start begging you to fuck me right here", said Sasha walking to the exit.

Dr Andre followed her out and they walked towards his black Mercedes Benz. He unlocked it, holding the passenger door open for Sasha. She got in and he shut it behind her, getting into the driver's seat. Dr Andre started the car up and drove out of the car park and towards his house and Sasha could feel her clitoris throb as she thought about the fun she'd had with Dr Andre and the fun they were about to have at his home. Dr Andre reached over to Sasha sliding his hand between her legs.

"Mmmm, you're soaking Sasha. God I can't wait to use my mouth, tongue and fingers on that pussy before I fuck you till your begging me to stop. I want to give you so much pleasure, you're so sexy and you drive me crazy! Feels so good when my cock's in that wet hole of yours and when I fuck that perfect ass. Oh god does it turn me on – you screaming with pleasure is so horny to me", said Dr Andre rubbing Sasha's pussy as he spoke making her moan with pleasure.

"Oh god doctor I need to cum so badly, make me cum for you", said Sasha.

"I've got a better idea let me see you make yourself cum",

said Dr Andre.

Sasha slid her hand down to her pussy. She gently rubbed her clitoris slowly at first then gradually faster. Her legs shaking as she brought herself to a shuddering climax. Her cum dripping down her thighs. She pushed her fingers in her pussy getting them wet then licked them clean.

"Oh Sasha that was horny. I'm going to have to pull over somewhere. I need to have you, my cock's so hard. I want to bend you over and give you a good hard fuck, making you scream with pleasure. There are some woods nearby. I'll park up and we can go there. I'm so hard and horny for you", said Dr Andre.

"Oh doctor all my fantasies are coming true with you. I've masturbated over being fucked by a hot doctor like yourself after he's given me a thorough examination. Let's go to the woods I want your cock doctor", said Sasha.

A short time later Dr Andre pulled up outside the woods. He got out and walked round to the passenger side, opening the door for Sasha. She got out and Dr Andre locked the car up before taking Sasha's hand and leading her into the woods. He found a secluded area near a large oak tree. He turned Sasha to face it, bending her over and pulling her dress up over her ass. He quickly unzipped his trousers, taking out his hard cock and ramming it in her pussy. She screamed with pleasure as he fucked her hard and deep, roughly pulling her hair as he pounded her pussy making her cum over and over again. Her cum dripped down her thighs and over his cock and balls. He grabbed her hips and fucked her harder than ever – pushing his cock deeper inside her pussy. He held on to the tree as he brought her to a shuddering climax, her legs shaking.

Dr Andre groaned as he reached his own climax, filling her with cum until it dripped down her thighs. He pulled out turning her to face him. Gently pushing her down on to her knees. She eagerly licked and sucked Dr Andre's cock clean. Suddenly Sasha and Dr Andre were aware of someone watching them. They heard the sound of a woman moaning. Sasha looked around, smiling as she saw Chantelle sat on the grass, her hand down her thong.

"Come join us Chantelle I don't mind sharing", Sasha. Chantelle walked over to Sasha and Dr Andre.

"I've been watching you both it got me so horny. May I lick his spunk out of your pussy please Sasha. I love the combined taste of spunk and pussy juice", said Chantelle, kneeling on the grass.

"Yes of course you can Chantelle", said Sasha laying down on the grass her legs wide open.

Chantelle eagerly licked Dr Andre's cum and Sasha's juices from her pussy, while Dr Andre knelt behind her and pulled her thong to one side, pushing his cock in her wet pussy. He fucked her hard and deep making her moan against Sasha's pussy. The vibrations making her cum filling Chantelle's mouth with her juices. She licked Sasha's pussy clean then pulled Sasha towards her kissing her passionately as Dr Andre pounded her wet pussy making her cum again and again until he reached his own climax. Filling her with his cum.

He pulled out and let Sasha and Chantelle suck him clean.

"Off you go now Chantelle. I want to get Sasha to mine. I know you get horny a lot go home and give that boyfriend of yours what he wants", said Dr Andre.

"Yes doctor I will be he'll be so hard and horny when I tell him what I've been up to", said Chantelle adjusting her thong before leaving Sasha and Dr Andre alone.

"Let's get to mine Sasha. I want to fuck you in every room. Give you the pleasure you deserve. I'll be your dream lover from now on. We'll have dirty weekends together and lots of great sex", said Dr Andre putting his cock away and zipping himself up. Sasha put her dress straight and followed Dr Andre back to his car.

"I can't wait you satisfy me completely like no other man could ever do. I've always had a high sex drive. I can go all night and I love a good fuck before breakfast", said Sasha licking her lips suggestively at Dr Andre.

He unlocked the car and opened the passenger door for Sasha. He started the car, driving towards his house smiling at Sasha as he drove. She smiled back at him. A while later they got to Dr Andre's house. Dr Andre unlocked the door and they walked in. He closed the door behind them locking it before pushing Sasha against the door, taking her dress off, unzipping his trousers and pulling them down to his ankles.

He wrapped Sasha's legs around his waist, sliding his cock in her wet pussy and fucking her hard and deep. She moaned with pleasure, bouncing up and down on Dr Andre's cock. He bent his head down to her breasts, hungrily licking, sucking, and biting her nipples as he fucked her harder and faster. She screamed with pleasure. Dr Andre moved his mouth from Sasha's nipples and up to her mouth. Kissing her passionately. She responded to his kiss, wrapping her arms around his shoulders. He walked upstairs his cock still deep in her wet pussy and went into his bedroom, taking her over to the bed. He laid her down on the bed and continued to pound her pussy, bringing her to climax over and over again. Her juices soaking the sheets. He finally reached his own climax, filling her with his hot, thick cum. He gently pulled out and turned Sasha over on to her stomach, getting her on all fours and parting her ass cheeks. He slid his cock in her tight ass, fucking her hard and deep making her scream with pleasure. Spanking her bare ass as he fucked her harder and faster, sliding his hand between her legs and rubbing her swollen clit. Gently at first then gradually harder and faster. Making her squirt everywhere as he continued to pound her tight hole, groaning as he climaxed, pumping her tight ass full of hot sticky cum until it dripped down her thighs. He pulled out, removing his fingers from Sasha's clitoris and laid down on the bed. Pulling her close and kissing her passionately.

"Oh doctor let's go into the bathroom next. I want to fuck in the shower. Want you to fuck me good and hard be rough with me", said Sasha licking her lips suggestively.

"Oh Sasha, that's a hot idea! Come on then my sexy lover, let's get wet", said Dr Andre getting off the bed and walking into the en-suite bathroom.

Sasha followed him. He switched the shower on and stripped naked while Sasha took off her boots. The two of them got into the shower. He turned her round so she was facing the shower screen, bending her over and parting her legs. He knelt down behind her parting her pussy lips and pushing his tongue inside. Licking her softly and slowly sucking on her clitoris. She moaned with pleasure grinding her pussy against his tongue.

"Oh god yes doctor, tongue fuck me! Make me cum in your mouth. Feels so good having your tongue in my wet pussy", said Sasha breathlessly.

Dr Andre began to tongue fuck Sasha's pussy hard and deep. Her legs shook as he expertly brought her to a shuddering climax with his tongue. Her juices filling his mouth. He licked her clean running his tongue over every inch of her pussy before standing up and pushing his hard cock in her wet pussy. Grabbing her hips and fucking her hard and deep. Making her scream with pleasure.

"Be rough with me doctor pull my hair. Spank my ass. Pull on my nipples. I love it rough", said Sasha pushing back against Dr Andre's cock taking the full length of it in her wet pussy.

Dr Andre spanked Sasha's ass and pulled on her hair and nipples as he pounded her wet pussy. Making her scream with pleasure. Her whole body shaking violently. She put her hand on the shower screen to stop herself from falling as Dr Andre brought her to a shuddering climax over and over again. Her juices gushing from her pussy dripping down her thighs and over his cock and balls. He pulled out and turned Sasha to face him, gently pushing her down on to her knees. She eagerly took his wet cock in her mouth, sucking and licking it clean. He put his hand on the back off her head, holding her head in place while he fucked her mouth. Filling her throat with his hot sticky cum. She swallowed every last drop and sucking him clean before allowing him to remove his cock from her mouth. He pushed her against the shower screen, wrapping her legs around his waist and rammed his cock in her tight hole. Fucking her hard and deep.

"Bounce on my cock Sasha! Take it all in that tight hole of yours! Milk my cock! I want to fill you with spunk!" said Dr Andre bending his head and taking Sasha's left nipple between his teeth gently pulling on it. She screamed with pleasure bouncing on Dr Andre's cock as he fucked her harder and deeper.

"Yeah that's it baby, take it all in your tight ass. Oh god I'm going to empty my balls in that slutty tight hole", said Dr Andre removing his teeth from Sasha's nipple.

He wrapped his arms around her kissing her hard and deep. Bruising her lips with his as he pounded her tight ass filling her with his hot sticky cum until it dripped down her thighs, mingling with her pussy juices. He gently pulled out of her ass and let Sasha put her legs down. Then he took her hand and helped her out of the shower. They got dried then they went downstairs and into the living room. Dr Andre laid on the sofa.

"Come and ride me Sasha you make me so horny baby. You're the best patient I've had other than your friend Yvonne and of course the wild and sexy Chantelle. I would love to have all three of my best patients in bed one day but right now I want to continue to pleasure you", said Dr Andre licking his lips at Sasha.

She straddled him pushing his cock in her wet pussy. She began to ride him bouncing up and down on his cock. She leaned over and kissed him passionately. He responded to her kiss sliding his hands down her back to her ass. He slid a finger down the crack of her ass cheeks and into her tight hole, fingering her as she bounced up and down harder and faster. Screaming with pleasure her legs shaking as she reached a shuddering climax. Her juices squirting everywhere. She continued to ride Dr Andre's cock. He slid his finger out of her ass, grabbing both ass cheeks and bouncing her up and down faster and harder, groaning as he reached his own climax. Pumping her pussy full of hot sticky cum. Dr Andre pulled out of Sasha's pussy and let her get off him. He took her hand and led her into the kitchen. He kissed her passionately pulling her close. She pressed herself against him.

"Oh doctor your an amazing lover. You satisfy me completely like no other man has ever done before. I can't get enough of you. I want you to fuck my ass again, bend me over the worktop and pound my ass. Maybe you can find something to fuck my pussy at the same time. That really gets me going", said Sasha.

Dr Andre turned Sasha to face the worktop bending her over it. He opened a draw taking out a rolling pin. He pushed it deep into Sasha's wet pussy before sliding his cock in her tight ass. He fucked both holes hard and deep, making her scream with pleasure. She held on to the worktop her legs shaking violently as Dr Andre brought her to a shuddering climax again and again until she flopped against him. He held her hips and pounded her tight hole, groaning as he reached his own climax, filling her with hot sticky cum. He pulled out and removed the rolling pin from her pussy letting Sasha suck it clean before putting it away. He scooped her up in his strong arms and took her upstairs to his bedroom – laying her on the bed they kissed passionately, caressing each other's bodies.

They spent the rest of that night and most of the following morning fucking in every position possible. They embarked on a sordid affair lasting two years until finally deciding to get serious. Sasha moved into Dr Andre's house. He fulfilled her every fantasy day and night. She shared him with Yvonne and Chantelle on occasion, enjoying the sensation of being pleasured by Dr Andre and two hot females. It drove her so wild, she couldn't get enough of her hunky doctor. No other man came close to him as a lover.

They would go away on dirty weekends. Spending most of it fucking in every area of their hotel room, sometimes going down to the bar and picking up another woman. Sasha loved to share Dr Andre. He brought his patients home sometimes introducing them to Sasha. She would show the women the delights of being pleasured by both a man and a woman. They all came back for more, most of them became regular patients. The word soon spread and they had women queuing up to be Dr Andre's next patient. Each of the women fully satisfied after each session. They would leave begging for more. Sasha was so happy she'd been introduced to Dr Andre. Her sex life was a lot more satisfying now and so much more interesting and varied. She never knew what her hunky doctor would want to do next. Life with him was exciting. The way she'd wanted her life to be for so long. He knew just how to make her cum and have her begging for more. They would fuck day and night between his sessions with his endless list of patients. Sasha worked with Dr Andre enjoying being with him. They would fuck at work as well as at home, involving his patients at all times. None of them complained at all. In fact they encouraged it. Getting Sasha to use various toys on them while Dr Andre fucked them at the same time. He would take turns with Sasha and his patients. In-between watching them pleasure themselves and each other.

As word spread they had to set up a clinic at Dr Andre's home making things even more interesting, as they could fuck and work at the same time. It was also more relaxing for the patients. Chantelle still worked on reception but she would join in their sessions on occasion when she wasn't teaching her boyfriend Wayne how to fuck her properly. He'd come into work and give her a good seeing to over the reception desk – not caring who was watching. Sometimes him and Chantelle would have steamy sex sessions with Dr Andre and Sasha. No matter if they had solo sessions three sums or foursomes, Sasha loved ever sex session she had with Dr Andre.

When they eventually got married they spent their honeymoon having group sex with a few willing Greek locals they'd met at a bar. It was the best holiday she'd ever had. She knew this was the start of things to come with her hunky doctor.

The Dominatrix

Adam had realised he was submissive while at school. It was a private school he was one of the youngest in his class and very shy. One of the older girls had decided to take advantage of his shyness. She invited him to her room one night where she had made him her slave. She had made him lick her shoes clean and spanked him hard several times. He went back to his room that night and masturbated. Adam had tried to find a woman to dominate him since then but none of them had been as good as Chloe so he had decided he would have to find a professional dominatrix. He'd looked through the ads in the back of a fetish magazine and found one for a 'Mistress Domina'. It read, "I will teach you the art of servitude submissive – Males wanted".

Adam rang the number provided and arranged a meeting with Mistress Domina at her home in London. He explained about his submissive fantasies. She told him to come to her house for a week or two and she would teach him the art of servitude.

"Yes mistress", said Adam in a shy voice he felt his cock grow hard in his boxers.

He went upstairs to his bedroom stripped naked and masturbated, fantasising about serving Mistress Domina. That weekend Adam packed a case with enough things to last him a couple of weeks then he grabbed his coat and walked out of his front door, locking it behind him. He put the case in the boot of his car before getting in and driving to Mistress Domina's house. His cock hard in anticipation of things to come. When he arrived at her house he knocked on the door and waited for her to answer. A few minutes later Mistress Domina opened the door dressed in a shiny black skin-tight sleeveless latex cat suit with a zip that went all the way down the front and between her legs, shiny black latex gloves and shiny black knee high PVC boots. Her long black hair was sleeked back into a ponytail. She looked Adam up and down a stern look on her face.

"So slave you wish to serve me is that correct?" said Mistress Domina a sly smile on her glossy red lips.

"Yes Mistress I will do anything you tell me. I will be your obedient slave", said Adam nervously.

Mistress Domina beckoned Adam into her home. He followed her like a faithful dog follows its owner. Mistress Domina went upstairs to her spare bedroom which had several wardrobes full of various fetish outfits, a large rack with whips, rope and canes etc. on it and a large Victorian style chest of drawers which she opened to take out a studded dog collar, a dog lead and a pair of skin-tight leather shorts. Mistress Domina ordered Adam to strip naked and put the shorts on. He obediently did it. Mistress Domina put the collar and lead onto him and got him to kneel on all fours. He did as he was told and she walked him like a dog into the master bedroom where she tied him to a metal ring at the side of her black metal four poster bed. Mistress Domina laid on the bed and unzipped her latex catsuit between her legs then she leaned over and opened the drawer of her bedside cabinet. She took out her 8 inch dildo and turned it on then she began to fuck herself with it. She could see Adam watching her with a bulge in his shorts. She stopped and got a pair of leather wrist cuffs. She put them on Adams wrists after placing them in front of him then she helped him out of his leather shorts. His cock was rock hard, she fastened a leather cock ring to the base of it. Then she got back on the bed and continued to fuck herself with her dildo. Adam watched as Mistress Domina quickly brought herself to orgasm, her juices running down her latex clad thighs.

She got off the bed after removing the dildo from her wet pussy, unfastening Adam's wrist cuffs and removing his cock ring then she sat on the edge of the bed, beckoning Adam towards her. He crawled towards her on his knees. Mistress Domina put her hands behind Adams head, pushing his face towards her wet pussy. He obediently started to lick her pussy, licking up every drop of her cum until she was clean. Mistress Domina ordered Adam to lay on the bed. He did as he was told. She fastened his wrists and ankles to the bedposts then straddled him, sliding his hard cock deep in her wet pussy. She started to ride him fast and hard, moaning with pleasure, grinding her pussy against his hard cock. Adam groaned his cock swelling in Mistress Domina's pussy. She stopped and got of him leaving him frustrated.

"I'm not letting you cum yet slave", said Mistress Domina getting back on top of Adam she started to ride him again a little slower this time, she rubbed her throbbing clitoris moaning with pleasure as she got faster and harder her legs shaking as she reached a violent orgasm.

"You may cum now slave", said mistress Domina.

Adam squirted his hot cum deep in Mistress Domina's pussy. She got off Adam and took of her catsuit. Then she turned off the light and got into bed at the side of Adam. Adam had enjoyed his first session with Mistress Domina. She was exactly how he wanted her to be very strict. He felt that he deserved to be treated like that. He was a worthless excuse for a man. He only lived to serve his mistress. He hoped that Mistress Domina might take him on as her permanent slave. It would be a dream come true for him. He'd been dreaming of it since his encounter at school. He spent many a night fantasizing about it and had many wet dreams about being a slave for a strict mistress.

The next morning Adam awoke to find himself unfastened. Mistress Domina had left him alone in the bed. He got out of bed and went to look for her. He soon found her taking a shower. He stood for a while, watching her lather up her beautiful naked body. She opened the glass door to get out of the shower and Adam grabbed a towel and handed it to her.

"You may dry me off slave", said Mistress Domina smiling at Adam.

"Yes mistress", said Adam taking the towel and gently drying Mistress Domina's wet body.

When she was dry he grabbed her satin dressing gown from the hook on the back of the bathroom door and helped her put it on. She fastened it then beckoned Adam to follow her. He did as she wanted. Following her like an obedient puppy. They went back into the bedroom.

Mistress Domina opened a large wardrobe and took out a pair of latex shorts and a latex mask. She put them on the bed along with a latex catsuit, a bottle of baby oil and a can of latex polish.

"I want you to oil me up and help me into my catsuit. then you can polish it for me slave", said Mistress Domina.

"Yes Mistress", said Adam taking her robe off then grabbing the bottle of baby oil he poured a little on his hands and began to oil her up then he helped her to get into her shiny black skin-tight latex catsuit.

Mistress Domina lay back on the bed. Adam put a little of the polish on a cloth. Then starting at her ankles. He began to polish her latex catsuit. Until it was really shiny.

"Good slave put on your outfit. then you can do some housework for me", said Mistress Domina.

"Yes mistress I am your faithful servant", said Adam putting on the shiny black skin-tight latex shorts and the shiny black latex mask which had holes for his eyes and mouth and air holes so he was able to breathe in it.

Mistress Domina went in her bedside cabinet drawer and took out a pair of latex gloves. She handed them to Adam. He obediently put them on then he followed Mistress Domina downstairs to the kitchen. She handed him a scrubbing brush and filled a bowl with warm soapy water then placed it on the kitchen floor.

"Scrub the floor slave", said Mistress Domina whipping Adam's latex clad ass hard with her leather whip.

"Yes mistress I will do anything to serve you", said Adam dipping the scrubbing brush into the warm soapy water and scrubbing the kitchen floor.

Mistress Domina followed him around the kitchen, whipping his ass as he continued to scrub the floor making sure he didn't miss a single spot. Adam wanted to please his mistress in the hope that she would let him become her live in slave. Once he had finished the floor he emptied the dirty water down the sink and waited for his mistress to give him another job to do. Mistress Domina handed him a can of polish and a duster.

"Polish my table slave. I want it to shine", said Mistress Domina.

"Yes mistress I will make it shine for you", said Adam walking into the dining room and spraying polish on the large mahogany dining table then polishing it with the duster.

Mistress Domina lay on the sofa fucking herself with a large black dildo. Adam felt his cock growing hard beneath his latex shorts as he noticed her playing while he continued to polish the dining table. Making it nice and shiny for his mistress hoping it would get her approval.

He loved to please his mistress in any way he could. He would be Mistress Domina's slave forever. Mistress Domina beckoned him over. Adam put the polish and the duster down and walked over to her.

"I want you to pleasure me with your tongue slave", said Mistress Domina licking her shiny red lips.

Adam knelt up on the sofa removing the dildo and started to lick Mistress Domina's wet pussy, pushing his tongue deep inside her.

She put her hands behind Adams head and wrapped her legs around his shoulders, pulling him closer. Grinding her pussy against his tongue, moaning with pleasure. Mistress Domina's legs began to shake as she exploded into a violent orgasm, filling Adams mouth with her juices. He licked it all up.

"Fuck my ass slave I'm horny. I need to be fucked hard and deep", said Mistress Domina getting on all fours her ass in the air.

Adam lubed her ass hole with her juices. Then pulled his shorts down and slid his hard cock into her tight hole. Grabbing her hips and fucking her hard and deep. She pushed her ass hard against his cock, moaning with pleasure as Adam fucked her harder and deeper.

"You may cum slave", said Mistress Domina breathlessly. Adam groaned with pleasure filling her tight hole with his hot cum it dripped down her latex clad thighs.

"Thank you slave, your mistress is pleased with you. I think we should make this a permanent arrangement", said Mistress Domina.

"Oh please mistress, let me be your live-in slave. I'll do anything", said Adam . Mistress Domina smiled at Adam.

"Do you agree to obey my every command slave?"

"Yes mistress I will do anything you want me to do and I

mean anything. I will be your faithful servant", said Adam.

"Very well slave you can be my live-in slave", said Mistress Domina pointing at the space in front of her. Adam knelt before Mistress Domina and kissed her feet.

"Thank you Mistress I am forever in your debt", said Adam.

Mistress Domina put Adam a collar and lead on and walked him like a dog to the basement which was kitted out like a dungeon. She walked him into a metal cage and fastened the cuffs. That were attached to it to his wrists and ankles.

"This will be your bed for the night slave", said Mistress Domina.

Adam spent the night dreaming of his mistress. He knew this was going to be good. It was a dream come true and he never wanted it to end. The next morning Mistress Domina walked downstairs to the basement dressed head to toe in shiny black latex. She had glossy red lipstick on her full lips.

"Morning slave. I hope you're ready for some more training. Your learning well. I'm pleased with you slave. I expect more of the same from you today. I'm expecting a guest later. She's a fellow fem dom. Her names is Tanya but you will refer to her as Mistress Tanya. You will obey us both", said Mistress Domina smiling as she unfastened Adam's wrists and ankles.

"Yes mistress I'm your willing slave. How may I serve you?" said Adam his head bowed.

"Lick my boots clean. I want them to be so shiny. I can see my reflection in them" said Mistress Domina.

Adam obediently knelt in front of his mistress and began to lick her boots, running his tongue over every inch of them, making sure they were nice and shiny. Mistress Domina looked down at Adam and smiled.

"Good slave now let's get you upstairs. Mistress Tanya will be here shortly. I'm sure she will be as impressed with you as I am", said Mistress Domina putting a lead on Adam she walked him out of the dungeon and upstairs taking him into the lounge.

"Kneel on the floor slave and assume the position", said Mistress Domina. Adam knelt on the floor head bowed arms behind his back a bulge in his latex shorts.

"I see your enjoying your training slave. You are not permitted to cum though until I say so", said Mistress Domina cuffing Adam's wrists so he couldn't touch his cock.

"I won't cum until you give me permission mistress. You're so beautiful and strict. I can't help but get turned on by you", said Adam.

"Your learning well slave. you know what will happen if you dare to cum without permission. I will test you soon when Mistress Tanya arrives, she's been known to make many slaves cum in their pants before now. I hope you will be the first to control yourself. She will be so pleased with you as well as me. I've had trouble with slaves before now. They can't control themselves. I have to punish them severely. it would be nice to find a slave who can serve me well. I'm hoping that you are what I've been searching for", said Mistress Domina walking out of the living room and leaving Adam alone.

He wanted to please his mistress so much. He hoped he would please her as well as Mistress Tanya. A while later Mistress Domina returned followed by a tall blonde haired women dressed in a shiny black skin-tight latex bather stockings and thigh high boots.

"Hello slave. My name is Mistress Tanya. Mistress Domina has told me all about you. I'm going to test you and see if you can control yourself for me. I'm hoping you can. Let's get that pathetic looking cock of yours out", said Mistress Tanya unzipping Adam's shorts and taking out his cock then she laid on the settee spreading her legs wide.

"Pass me a large fat dildo Mistress Domina, and you slave look at me while I pleasure myself. Maybe I'll even have a little fun with your mistress. She's hot isn't she? I want to taste that juicy wet pussy of hers and suck on those tits. Mmmm, I'm getting wet just thinking about it", said Mistress Tanya teasing Adam as he watched her.

Mistress Domina got a large fat dildo from a draw. She took it over to Mistress Tanya, passing it her while she unzipped her latex catsuit exposing her breasts and pussy. She slid her latex clad fingers in her wet pussy fingering herself hard and deep while Mistress Tanya fucked herself with the dildo.

The two women moaned with pleasure, watching Adam's cock twitching as he watched them pleasuring themselves.

Wishing he could join in. He tried to control himself. His balls filled with cum.

"He's doing so well Mistress Domina. My other slaves had all covered themselves in their own cum by now come here slave", said Mistress Tanya beckoning Adam over to her he shuffled over to her and knelt in front of her.

"How may I serve you Mistress Tanya?" said Adam.

"Lick my pussy slave make me cum. Do a good job and I will allow you to empty your balls otherwise it's the cane for you", said Mistress Tanya removing the dildo from her wet pussy and sucking it clean then she put it down.

Adam obediently began to lick Mistress Tanya's wet pussy, pushing his tongue deep inside. She moaned with pleasure, grinding her pussy against his tongue.

"Oh god yes slave tongue fuck me. I'm going to cum. Mistress Domina I think we should let our slave cum now unfasten him", said Mistress Tanya breathlessly.

As Adam tongue fucked her hard and deep. Bringing her to a shuddering climax. Her juices filling his mouth. He licked her clean running his tongue over every inch of her wet pussy. Getting every last drop of her cum while Mistress Domina unfastened his wrists.

"I'll handle him now Mistress Tanya. He's been such a good slave. he deserves a treat. It's my turn to use my slaves tongue. He's good with it as well as his cock. He serves me well. I'm not willing to give him up.

I will however lend him on occasion. He's too good a

slave to let go off", said Mistress Domina.

"As you wish Mistress Domina. Now slave, stop licking my pussy and prepare for your treat from Mistress Domina. I know you will enjoy it you deserve it. You've done so well", said Mistress Tanya gently pushing Adam away. Mistress Domina knelt next to Adam.

"On your back slave", said Mistress Domina.

Adam obediently laid on his back while his Mistress knelt between his legs taking his cock in her mouth. She sucked it hard and deep, wanking him into her mouth until he pumped her mouth full of hot sticky cum. She swallowed every last drop, sucking him clean then she walked over to Mistress Tanya, pulling her close and kissing her passionately, sharing Adam's cum with her. She kissed her back. Her hands wandering over Mistress Domina's body.

"Thank you mistress so much. I needed that so badly. I'm so happy that I've pleased you both. I am your willing slave for as long as I'm needed. I'm willing to do anything you ask of me. No matter how humiliating it is. I will become the best slave you've ever had. I'll take my punishments without a whimper no matter how painful they are. I was born to be a slave. I've always been submissive. I'm not worthy of being anything else", said Adam looking directly at Mistress Domina and Mistress Tanya as he spoke.

"Very well said slave I think we should get you down to the dungeon and give you a little pain. you've had enough pleasure for one day. It's time you experienced some extreme pain. if you're going to be my slave. I expect you to handle pain. as well as experiencing pleasure when you've been good", said Mistress Domina walking Adam out of the living room and back downstairs to the dungeon followed by Mistress Tanya.

She helped Adam out of his latex shorts then made him lay on the floor of the dungeon. She put his arms above his head and cuffed his wrists together then she walked over his chest in her stiletto boots before pressing down on his cock and balls. He bit his lip to stop himself from screaming. The pain was extreme but yet it aroused him. Pre-cum dripped from his cock.

Mistress Domina walked over to a chair made from black latex. She sat down and took of her boots before walking back over to Adam. She sat down next to him rubbing his cock with her latex covered feet, teasing him, then she used both feet to wank him off until he covered her latex clad feet in his sticky cum. She pushed her feet against Adam's lips. He licked them clean, tasting his own cum as well as the latex.

"Good slave Mistress Tanya your turn now. Show him what real pain feels like. Choose your instrument of torture", said Mistress Domina smiling.

Mistress Tanya chose a long leather whip with wire on it. She stood over Adam and gave him sixty strokes of the whip. Each one harder than the one before covering his body with red welts. She stood back and admired her work.

"Well done slave – you took your punishment! without so much as a whimper. Let's see how far you will go to please myself and your Mistress. Open your mouth wide ready to drink our golden nectar slave then you will lick us clean", said Mistress Tanya.

Adam obediently opened his mouth wide for his Mistresses. They took turns squatting over his face and pissing in his mouth. He swallowed it then licked their pussies clean.

"Good slave I think that's enough for now", said Mistress Domina unfastened Adam's wrists and helping him up. She took him over to the metal cage he'd slept in the night before helping him in and cuffing his wrists and ankles then she shut the door.

"I will leave you now slave with your mistress. I intend to borrow you on occasion there's a domes and subs meeting this weekend in London. I trust you will be taking him Mistress Domina?" said Mistress Tanya making her way out of the dungeon.

"Of course Mistress Tanya he's worthy of going with me. I can't wait to show him off to the other fem domes. I'll let him rest now he needs his energy to serve me. I will see you this weekend. I look forward to meeting your other slaves", said Mistress Domina giving Mistress Tanya a passionate kiss before the two of them left the dungeon leaving Adam alone in the cage. His cock rock hard. The idea of being in the company of other fem domes as well as his mistress and Mistress Tanya excited him yet at the same time he was nervous he hoped he would be up to scratch. He knew he had pleased both Mistress Domina and Mistress Tanya but he would have to please more than just them at the meeting otherwise his mistress wouldn't be at all pleased. He knew that if he displeased her or Mistress Tanya. He would be in for severe punishment which was not what he wanted at all.

Later that day after what seemed like an eternity Mistress Domina walked into the dungeon dressed in a black skin-tight latex bather, stockings, elbow length gloves and thigh high boots. She had a leather riding crop in hand and a sly smile on her face as she walked towards Adam opening the cage door.

"Ready for some more training slave?" said Mistress Domina helping Adam out of the cage.

"Yes mistress I'm ready for more training. I want to the best slave I can possibly be", said Adam his head bowed. Mistress Domina walked Adam to the middle of the dungeon.

"On all fours slave I want you to crawl around the dungeon for me on all fours while I follow you whipping you with my riding crop. I don't want a peep out of you. I will make sure that pale ass of yours is red raw by the time I'm finished with you", said Mistress Domina.

Adam obediently got on all fours and began to make his way around the dungeon. Mistress Domina walked behind him. Raising the riding crop high in the air and bringing it down hard on Adam's bare ass. Giving him 60 strokes in total. Each one harder than the one before. His ass was red raw by the time Mistress Domina had finished with him. She smiled at him standing in front of him.

"What do you say to your mistress?" said Mistress

Domina.

"Thank you Mistress", said Adam kissing his mistresses boots as a sign of his respect for her.

"Good slave you did well get up and come with me to my bedroom, your mistress needs satisfying by her slave sexually. You have earned your treat, I hope you will please me as much as you did before. This time though it's on my terms. I am still in control so you only cum when I say you can. I am always in charge in the bedroom no matter who I'm fucking. It's just the way I like it", said Mistress Domina.

"As you wish Mistress just being able to fuck you is an honour in itself. You being in control is the way I like things. Your my mistress you're in control of every inch of me including my cock and I only cum when you say I can. It's the way I like it I've been submissive for as long as I can remember. When I was at school one of the older girls made me her slave. She made me lick her shoes clean and dominated me. I've had girlfriends since then but up until I met you none of them compared to Chloe", said Adam getting up and following Mistress Domina upstairs to her bedroom.

"That name rings a bell slave. There's a mistress Chloe that attends the monthly domes and subs meetings. What does she look like?" said Mistress Domina opening her bedroom door.

"She's quite tall Mistress around 5"9 maybe even 6 ft. she's got long dark brown hair, blue eyes, large breasts. She developed early and if I remember rightly she's got a love heart tattoo on her left ass cheek", said Adam looking directly at his mistress as he spoke.

"That's Mistress Chloe she's a very popular Mistress among the sub community. makes thousands from being a professional fem dom. I wonder if she will remember you. we will find out when we got to the meeting this weekend. I'm sure she will when she sees you although it's been a long time, right now though I want you to get on that bed for me slave. It's time for your treat", said Mistress Domina.

Adam obediently got on the bed for his mistress his cock hard. The mere mention of Chloe's name making him hard. The thought of seeing her again was exciting, he hoped she would remember him. He'd seen her since school but only for a quick chat as he'd been with one of his many girlfriends at the time.

Mistress Domina joined Adam on the bed, cuffing his wrists and ankles to the bedposts. She straddled him, pushing his cock in her wet pussy as she began to ride him slowly moving back and forth on his cock, moaning with pleasure. She began to speed up a little, grinding her clitoris against his cock teasing herself before starting to bounce up and down fast and hard. She pulled her bather down over her breasts, running her hands over them and lifting each one up licking and sucking her nipples while she bounced up and down harder and faster, screaming with pleasure. Her legs shaking as she reached a shuddering climax. She continued to ride him faster and harder, making herself cum over and over again.

"You may cum now slave", said Mistress Domina unfastening Adam's wrists he grabbed her ass and began to fuck her hard and deep. Groaning as he reached his own climax. Pumping her pussy full of hot sticky cum.

"Thank you Mistress so much. You don't know how much I've wanted to fuck you again after the first time, you are amazing in bed. No other woman other than Chloe has ever turned me on the way you do, being told I can't cum until I'm told to drives me wild with desire. You know how to get me off", said Adam.

"You're welcome slave, I'm not done with you yet though. It's time for you to fuck my ass while I fuck my pussy with a nice big fat dildo", said Mistress Domina unfastening Adam's ankles before getting a large dildo from her bedside cabinet.

She got on all fours sliding the dildo in her wet pussy before spreading her ass cheeks. Adam knelt behind his mistress and pushed his cock in her tight hole, fucking her hard and deep while she fucked her pussy with the dildo, screaming with pleasure, pushing her ass back against Adam's cock.

He fucked her harder and deeper trying his hardest to control himself as his mistresses tight hole squeezed his cock.

"Cum slave. Fill my ass with your hot sticky cum", said Mistress Domina.

Adam fucked Mistress Domina harder still, groaning as he reached climax filling her tight hole with his hot sticky cum. He gently pulled out then laid on the bed watching his mistress bring herself to another shuddering climax with her dildo. Her juices squirting everywhere.

She removed the dildo and squatted over Adam's face, leaning over and taking his cock in her mouth – sucking it clean while he licked her pussy clean. Then she got off him and laid down on the bed.

"I will allow you to sleep in my bedroom tonight slave. You will sleep on the floor though at my side of the bed", said Mistress Domina.

"Yes mistress as you wish", said Adam getting off the bed and walking round to Mistress Domina's side.

He laid down on the floor and got himself comfortable while his mistress covered herself with the duvet and they both fell asleep. That night as he slept Adam dreamed about Chloe or Mistress Chloe as she was known on the S+M scene. In his dream she had him cuffed to a metal rack. He was fully naked. She whipped him giving him 80 strokes of the whip, each one harder than the one before. She made him lick her boots clean as a thank you before making him watch as she used a strap-on dildo on Mistress Domina. The two women moaned with pleasure. Driving him crazy his cock leaking pre-cum. Afterwards Mistress Chloe and Mistress Domina took turns allowing him to lick them clean. The next morning Adam woke up rock hard. After his dream about Mistress Chloe. He sat up looking up at his mistress. She stared down at him smiling.

"Good morning slave time for some more training. I think we should get you doing some cleaning again. This time you will be naked the whole time. I'll put a cock ring on you. so that your cock stays hard for me. Oh, and I'll be just wearing my latex bather stockings and thigh high boots. I don't want you to cum though. I know I'm distracting but I'll have my whip with me so I'm hoping you will behave yourself", said Mistress Domina getting out of bed.

She pulled her latex bather back up over her breasts then put on her thigh high boots before walking round to Adam helping him up she made him stand next to the bed while she got a cock ring and a whip out of her wardrobe. She put the cock ring around his hard cock then she got hold of his lead and walked him out of her bedroom and downstairs to the kitchen. She opened a cupboard and got a bowl and a scrubbing brush. She filled the bowl with warm water and added a little floor cleaner then put it down on the floor.

"Get on your hands and knees slave and scrub the floor clean. I want to see my reflection in it", said Mistress Domina a sly grin on her face as she spoke to Adam.

Adam obediently got on his hands and knees and began to scrub the kitchen floor, crawling around like a dog, making sure he got every inch of it clean while his mistress followed him whipping his bare ass as she did. He tried not to get distracted despite the way his mistress was dressed, her pussy on display for him. She teased him squatting in front of him and rubbing her wet pussy for him and spreading her pussy lips. He couldn't help but stare. Knowing he'd had his cock in that warm hole last night.

"Good slave it's looking very shiny. let me give you more to clean slave", said Mistress Domina squatting in front of Adam her legs wide open. She began to rub her clitoris fast and hard until she squirted all over the floor Adam obediently cleaned it up.

"Good slave follow me you can clean the dining room next. I've got a special way for you to clean that floor which doesn't involve a scrubbing brush. Maybe I'll get one of my toys and pleasure myself till I cum on the floor then you can lick it all up with your tongue. Humiliation is part of a slaves training. I am in control of you", said Mistress Domina smiling at Adam.

He followed her into the dining room. The idea of licking up her cum excited him. Despite the humiliation he'd do anything to please his mistress. No matter how humiliating it was. He got off on being humiliated anyway. His cock got harder sticking out like a sore thumb. Mistress Domina got a large fat dildo out of a drawer in the dining room and laid on the floor, spreading her legs wide and sliding it in her wet pussy. She began to fuck herself with it, rubbing her clitoris at the same time. She moaned with pleasure. Her legs shaking as she quickly brought herself to a shuddering climax. Her cum squirting out all over the floor. She kept going making a nice pool on the floor.

"Lick it up slave get every last drop of it up. then you can lick my pussy clean", said Mistress Domina.

"Yes Mistress", said Adam licking his mistresses cum off the wooden floor getting every last drop. Then he licked her pussy clean, running his tongue over every inch of it making sure it was fully cleaned.

"Good slave, now polish the table while I go and attend to some business. I'll be back to inspect your work. I expect it to be shiny", said Mistress Domina getting a duster and some polish out of a cabinet and passing them to Adam.

"It will be so shiny mistress. I live to please you in any way I can", said Adam looking directly at his mistress.

She smiled at him then left. Adam got to work polishing the large mahogany dining table making sure it was nice and shiny for his mistress. A while later Mistress Domina returned. She looked at the dining table smiling.

"Good work slave as always. I've decided that we should set off tonight to go to the doms and subs meeting. Mistress Chloe will be going down to London tonight as well. She's be staying in the same hotel as us so no doubt we will see her at some point. She remembers you and looks forward to seeing you again. She wants to see how submissive you really are. She's really looking forward to it", said Mistress Dominique.

"I look forward to seeing her too mistress. It's been so long I'm hoping I can impress her. Until I met you she was the only dominant female that has lived up to my fantasies. I hoped that she would become my full time mistress but we lost contact I tried to fulfil my fantasies with numerous girlfriends, but none of them were as good as Chloe. That was until I met you mistress", said Adam.

"Well slave I'm sure she will be watching you closely to see how you perform as a slave. I realise that I may lose you but I'm willing to accept that. Mistress Chloe is a very good friend of mine and an occasional lover. We like to tease our slaves to test them to see how good they really are, like me and Mistress Tanya did yesterday. She's hot slave. I can understand why your besotted with her. She's also a very good mistress. She knows how to dominate her slaves and how to train them. She's trained some of my more difficult slaves both male and female, one of them ended up becoming her slave. Anyway let's get dressed and pack a case ready to go down to London. We don't want to get caught up in the rush hour traffic", said Mistress Domina getting hold of Adam's lead and walking him out of the dining room and upstairs to her bedroom.

She got changed into her latex catsuit and latex mask. Then she helped Adam into his latex shorts before getting a large suitcase and packing a few clothes for herself, a selection of toys, whips, canes ,and a riding crop as well as cuffs. She zipped up the case and passed it to Adam. He carried it for his mistress and the two of them walked out of the bedroom and downstairs, walking outside where a limo was waiting. Adam put the suitcase in the boot, then got into the limo with his mistress. He knelt at her feet his arms behind his back. The limo driver set off towards London. Later that day they arrived. The limo parked up outside the hotel. They got out and Adam got the suitcase out of the boot and headed into the hotel, getting their key from reception, then upstairs to the room. Adam's face lit up as he saw Mistress Chloe coming out of the room next door to them. A sly smile on her face as she noticed them.

"Nice to see you again Adam, or should I say slave. Mistress Domina has told me all about your training. I want to observe you at some stage if I can. In fact may I borrow him for a while Mistress Domina? My slave has let me down so I need a slave. I'll explain that we've come together anyway", said Mistress Chloe.

"Of course Mistress Chloe. Slave put the case in our room then you will go next door to Mistress Chloe's room for an hour or so", said Mistress Domina.

"Yes mistress", said Adam opening the room door and taking the suitcase in. He put it into the bedroom for Mistress Domina then he went into Mistress Chloe's room.

He couldn't keep his eyes off her, dressed in her skin-tight latex corset, stockings, and thigh high boots – large firm breasts threatening to spill out over the top of the corset.

"So slave I hear your quite submissive. Mistress Domina is very pleased with you. I know from past experience that you love to please your mistress. I know your besotted with me and that Mistress Domina is willing to let you go. If I decide to become your full-time mistress which if you perform like I think you're going to then I will anyway. Come in slave you will do as I tell you. No questions asked", said Mistress Chloe.

"Yes Mistress as you wish I will be your obedient slave. I've been wanting to be your slave for so long", said Adam following Mistress Chloe into her room. She took hold of his lead and walked him into the bedroom then sat on the edge of her bed and made him kneel in front of her.

"Lick my boots clean slave", said Mistress Chloe getting a whip off her bedside cabinet. She raised it high in the air as Adam began to lick her boots clean bringing it down hard on his latex clad ass. He didn't make a sound just continued to run his tongue over every inch of her boots.

"Good slave, Mistress needs some attention. Come up

here and get that tongue of your in my pussy. Make me cum slave", said Mistress Chloe.

Adam got up of the floor and got on to the bed, kneeling between Mistress Chloe's legs. He began to lick her wet pussy, making her moan with pleasure. She reached down pushing his face against her pussy. He licked her harder and deeper, making her scream with pleasure. Her legs shaking as he brought her to a shuddering climax. Her juices filling Adam's mouth. He licked her clean getting every last drop of her cum.

"Good slave, god you are good. Will you be my full-time slave and lover? I love to dominate both in and out of the bedroom. You will be perfect for me", said Mistress Chloe smiling down at Adam.

"Of course I will Mistress Chloe. I've fantasised about this moment for years mistress", said Adam.

"Very good slave that's settled. Right, kneel on the floor and assume the position", said Mistress Chloe.

Adam got off the bed and knelt on the floor head bowed arms behind his back. Mistress Chloe got a set of leather cuffs out of her bedside cabinet. Then she walked over to Adam kneeling on the floor and cuffing his wrists.

"I'll go and let Mistress Domina know that you will be staying in my room tonight. I'm not done with you just yet", said Chloe walking out of her room and heading to Mistress Domina's room.

For the rest of that night Mistress Chloe fulfilled Adam's

submissive fantasies using whips, canes and riding crops on him as she dominated him completely, not allowing him to cum until she was ready for him to do so. Adam loved every minute of it. He was completely besotted with Mistress Chloe and had been for years. She allowed him to fuck her several times that night but each time she was in control. She told him when to cum and how hard to fuck.

The next day at the meeting both Mistress Chloe and Mistress Domina were impressed with Adam. He allowed them to take turns, whipping him and torturing his cock and balls, standing on them and using whips on him. He never made a sound despite the extreme pain.

All the other fem-domes were very impressed with him asking him to show their slaves how it was done. He went to each of their houses helping them to train their slaves before going back to Mistress Chloe. He still saw Mistress Domina on occasions, despite being the property of Mistress Chloe. She had him collared and asked a tattooist to put a tattoo on Adam saying 'Property of Mistress Chloe'. She made an exception with Mistress Domina as she was her lover. They shared Adam on occasions which he loved.

Having two beautiful woman dominate him was his ultimate fantasy. His life centred around Mistress Chloe now. He couldn't help but get aroused by her, she turned him on so much. Being able to get the chance to fuck such a beautiful woman was an honour in itself. She was his dream mistress.

He spent the rest of his life serving her in any way she saw fit – sexual or otherwise. He would do anything.

His Personal Secretary

I had got an interview for a job as personal secretary for an erotic fiction writer. He had asked me to go to his studio flat in London so he could see how suitable I was for the job. I arrived at his studio flat and knocked on the door. He answered looking very handsome in tight white jeans and a shirt unbuttoned to show off his tanned chest.

"Please come in and I'll start your interview", he said in a posh yet sexy voice. I felt nervous but I hoped I would be good enough for the job. We went to his office and he asked me to sit down.

"So how badly do you want this job?" he said smiling at me his eyes wandering up and down my body.

"It's my dream job I'll do whatever it takes. the money is good and it's near where I live", I said. He smiled at me and licked his lips with the tip of his tongue.

"Have you read any of my books? There not to everyone's taste. They are of an extreme nature", he said.

I couldn't help noticing a rather impressive bulge in his jeans. I could feel my thong getting damp.

"I've read all your books, I really enjoyed them. I love the explicit content. It would be an honour to work for you", I said.

"I need a secretary to arrange my appointments etc. also she needs to be able to cope with any situation. Show me how badly you want this job", he said.

I knelt under the desk unzipped his jeans and took out his thick tanned cock. Taking it in my mouth and sucking it deep and hard, while gently wanking him. He typed on his laptop as I sucked and wanked his cock, moaning softly. After a few minutes he pulled me up, bent me over his desk dragged my jeans and my thong down to my ankles and spanked my ass hard before fucking me really softly then hard until I arched my back and orgasmed violently as he pumped his hot cum in my warm wet pussy. Afterwards I pulled my jeans and thong back up and sat down.

"You've got the job. You will be my personal secretary. you start first thing tomorrow", he said smiling at me.

I was almost speechless for a few minutes.

"Thanks. You won't regret this I promise", I said as I grabbed my things and left his flat.

That night I had a hot shower thinking about what had happened earlier. I couldn't wait to start my new job. I went to sleep dreaming of my hunky boss. The next day I woke up early and got out my clothes ready for my first day as personal secretary. I chose a short black skirt, white blouse, black lace top hold-ups, tiny black thong and matching bra, black suit jacket and black court shoes. I headed to my job feeling excited and a little wet between my legs.

When I arrived my hunky boss was waiting at the front door for me in jeans, a shirt, and dark shades. He looked so hot and he had a wicked look in his eyes. I wondered what he had in store for me today. He gestured for me to go in. I felt his hand on my ass as we went into his office.

My clitoris throbbed. I sat at my desk next to his. Crossing my legs, deliberately to tease him, knowing he would be able to see the tops of my stockings. He looked over at me licking his lips suggestively then he continued typing his latest story. I got on with typing, trying my hardest not to be distracted by the growing wetness between my legs. At lunchtime he insisted on taking me out for a meal. We flirted shamelessly. When we got back to his flat we kissed passionately then he took my hand and lead me into his office. Whispering in my ear that he had a treat in-store for me. I couldn't wait to find out what it was.

"Put your hands on my desk", he said.

I did as I was told. He blindfolded me and spread my legs wide apart, lifting my skirt over my hips and taking my thong off. Then he licked up the backs of my thighs and over my ass. He pulled my cheeks apart as I moaned softly. Putting his face close to my tight hole and smelling it. Then he licked deep inside my ass hole until I'm close to coming. Then my soaking wet pussy, then my clitoris and back to my ass hole. I arch my back, as I'm about to cum. He stops and fingers both my holes, making me lick his fingers tasting the amazing cocktail of both holes. He slips his cock deep in my pussy, pulling my hair and fucking me until I'm about to cum. Then stops makes me suck his big cock. Then turns me around again slipping his cock into my impossibly tiny ass hole. Fucking me hard and playing with my clitoris until I explode into orgasm. Feeling his hot cum pumping deep inside my ass so deep it was frightening. Afterwards I bent down to get my thong.

"Leave it off baby I want access to all your holes", he said.

I sat back at my desk his cum running down my thighs. I knew that there and then that this was going to be an exciting place to work. As I headed home that night I couldn't help but wonder what my boss had planned for me next.

The next morning I got up and had a shower before getting dried and going back into my bedroom. I opened my wardrobe and looked at my clothes. I decided on a short black skirt and a white almost see through blouse. I opted to go commando beneath my skirt. I put my black lace bra on knowing he would see it through my blouse. I left a couple of buttons open on my blouse then put fishnet hold-ups on before putting on my skirt and my black shoes. Then I set off out of my house and went to work as I walked in he smiled at me and beckoned me over to him. I walk over to him. He put his hand beneath my skirt rubbing my wet pussy.

"Good girl for remembering", he says licking his lips at me as he removes his hand from my pussy and lifts my skirt up turning me round so I'm facing his desk.

He bends me over it before unzipping his trousers and taking out his cock. He rams it in my wet pussy grabbing my hips and fucking me hard and deep. I moan with pleasure grinding my pussy against his cock. He pushes my head down, making my ass stick up in the air and pushes his cock deeper inside me. Fucking me so hard that I start to squirt over his cock and balls. He reaches round ripping my blouse open and pushing my bra up over my breasts. Roughly squeezing them as he pounds my pussy. I scream with pleasure holding on to the desk. My legs shaking as he brings me to a shuddering climax. My cum covering his cock and balls and dripping down my thighs. He groans loudly as he reaches climax pumping me full of cum until it leaks out of my pussy, dripping down my thighs. He gently pulls out and turns me round, pushing me down on to my knees. I take his wet cock in my mouth. Sucking and licking it clean.

"Sit at your desk baby I will give you a proper seeing to later. I just needed to fuck you. I want you to go without underwear from now on, in fact tomorrow just wear a long coat, stockings and shoes please. I want access to that body of yours at all times", he said a sly grin on his face.

"Anything you say sir I want to keep my job. It's the most exciting one I've had in years", I said before pulling my skirt back down and putting my bra straight he stops me.

"Leave them as they were", he says pushing my skirt back up and pulling my bra back up over my breasts.

I walk over to my desk and sit down trying to concentrate on my work despite having his cum dripping down my thighs. He watches me as he puts his cock away and zips up then he sits at his desk and works on his latest masterpiece. Later that day he walks over to my desk.

"Bend over for me let me taste that pussy and ass and smell your divine aroma. you horny little slut", he said.

I bend over my desk for him spreading my legs wide for

him. He kneels on the floor pressing his face against my pussy inhaling deeply before running his tongue over my pussy and down to my tight hole. He goes from one to the other driving me wild. I moan with pleasure. My legs shaking as he quickly brings me to a shuddering climax. My juices squirting into his mouth. He licks me clean then stands up and turns me to face him pulling me close. He kisses me passionately sharing my taste with me as he pushes me on to the desk ripping my bra off and pulling my skirt off. Then he gets on top of me, putting my legs over his shoulders and sliding his cock in my wet pussy. He leans over me, his mouth descending on my nipples. He licks, sucks, and bites them as he slowly slides his cock in and out of my pussy.

"Fuck me please! I want it hard and deep", I say breathlessly.

He begins to fuck me harder. I moan with pleasure. Meeting his every thrust. He fucks me harder still. Making me scream with pleasure. His balls slap against my ass as he pounds my pussy bringing me to climax over and over again until I'm begging him to stop. He pumps me full of hot sticky cum.

"Let's go to mine baby we can have a nice relaxing bath. In fact I want you to stay over at least for a couple of days. I can't get enough of you your the perfect little slut", he said gently removing his cock from my pussy.

He puts his cock away and zips himself up before helping me off the desk and helping me into my skirt. Then he puts his coat around my shoulders and we leave his office. He locks up and walks me over to his BMW.

"Your car will be safe here I'll drive us back to mine. I want that skirt up over your ass when you get in baby", he said unlocking the car.

He opens the passenger side door for me. I get in and push my skirt up over my ass. He shuts the door behind me and walks round to the driver's side and gets in shutting the door behind him. We put our seat belts on and he starts the car up. Leaning over and sliding his hand between my legs. He starts to finger my wet pussy making me moan with pleasure. He keeps going, finger fucking me hard and deep until I cum over his fingers. He slides them out and pushes them in my mouth. I eagerly lick and suck them clean. He removes them and sets off towards his flat smiling at me as he drives.

"Keep those legs open for me baby. you make me so hard", he said grabbing my hand and placing it on his crotch.

I gently rub his cock through his trousers as he drives towards his flat. He removes my hand and unzips his trousers. Taking out his hard cock. He parks up in a lay-by and pushes my head down on to his cock, pushing it deep in my mouth. I suck it hard and deep. He put his hand on the back of my head, holding it in place as he begins to fuck my mouth. He groans as he reaches climax, filling my throat with his hot sticky cum. I swallow every last drop and suck his cock clean.

"Good little slut, oh god you make me horny baby. I want to fill every hole with my spunk till its dripping from you. I want to piss over your face tits and pussy and cover you with my spunk. You're such a horny little slut", he said removing his cock from my mouth and putting it away he zips his trousers up and sets off again.

"Mmmmm, I'd love that so much. You make me so horny. This is the best job I've ever had and you're the best boss I've ever had", I said smiling back at him.

"Please call me Paul. I think it's time you referred to me by my proper name or you can call me daddy if you're up for role-play. You can be my sluttish step-daughter. I've got outfits back at my flat. I bought them specially for you", said Paul licking his lips suggestively.

A while later we arrived outside Paul's flat. He parked up and we got out. He locked the car up then we walked up to the front door of the building. He unlocked it and we walked in getting into the lift. He pressed the button for the 5th floor and the lift slowly made its way up. We got to the 5th floor and walked to his flat. He took me straight into the bedroom, helping me undress then he undressed himself and we went into the en-suite bathroom. He ran us a hot bath and helped me in first before getting in with me, pulling me close and kissing me passionately. I responded to his kiss, pressing myself against him. He ran his hands over my body, working his way down to my pussy. Teasing me with the tips of his fingers before grabbing a cloth and some shower gel. He washed my wet naked body, paying extra special attention to my breasts and pussy then handed me the cloth. I washed his body paying extra special attention to his cock and balls. After washing we got out then dried each other with a large soft white towel before walking back into his bedroom. He opened his wardrobe and took out a short tartan skirt, a tight white vest top, and a pair of black knee high boots and put them on the bed.

"Put these on then put your hair in pigtails baby. I'll go into the room and wait for you. I want you to tease me. Drop something on the floor and bend over to pick it up giving me a good view of that wet shaven pussy of yours. I want you to rub it for me tease me. Leave your bra off and get the large dildo out of the bedside cabinet draw so you can use it to tease me by fucking yourself with it and begging me to fuck you. Call me daddy though. I'll be your horny step-dad your my horny teenage slut of a step-daughter. You need a man's cock, you've seen mine before. when you've walked in on me in the bathroom accidentally", said Paul walking out of the bedroom and heading into the living room.

I put the vest top skirt and boots on then I put my hair in pig tails before getting the dildo out of the bedside cabinet draw. Then I grab a handkerchief taking it with me into the living room where Paul's sat on the sofa pretending to watch TV. I walk in and drop the handkerchief on the floor, bending over to pick it up, making sure he gets a good view of my pussy. I reach between my legs and rub my wet pussy, moaning softly. I look back at him making sure he's watching me. He looks at me then looks back at the TV. I walk over and sit next to him my legs wide open. I lay back and push the dildo in my wet pussy.

"Oh daddy I want you to fuck me. I need a man's cock like yours. It's so big and hard. Not like the boys cocks I've had at college", I said breathlessly as I fucked myself with the dildo.

"You're a horny little slut aren't you? tell me what you are and what you need", said Paul.

"I'm a horny little slut I need cock daddy", I said fucking myself harder and deeper.

He rubs his hard cock through his trousers then unzips them taking it out. I lick my lips as I look at his hard cock.

"You want daddy's cock don't you? You horny little slut", said Paul

"Yes daddy I do. I need daddy's big hard cock in my wet pussy, my tight ass, and my mouth", I said.

"Suck daddy's cock slut. show him how much you want his cock", said Paul.

I lean over and take his cock in my mouth. Sucking it deep and hard. He groans softly putting his hand on the back of my head, pushing me further down on to his cock. I deep throat him.

"Good little slut, that's it take daddy's cock in your mouth. I'm going to fill that mouth of yours with spunk. till it drips down your chin", said Paul.

I continue to deep throat him. He fucks my mouth hard and deep, groaning as he reaches climax filling my mouth with cum till it drips down my chin. I swallow every last drop, sucking him clean before scooping the remainder of his cum off my chin and sucking my fingers clean.

"Now it's time to take daddy's cock in that wet pussy. Bend over the settee for me horny little slut", said Paul. I get up off the settee and turn round to face it bending over for him.

He stands behind me and grabs my hips, ramming his cock in my wet pussy. I scream with pleasure as he fucks me hard and deep. His balls slapping against my ass. He roughly pulls my hair as he pounds my wet pussy harder and faster. I hold on to the settee my legs shaking as he brings me to a shuddering climax. He keeps going, fucking me so hard that we both piss and cum at the same time. He continues to fuck me, filling me with his cum till it drips down my thighs. He pulls out of my pussy and spreads my ass cheeks, ramming his cock in my tight hole. He fucks me hard and deep, grabbing the dildo and pushing it in my wet pussy. He fucks both holes hard and deep, making me scream with pleasure. My juices squirting everywhere. He fucks both holes harder and deeper. Groaning as he reaches climax again. Pumping my ass full of his hot sticky cum till it drips down my thighs. He gently pulls out and turns me round to face him, kissing me so passionately my legs go to jelly. I collapse on to the sofa he lays on top of me. Pushing my vest top up over my breasts. He licks, sucks, and gently bites my nipples. Making me moan with pleasure.

"Oh god that was so good daddy. You're so much more experienced. than the boys I've fucked at college", I said smiling at Paul.

"You're a horny little spunk loving slut aren't you baby? you can't get enough of my cock and my spunk you love it don't you?" said Paul.

"Yes I do daddy – oh god your cock feels so good! It's so

big and hard and I love being filled with your spunk", I said reaching between his legs and stroking his cock.

He moans softly, sliding his hand between my legs and fingering my wet pussy. He leans over and sucks my tits while he finger fucks me. I moan with pleasure, wanking him harder and faster his body arches as he reaches climax. His cum squirting everywhere. He finger fucks me harder and faster until I cum over his fingers. He stops sucking my tits and removes his fingers from my wet pussy, pushing them in my mouth. I eagerly lick and suck them clean.

"Good slut now lay back on the settee legs wide open for me so I can pound that juicy wet cunt of yours again. Daddy wants to spread those cunt lips", said Paul.

I laid back on the sofa my legs wide open. He gets on top of me ramming his cock in my wet pussy. I scream with pleasure as he fucks me hard and deep, stretching my pussy lips with his hard fat cock. He leans over and kisses me hard and deep, bruising my lips with his. I kiss him back dragging my nails down his back making him fuck me harder than ever. His balls slapping against my ass as he pounds my pussy making me cum over and over again. My juices covering his cock and balls and dripping down my thighs. He continues to fuck me until he reaches climax filling my pussy with cum till it drips down my thighs. He pulls out and gets me to kneel in front of him. He pushes my head down on to his cock and I suck his cock clean. Then we go upstairs to his bedroom and get into bed together. Kissing and cuddling until we fall into a blissful sleep.

That night as I sleep. I dream about Paul fucking me in different locations and getting strange men to join in. Filling me with their cum and making me suck there cocks. My pussy gets wet as I think about it, knowing it would be a huge turn on for me and a fantasy come true. The next morning I woke to find myself alone in the bed. There was a note on the pillow next to me and an outfit had been laid out for me consisting of a short denim skirt, a low cut top and a pair of black thigh high boots. the note read.

"Have a shower and make sure you shave your pussy nice and smooth then put on the outfit I've put out for you and come down to see me xxxxx Paul".

I got out of bed and went into the en-suite bathroom. I switched on the shower and got in. Getting a soft cloth and some shower gel. I put a little shower gel on to the cloth and washed my body then got a razor and some shaving gel. I put some shaving gel on to my pubic area then used the razor to shave myself, making it nice and smooth before washing off the remainder of the soap. I got out and dried off then went back into the bedroom and put on the top, skirt, and boots on before walking downstairs and looking for Paul. I found him in the living room. He was sat on the sofa holding a large fat cigar in his fingers.

"Good morning baby, you look so hot in that outfit. Show me your cunt let me see how smooth it is", he said smiling.

I lifted up my skirt showing him my shaven pussy. He beckoned me over to him. I walked over to him standing in front of him and reached between my legs, running his hand over my pubic area.

"Mmmmm, nice and smooth baby. Keep it that way from now on please", said Paul licking his lips as he unfastened his dressing gown revealing his hard cock.

"I will Paul, anything to please you", I said licking my lips as I gazed at his cock. He pushes me on to my knees and pushes my head down I take his cock in my mouth sucking it deep and hard.

"Good slut suck my cock and finger your cunt for me. Get it nice and wet ready for my big fat hard cock", said Paul.

I sucked his cock deeper and harder while fingering my pussy getting it nice and wet ready for his cock. He began to fuck my mouth holding my head in place as he fucked my mouth hard and deep. His body arched as he reached climax – filling my throat with his hot sticky cum. I swallow every last drop. Sucking his cock clean. He slowly removes his cock from my mouth and stands up, putting his cigar on the table next to him. Then he helps me up. I remove my fingers from my pussy. He bends me over the settee pushing my head down so that my ass stuck up in the air then he rammed his cock in my wet pussy, grabbing my hips and fucking me hard and deep. I moan with pleasure. Grinding my pussy against his solid cock.

"Ride my cock you dirty little whore", said Paul pushing his cock ball deep in my pussy.

I began to ride his cock screaming with pleasure as he fucks me harder and deeper. Spanking my ass as he fucks me. His balls slapping against my ass. I feel my juices running down my thighs. He lifts up my top and reaches round, pulling on my nipples as he pounds my pussy so hard that we both cum and piss at the same time. He pulls out of my pussy and turns me over, wanking over me until he covers my tits and pussy with his cum. Then he gets his cigar and a lighter and walks out of the room without saying a word. I lay on the settee covered in his cum, wondering where he's gone. A while later a tall dark haired woman with large firm breasts walks into the lounge. She kneels in front of me her short skirt barely covering her pussy and her top barely concealing her tits. She begins to lick Paul's cum of my pussy. I moan softly as her kitten like tongue rubs against my clitoris.

"My names Lily. I'm a friend of Paul's. He told me he had a new slut on the go and asked me to come and have some fun with you. Mmmm, his spunk tastes so good. Can I taste your cunt please? I want to eat his spunk and your juices from it so bad", said Lily rubbing her own pussy as she spoke.

"Mmmm, please do Lily lick up every drop from my pussy. Then you can lick it off my tits", I said breathlessly.

Lily gently parted my pussy lips and began to lick my pussy. I moaned with pleasure, grinding my pussy against her tongue, making her push her tongue further inside. She licked me harder and deeper, running her tongue over every inch of my pussy, making sure she got every last drop of Paul's cum and my juices. She got up and straddled me, licking his cum off my tits. Before kissing me passionately. I suck her tongue enjoying the combination of my juices and Paul's cum. I smile as I see him watching us from the doorway. He walks in and kneels on the floor running his tongue over my pussy then works his way up to Lily's pussy and her tight hole. Going from one to the other driving us both wild until we cum together our juices combining. He licks us clean then he stands up.

"Let's go my sexy little sluts. I've arranged for some male friends of mine to meet us in the woods. They will have so much fun with you too", said Paul.

Lily gets off me and we follow Paul out of the living room. He's now fully dressed in tight black jeans, black shoes, and a black polo neck jumper. His long hair sleeked back in a ponytail. We walk out of his flat and get into the back of his car. He shuts the door behind us and gets into the driver's seat, starting the car up and driving towards the woods.

A while later we arrive at the woods. He parks up and we all get out heading into the woods to a secluded area. We all sit down on the grass and wait for Paul's friends to join us. We don't have to wait long – a group of men soon join us. The youngest two lay me and Lily down on the grass and undress themselves before getting on top of us, pinning us down as they ram there cocks in our little wet pussies and fuck us hard and deep. We both moan with pleasure. The other two men kneel next to us and make us suck their cocks. Fucking our mouths hard and deep until they cum deep in our throats. We swallow every drop. Sucking them clean while the youngest two men pound our wet pussies hard and deep. The fun continues for the rest of the afternoon. The four men and Paul take turns to fuck us in all three holes, filling us with their hot cum before the five of them strip us naked and wank over us, covering us with their loads of cum. Me and Lily take turns to lick the cum off each other tits and pussies then we share a passionate kiss, sucking each other's tongues, sharing sticky cum with each other. Then Paul takes me and Lily home with him while his friends get dressed and go their separate ways.

Suddenly I wake up in my own bed realising this had all been a very dirty dream. My pussy's soaking wet and my clitoris is throbbing. I grab my trusty dildo and lay back, ramming it in my pussy, closing my eyes, imagining the dildo is Paul's cock – hoping that one day my dreams and fantasies would come true.

The Training of Jenifique Cullen

Jenifique heard the familiar sound of her master's footsteps as she knelt naked on the cold floor of the dungeon he kept her in when she wasn't needed. She was busy shining her master's black boots as best she could. She hoped her master would be pleased with her. She'd been his slave for two whole weeks now. He was training her in the art of complete subservience and obedience. The dungeon door opened and her master walked in dressed in tight black leather trousers and black polo neck sweater – a fat cigar in one hand and a whip in the other.

"Good morning slave, I see you're obeying my orders. Let me inspect your handiwork", said Master Dominic walking over to Jenifique and kneeling next to her. He picked up his boots inspecting them.

"Good work slave, now let's see how your other skills are coming along. Open wide", said Master Dominic as he unzipped his leather trousers taking out his large fat cock.

Jenifique obediently opened her mouth wide for her master. He forced his cock in her mouth until the tip nudged against the back of her throat.

"Suck it slave, show your master what a good little slut slave you are", said Master Dominic.

Jenifique obediently began to suck her master's cock hard and deep. He held her head in place and began to fuck her mouth. She swallowed and breathed slowly so she didn't gag as he fucked her mouth harder and faster. His body arching as he climaxed, groaning loudly as he filled her throat with his hot sticky cum until it dripped down her chin. She swallowed every last drop, sucking him clean before he slowly removed his cock from her mouth.

"Good little slut slave, you're learning well. I'm pleased with you. I think you deserve a little treat but I want you to beg for it. Beg for your master's cock. Beg me to fuck that tight wet cunt of yours and that tight hole", said Master Dominic, a sly grin on his face.

"Fuck me master please, I beg you. Fuck my cunt and my throbbing ass. I'll do anything you ask of me", said Jenifique getting into the 'Fuck Me!' position on her back legs wide open bent at the knee.

"Come on slave, you can do better than that. Here, show me what you want me to do with my cock. Use this", said Master Dominic passing Jenifique a large fat real feel dildo modelled from his own cock. Jenifique took the dildo in both hands ramming it in her wet, waiting pussy.

"Fuck me master, fuck me good and fucking hard. Fuck my juicy wet cunt with that magnificent cock", she said, fucking herself with the dildo, her pussy lips stretching to accommodate its girth.

"Better slave! I'll fuck you all right. You little slut slave! But first I need you restrained, you know how I love you to be helpless while you take my cock", said Master Dominic getting two sets of cuffs.

Jenifique knew only too well how much her master loved

her to be helpless. The first time they'd met he'd cuffed her to his bed while he fucked both her holes then her mouth. She knew then that it would be like this every time. She'd learned to love it, enjoying the feeling of being helpless as she took her masters cock.

Master Dominic cuffed Jenifique's wrists and ankles then stripped naked and knelt in front of Jenifique, removing the dildo from her pussy and replacing it with his cock. Ramming it in her wet pussy and fucking her hard and deep. She moaned with pleasure taking every, every inch of her master's cock in her wet pussy.

"Yes that's a good little slut slave! Take your master's cock, grip it with your pussy", said Master Dominic.

Jenifique gripped Master Dominick's cock with her pussy, holding it tightly as he fucked her harder, faster, deeper. Making her scream with pleasure...

"Don't you dare cum yet slave", said Master Dominic pounding Jenifique's pussy harder still his cock ball deep in her wet pussy.

"Please may I cum now master? I can't hold on much longer", said Jenifique breathlessly.

"You may cum now slave. Cover your master's cock with your cum while I pump you full of spunk", said Master Dominic fucking Jenifique even harder.

She screamed with pleasure covering her master's cock with her cum while he pumped her pussy full of his hot sticky cum till it dripped down her thighs. He pulled out and knelt near to her face.

"Suck it clean slave before I fuck that tight hole", said Master Dominic.

Jenifique obediently sucked her master's clean then he removed his cock from her mouth, unfastened her wrists and ankles, and got her on all fours, pulling her arms behind her back and cuffing her wrists. He pushed her head down so that her ass was high in the air then he spread her ass cheeks wide, grabbing a bottle of baby oil and pouring a little into her tight hole. He rammed his cock in her tight ass, fucking her hard and deep. She screamed with pleasure. He roughly pulled Jenifique's long black hair as he pounded her tight hole. Jenifique screamed with pleasure.

"Oh god yes master, pound my tight ass. Treat me like the little slut slave I am", said Jenifique breathlessly enjoying the way her master's fat cock stretched her tight asshole.

Master Dominic pounded Jenifique's tight hole. Pushing his cock deeper inside her tight hole until his balls slapped against her pussy as he fucked her harder still, groaning as he climaxed, filling her tight hole with cum until it dripped down her thighs. He pulled out and unfastened her wrists turning her round to face him.

"Kneel in front of me slave and open wide. It's time for a spunk shower", said Master Dominic holding his cock with his hand making a fist.

Jennifer obediently knelt in front of her master mouth wide open while her master stood over her and wanked his cock hard and fast until he squirted his cum over her face and tits, some of it going in her hair and some in her mouth. He continued until he'd emptied his huge balls.

"What do you say slave?" said Master Dominic smiling.

"Thank you master for giving me a spunk shower. I deserve to be covered with your spunk", said Jenifique.

"Good little slut slave. I will put you in the bath now slave then you will go in your cage. I've got business to attend to. I'll get Mistress Gwen to watch over you while I attend to business", said Master Dominic helping Jenifique up and taking her out of the dungeon and upstairs into the bathroom.

He put the plug into the large oval shaped bath and ran Jenifique a hot bath, pouring in a little bubble bath. He helped Jenifique into the bath, getting a soft cloth and pouring a little shower gel on it. He began to wash Jenifique's body before rinsing the soapsuds off. He washed her face and washed her hair, getting every drop of his thick spunk out of it before helping her out and drying her with a large soft white towel.

Taking her into the master bedroom, he made her kneel on the floor while he opened the large wooden wardrobe and taking out a black PVC bondage bra consisting of several straps and buckles. It had a matching thong which left her pussy and most of her ass cheeks exposed. He put the bra and thong on the bed then helped Jenifique up, sitting her on the bed and getting a hairbrush.

He brushed her long black hair then helped her to get the

thong and bra on. He put a dog collar and led on her, taking hold of the lead and walking her out of the bedroom and back downstairs to the dungeon. He walked her over to the centre of the dungeon and made her kneel. "Assume the position slave", said Master Dominic. Jenifique knelt with her arms behind her back her head bowed.

"Good slave I will leave you now. Mistress Gwen will be with you shortly to watch over you and make sure you continue to behave. Do as she instructs you without question is that clear?" said Master Dominic.

"Yes master, crystal clear. I am a willing slave to both you and Mistress Gwen", said Jenifique.

"Good slave. I'll check on you later once I've finished", said Master Dominic before leaving Jenifique alone in the dungeon.

A while later Mistress Gwen walked into the dungeon dressed as always in her shiny black skin-tight latex catsuit and thigh high boots. Her long blonde hair in a high ponytail. She walked over to Jenifique.

"Look at me slave", said Mistress Gwen. Jenifique lifted her head and looked at Mistress Gwen.

"Good girl, now kiss my boots as a sign of your respect for your mistress", said Mistress Gwen.

Jenifique knelt at her mistress's feet and kissed her boots as a sign of respect. Looking up at her mistress knowing it would please her mistress to have eye contact.

"Good girl, now let me see these skills of yours!"

Mistress Gwen unzipping her catsuit between her legs revealing her smooth shaven pussy.

"Lick my pussy slave, make your mistress cum like you made your master cum. Then I'll get my new strap-on with its real feel dildo modelled from your master's magnificent cock as all the dildos are", said Mistress Gwen laying down on the stone floor, legs wide open bent at the knee.

Jenifique began to lick her pussy, spreading her pussy lips and pushing her tongue deeper inside, making her mistress moan with pleasure. She rubbed her pussy against Jenifique's tongue.

"Oh god yes slave, lick me deeper harder. I'm going cum, you're learning well slave. Mistress is pleased with you", said Mistress Gwen breathlessly.

Jenifique licked her mistress's pussy harder and deeper. Sensing her mistresses impending climax. She began to tongue fuck her harder and faster. Her mistress's legs shook violently as she brought her to a shuddering climax. Her juices filling Jenifique's mouth. She licked her clean making sure she got every last drop.

"Good girl now get on all fours for me slave", said Mistress Gwen getting up of the floor and walking over to a small cupboard, opening it and taking out a strap-on with a large real feel dildo which was the same length and girth as Master Dominick's cock.

It had been modelled on his cock as all the dildos were.

She put it on and walked over to Jenifique who was already on all fours for her mistress. She knelt behind her sliding her thong to one side before sliding the dildo in her wet pussy and fucking her hard and deep, making her moan with pleasure. Jenifique heard her master's footsteps as her mistress continued to fuck her wet pussy. She knew he would be pleased. He walked into the dungeon smiling as he looked at his slave being fucked by her mistress. He stood and watched for a while before walking over a whip in his hand.

"I think my slave needs a little pain to go with her pleasure", said Master Dominic raising the whip high in the air before bringing it down hard on Jenifique's bare ass he gave her 60 strokes of the whip, each one harder than the last. She took each one without so much as a plea for mercy wanting to please her master and mistress well.

"Well done slave. Now to thank your master. Open your mouth and take my cock – deep-throat me until I fill that throat with man spunk then afterwards you will take my cock in your ass, this time without lubrication other than your saliva", said Master Dominic kneeling in front of Jenifique and unzipping his trousers taking out his cock.

Jenifique obediently opened her mouth, taking every inch of her master's cock – Deep-throating him while her mistress fucked her pussy harder and deeper. Bringing her to a shuddering climax. Mistress Gwen removed the dildo and stood up.

"I will leave you alone now. I have things I need to attend to anyway", said Mistress Gwen wiping the dildo clean before taking the strap-on off and putting it away. She made her way out of the dungeon.

Jenifique continued to deep-throat her master until he climaxed, filling her mouth with his sticky cum. She swallowed every last drop, sucking him dry then allowed her master to pull out of her mouth. He got up and walked around to the back of her, kneeling on the floor and gently parting her ass cheeks, ramming his cock in her tight hole. She screamed with pleasure, taking every inch of her master's cock without hesitation.

"Good little slut slave, you have earned a night in your master's bed tonight for being such a good slave", said Master Dominic, fucking Jenifique's tight hole harder and faster, groaning as he reached a second climax, pumping her ass full of hot sticky cum till it dripped down her sweaty thighs. He gently pulled out and helped Jenifique to her feet.

"Thank you master so much. It's an honour to be allowed to spend a night in my masters bed", said Jenifique.

"You're welcome slave. As I said, you've earned it. Although as you know, it will be on my terms slave", said Master Dominic taking Jenifique out of the dungeon and upstairs to the master bedroom. He helped her on to the bed and cuffed her wrists and ankles to the bedposts then laid down next to Jenifique.

"Goodnight slave. You will continue your training tomorrow. I think you need a little more domination", said Master Dominic.

"Goodnight master. I will be your willing slave as always. I live to please my master and my mistress", said Jenifique closing her eyes.

That night as she slept, she dreamt of her master and mistress dominating her using a variety of whips. They had her crawl round on all fours for them. They whipped her ass as she crawled around for them then Mistress Gwen got a specially designed dildo with a tail attached and put a harness over her – making her like a human pony. Mistress Gwen sat on her back and made her walk around the room on all fours, using a riding crop on her bare ass as she did. The next morning Jenifique woke up to her master unfastening her cuffs.

"It's time for more training slave. Mistress Gwen is waiting downstairs for us. Let's get you ready", said Master Dominic getting off the bed and walking over to the wardrobe.

He opened it and took out a pair of black latex stockings and a matching latex collar with a large metal D-Ring.

"This is all you will be wearing. Mistress Gwen wanted the rest of your body exposed. You will be allowed footwear. Mistress Gwen has them downstairs with her. She will help you put them on. I will get these off", said Master Dominic taking off Jenifique's bra and thong along with her collar and lead.

He poured a little baby oil on his hands and rubbed it on to her thighs and legs before helping her put the latex stockings on then he fastened the matching latex collar around Jenifique's neck before attaching it to the lead. He helped Jenifique off the bed and walked her out of the master bedroom and downstairs to the dungeon where

Mistress Gwen was waiting.

"Come and sit down slave so I can help you put these special boots on – the bottoms are shaped like hoofs. You're going to be my pony today. I've also got you a nice tail", said Mistress Gwen holding a small dildo with a long black horse like tail attached to it.

Jenifique sat on the floor next to Mistress Gwen. She helped her to put the special boots on then got her on all fours and parted her ass cheeks, pushing the dildo deep inside. She put a harness over Jenifique's head, putting the metal bit into Jenifique's mouth.

"Now pony slave, you're ready to go", said Mistress Gwen clipping a set of reins on to Jenifique's harness then put a saddle on her before straddling her.

"Giddy up horsey", said Mistress Gwen whipping Jenifique's bare ass with a riding crop.

Jenifique moved slowly around the dungeon, her pussy throbbing as her mistress continued to whip her with the riding crop harder leaving red welts on her pale skin.

"Good pony slave, do another two trips around the dungeon then you can have a drink. Master Dominic you know what to do", said Mistress Gwen smiling at Master Dominic.

"Of course Mistress Gwen, I'll go and prepare her drink now", said Master Dominic walking out of the dungeon. Jenifique did two more trips around the dungeon her juices running down her white thighs.

"Well done pony slave time for your drink", said Mistress Gwen getting, off Jenifique and removing her reins and harness.

She helped her out of the hoof boots and into a pair of black stilettos before making her kneel on the floor, head bowed, arms behind her back. A few minutes later Master Dominic walked back into the dungeon carrying a small bowl filled with his semen. Jenifique realised that this was the drink Mistress Gwen had been talking about.

Master Dominic put the bowl on the floor in front of Jenifique.

"Drink slave you need it after that session", said Master Dominic.

Jenifique bent her head and began to drink from the bowl. Mistress Gwen knelt beside her, holding her hair out of the way. Running her hand over Jenifique's ass before removing the dildo from her tight pink hole. She got her to kneel on all fours then got a larger dildo and a butt plug. She pushed the large fat dildo in Jenifique's tight hole and pushed the butt plug in to keep the dildo in place.

"Now slave, once your finished drinking I think we need to punish that pussy of yours. I noticed you climaxed while I was whipping you. I didn't give you permission to do that", said Mistress Gwen.

"I'm sorry Mistress, I tried to stop myself but the pain turns me on so much. I couldn't control myself", said Jenifique, tears in her eyes as she continued to drink her masters cum, licking the bowl clean.

"Right slave get up and come with me to the rack. I will need to put you on there so that me and Master Dominic can punish you", said Mistress Gwen.

Jenifique got up and followed Mistress Gwen over to a metal rack. She helped her on to the rack and fastened her wrists and ankles into the leather restraints. She began to whip Jenifique's pussy with the riding crop before getting a cat 'O' nine tails raising it high in the air and bringing it down hard on Jenifique's pussy making her squeal.

"Quiet slave. Master Dominic take over. I think she needs your expertise. I will go and see to my live in slave back at my place", said Mistress Gwen leaving Jenifique in the hands off her master.

Jenifique knew that pain would be the order of the day. Master Dominic took the whip and gave her 60 strokes of the whip before pushing a large fat dildo up her pussy and leaving her to think about what she had done while the dildo stretched her pussy lips to the maximum. She tried to control herself as best she could as the vibrations drove her wild. Her juices trickling down her thighs. She wanted to please her master so much. Wanted to show him she could control herself. A while later Master Dominic walked back into the dungeon. He walked over to Jenifique and gently removed the dildo from her wet pussy.

"You have done well slave – so far. Let me see how well you do controlling your orgasms when I give you a good hard fuck. I will switch the dildo in that tight ass of yours on, just to make things a little more difficult for you", said Master Dominic unfastening the leather restraints holding

Jenifique on to the metal rack.

He helped her down and got her to kneel on all fours for him. He knelt behind her and removed the butt plug in her tight hole before gently pulling the dildo out and switching it on. Then he pushed it back into her tight hole. He put the butt plug back in to keep the dildo in place before gently parting her legs. He unzipped his trousers and took out his hard cock, ramming it in her wet pussy, grabbing her hips and fucking her hard and deep. She moaned with pleasure. Taking every inch of her master's cock.

"Good slut, slave take it all in that juicy wet cunt of yours. But don't you dare cum until I give you permission to do so", said Master Dominic.

"I will control myself for you master. I live to please you in every way I can", said Jenifique breathlessly as her master continued to pound her pussy.

He roughly pulled her hair as he pounded her pussy harder and deeper. Making her scream with pleasure, her juices dripping down her quivering thighs.

"Good little slut squeeze my cock with those pelvic muscles. Milk my cock, I want to fill that cunt of yours with my hot spunk until it drips out of your pussy and down your legs", said Master Dominic pushing his cock deeper inside Jenifique's wet pussy until the tip rubbed against her G-spot as he fucked her harder and deeper.

Jenifique gripped her master's cock with her pelvic muscles, milking his hard cock. He groaned as he reached climax. Pumping her hungry pussy full of hot sticky cum.

"Cum for me little slut slave. Cover your master's cock and balls with your cum. let go I want you to squirt for me", said Master Dominic.

Jenifique let herself go her juices squirting out over her master's cock and balls. Mixing with his cum. She flopped against her master her legs shaking.

"Well done little slut slave. I will take you upstairs and let you lay on the bed. I'll leave you as you are with my spunk dripping from your dirty cunt. My other slave Jessica will come and clean you up. You two will have fun together. She's a good little slut slave. I am hoping you two will work together to please your master and your mistress. She loves to use female slaves on occasions as well as male slaves and I love to use two female slaves at the same time on occasions. Having you both sharing my cock will be so good but you must behave yourself to be able to do that. If you allow yourself to be pleasured by Jessica and you pleasure her, that will please me and Mistress Gwen. I've set up a camera in there so she can watch the tape later", said Master Dominic gently pulling out of her pussy.

He turned her round to face him and got her to suck his cock clean. Then he helped her up and took her upstairs to the master bedroom, getting her to lay on the bed. He walked towards the door.

"Jessica will be with you shortly. I will come and get you later slave. Behave", said Master Dominic walking out of the bedroom.

"I will master. I'll do anything to please both you and Mistress Gwen. My life revolves around pleasing you both", said Jenifique getting herself comfortable on the bed while she waited for Jessica.

A while later a tall slim girl with long blonde hair and blue eyes walked into the master bedroom, naked except for her latex collar. She had pierced nipples which Jenifique found rather attractive.

"Hi you must be Jenifique. Master told me all about you. I can't wait to have fun with you and our master and mistress", said Jessica getting on the bed and laying next to Jenifique. Her hands wandering over her breasts and down towards her pussy making her moan softly.

"Lick my pussy clean Jessica. That will please my master. We could 69 so that I'm pleasuring you at the same time", said Jenifique.

Jessica squatted over Jenifique's face leaning forward and licking her pussy, running her tongue over every inch of it before pushing her tongue inside, licking up every drop of her masters cum from Jenifique's pussy while she licked hers.

They moaned in unison, bringing each other to climax over and over again. Both unaware that Master Dominic and Mistress Gwen were stood in the doorway watching them, smiling at them pleased with their slaves as they pleasured each other. Their legs shaking as they reached a shuddering climax, filling each other's mouths with their wet juices.

They licked each other's pussies clean. Jessica got off Jenifique and laid beside her, pulling her close and kissing her passionately. Jenifique responded to her kiss. Sucking each other's tongues, sharing cum and sweet cunt juice before gently pulling away from each other as they noticed their master and mistress walking into the bedroom.

"You have both done very well indeed slaves. Let's get you both cleaned up and get you dressed appropriately then we will take you downstairs to the dungeon and continue with training. Jenifique needs a little more training. You are a little more experienced Jessica. I expect you to show Jenifique how it's done", said Mistress Gwen.

"Yes mistress as you wish", said Jessica getting off the bed along with Jenifique.

They followed Mistress Gwen and Master Dominic into the bathroom. Their master smiled as he ran them a hot bath pouring a little bubble bath in before helping both girls in. He helped Mistress Gwen wash their naked bodies clean before helping them out and drying them off. They took them back into the master bedroom and got them to sit on the bed while they got out matching black latex bathers and stockings. Mistress Gwen poured a little baby oil on her hands and oiled up their thighs and breasts before helping them into their outfits.

That day Jenifique's training continued. She learned the art of submission and complete servitude enabling her to serve her master and mistress in every way possible. They took her and their other slaves to several subs and doms meetings and parties – showing off their latest slave. The other masters and mistresses were impressed with Jenifique's complete submissive nature. She would do anything her master and mistress told her to do without question and took her punishments without so much as a whimper. She became so popular that she was often asked to train other slaves along with Jessica who became her playmate. They would serve their master and mistress, pleasuring them as well as being pleasured by them for their good behaviour. They were allowed their own room to sleep in at night although sometimes they would remain restrained but it was all part of their slave training. They both learned to love the pain and gained immense pleasure from it. They learned to control their climaxes and were able to please their master. Milking his cock with their pelvic muscles and learning to deep-throat him properly without gagging on his superior fat cock as well as taking his cock in their tight holes which over time were stretched with various sized dildos so that it was easier for him to push his cock fully inside their tight holes. They lived to please their master as well as their mistress, loving the different methods they used to train them and the different ways they pleasured their slaves. Master Dominic love to be rough with them where as Mistress Gwen was a little more gentle with her touch.

She loved using the various toys as well enjoying watching her slaves squirm as she pushed them to their limits.

One Slave Two Mistresses-
A Fem-Dom Story

For as long as he could remember Daniel had been submissive. He'd found himself visiting dominatrices to help his submissive fantasies. He had met his current mistress Natalia or Mistress Natalia through an advert in an S+M magazine. She had introduced him to her lover and fellow fem dom, Dana. The two women dominated him on a regular basis. He paid them hundreds of pounds for the pleasure. A few months ago Mistress Natalia had bought a mansion style house with the money her rich husband had given her after their divorce and had converted the basement into a dungeon. She'd insisted that Daniel become her and Mistress Dana's live in slave. He had jumped at the chance. He'd packed in work knowing he could easily work from home when he got the chance and anyway he'd been keeping a diary since he'd first met Mistress Natalia and Mistress Dana, he would one day turn it into a book. Mistress Natalia and Mistress Dana had been training Daniel since he'd moved in with them in the art of subservience. One morning Daniel heard the familiar sound of his mistress's footsteps as they walked downstairs to the dungeon. His cock went instantly hard. He knew he would be punished. However, he couldn't help himself they were so beautiful.

"Morning slave. I see you're pleased to see us. You know better than to get that pathetic cock of yours hard without our permission. Get up slave, you will go on the rack while me and Mistress Dana punish you", said Mistress Natalia.

Daniel got up and let Mistress Natalia clip a dog lead on to his collar. She walked him over to the metal rack and fastened him into it then got a cat 'O' nine tails whip raising it high in the air and bringing it down hard on his cock. He screamed at the pain but Mistress Natalia continued until she decided he'd had enough.

"Now slave, tell me and Mistress Dana why your pathetic cock was erect without permission", said Mistress Natalia pulling her lover close and kissing her passionately while she waited for Daniels response.

"You're both so beautiful, I can't help but get aroused Mistress Natalia. What I wouldn't give to be able to pleasure you both. It would be a dream come true however I was born with this pathetic excuse for a cock", said Daniel his head bowed as he spoke.

"Very well, said slave. If you're good maybe one day we will allow you to do that. Until then I think we should torture you. Let you watch helplessly as we get fucked by our well endowed lover Dane. He's on his way here so it won't be long. Dana babe, go and check see if he's arrived while I stay here with our slave. I want to tease him a little before our lover arrives", said Mistress Natalia smiling at Dana. Mistress Dana left the dungeon and went upstairs to check if Dana had arrived leaving Daniel in the capable hands of Mistress Natalia.

"Now slave I know you find me very attractive don't you?" said Mistress Natalia slowly unzipping her shiny black skin-tight latex catsuit revealing her large firm breasts.

"Y.. yes Mistress Natalia. You're a beautiful woman", said Daniel stammering his eyes fixated on Mistress Natalia's breasts.

She sat down on a large leather chair spreading her legs, unzipping her catsuit further down revealing her smooth pussy and pierced clitoris. She ran her latex covered fingers over her breasts, teasing her nipples with her fingers before moving one hand between her legs and rubbing her fingers over her wet slit. Moaning softly, then she slid two fingers into her pussy, fingering herself while Daniel watched helplessly. She stood up and walked over to him. Turning a handle so that he was laying face down. Then she pressed her wet sticky fingers against Daniels lips. He opened his mouth.

"Suck it clean slave this is the nearest you will get to tasting my pussy – for now anyway", said Mistress Natalia. Daniel obediently sucked Mistress Natalia's finger. Enjoying the combined taste of her juices and the latex.

"Good slave I see your enjoying yourself", said Mistress Natalia noticing his erection she teased him grabbing hold of it.

"Please Mistress Natalia stop before I cum", said Daniel pleading with Mistress Natalia as she tightened her grip on Daniels cock moving her hand up and down.

"You will cum slave but not yet", said Mistress Natalia releasing her grip on Daniels cock. Smiling as she saw Dana and their lover Dane walking into the dungeon. Dane had his hands all over Dana as they walked towards her smiling.

"Hello again big boy come here. Let me show my slave Daniel what a real man's cock looks like", said Mistress Natalia. Dane walked over to Natalia unzipping his jeans and taking out his long fat cock. Mistress Natalia bent over next to Daniel.

"Fuck me Dane, show how him how it's done", said Mistress Natalia.

Dane stood behind Natalia ramming his cock in her wet pussy and fucking her hard and deep. She moaned with pleasure taking every inch of his cock in her wet pussy while Daniel watched unable to do anything. He knew that Dane could satisfy her more than he ever could. Dane continued to fuck Mistress Natalia grabbing her hips and pounding her pussy, making her scream with pleasure while Mistress Dana watched them. Her fingers busy in her wet pussy. She grabbed a large dildo and began to fuck herself with it, moaning with pleasure as she brought herself to climax over and over again. Mistress Natalia got Dane to fuck her even harder. Her legs shaking as she reached a shuddering climax. Her juices squirting out over Danes cock and balls.

He pulled out and turned her to face him. She knelt in front of him sucking his cock clean. Then she beckoned Mistress Dana over. She walked over kneeling in front of Mistress Natalia, licking her pussy clean. She stood up pulling her close and kissing her passionately, sharing cum with her. She pulled away and let Dane bend her over. He rammed his cock in her tight ass, fucking her tight hole while she fucked her pussy with the dildo. Screaming with pleasure. Mistress Natalia walked over to Daniel.

"I bet you would love to fuck me like that wouldn't you?" said Mistress Natalia straddling Daniel her pussy inches from his cock she smiled at him.

"Yes Mistress Natalia I'd love to fuck you so much", said Daniel looking directly at his mistress while he spoke to her.

"Beg me to let you fuck me", said Mistress Natalia.

"Please Mistress Natalia let me fuck you. I want to please you so much", said Daniel his cock getting harder as Mistress Natalia moved down towards his cock.

"Do you promise to make me cum slave? I expect only the best from my slaves", said Mistress Natalia.

"I promise to make you cum. let me fuck you please Mistress Natalia", said Daniel.

"This once then but if I'm not satisfied you will never fuck me again is that clear?" said Mistress Natalia.

"Crystal clear Mistress Natalia unfasten me please", said Daniel.

Mistress Natalia got off Daniel and unfastened him. Helping him down off the rack. She took his hand and took him upstairs to her bedroom. She laid on the bed on the bed for him licking her lips.

"Come get me slave", said Mistress Natalia.

Daniel joined his mistress on the bed, getting on top of her and putting her legs over his shoulders. Pushing his cock in her wet pussy. Fucking her hard and deep. She moaned with pleasure.

"Oh god yes, slave fuck me harder, you're good. Your cock's actually quite fat. Feels good in my wet pussy. Play with my tits slave, I know you want to. You've earned it", said Mistress Natalia grabbing Daniels hands and placing them on her breasts.

He caressed them as he fucked her harder and deeper. Making her scream with pleasure. She bounced on his cock. Her legs shaking as Daniel brought her to a shuddering climax. Her juices covering his cock and balls.

"Oh slave you may cum now god your good", said Mistress Natalia breathlessly.

Daniel fucked Mistress Natalia harder, faster, deeper until he reached his own climax, filling her wet pussy with his cum he gently pulled out and laid on the bed.

"Let's go and join Mistress Dana now slave. I'm sure she will be missing us", said Mistress Natalia getting off the bed and walking out of her bedroom. Daniel followed her and they went back down to the dungeon. Where Mistress Dana was busy riding Danes cock. Moaning with pleasure.

"Oh babes your enjoying that aren't you? I've just tried out our slaves cock. He's good in bed he made me cum so much. He's been a good boy I think maybe I should give him another treat. What do you think?" said Mistress Natalia licking her lips as she watched Mistress Dana bouncing up and down on Danes cock her pussy lips stretched to the limit.

"Yes I think you should give his cock a suck while he licks your pussy. Make him taste his own cum as well as yours", said Mistress Dana. Mistress Natalia got Daniel to lay on the floor then she squatted over his face leaning forward and sucking his cock.

"Lick Mistress Natalia's pussy slave, taste your own cum, there's a good boy", said Mistress Dana.

Daniel obediently licked Mistress Natalia's pussy tasting his own cum and Mistress Natalia's juices at the same time while Mistress Natalia sucked his cock.

"Please may I cum Mistress? My balls are going to explode if I don't cum soon", said Daniel.

"You may cum slave", said Mistress Natalia wanking Daniels cock into her mouth while she sucked his cock deep and hard. His body arched as he reached climax filling his mistresses mouth with his hot sticky cum. She greedily swallowed every last drop of his cum, sucking him clean.

"Lick me harder and deeper slave. Make me cum in your mouth", said Mistress Natalia.

He obediently licked his mistresses pussy harder and deeper, making her moan with pleasure. Her legs shaking. As he brought her to a shuddering climax. She filled her slaves mouth with her juices. He licked her clean. Mistress Natalia got off Daniel and helped him up, walking him over to a large metal cage, helping him inside and cuffing his wrists behind his back. Then she walked out locking the cage door., smiling at Daniel as she walked towards the door leading out of the dungeon.

"You will stay here until I need you again slave. What do you say to your mistress?" said Mistress Natalia.

"Thank you Mistress Natalia", said Daniel.

"Good slave I'm pleased with you today", said Mistress Natalia before walking over to Mistress Dana kissing her passionately. Sharing cum with her while running her hands over her body.

"Let's go upstairs the three of us. Daniel will be fine on his own", said Mistress Natalia gently pulling away from Mistress Dana and taking her hand leading her out of the dungeon.

Dane followed them and they went upstairs to Mistress Natalia's bedroom leaving Daniel alone for the rest of the day and all of that evening. That evening Daniel dreamt of more training sessions involving CB torture sessions, and lots of pain. Something which he quickly learned could turn to pleasure for him. He adored both of his mistresses and hoped to one day pleasure them both at the same time. He'd had many dirty dreams about it, all of which had him waking up with a hard cock pre-cum leaking from it. He knew he would have to earn such a pleasure. He vowed to be the best slave for his mistresses.

The next morning Mistress Natalia and Mistress Dana came down to see Daniel dressed in matching shiny black skin-tight latex catsuits and thigh high boots. They walked over to his cage. Mistress Natalia unlocked the cage walking in and unfastening him.

"I hope you're ready for some training. From now on you will be dominated severely and experience more pain than pleasure. It's time for the real training to begin. On all fours slave! You will crawl around on your hands and knees!" said Mistress Natalia.

"Morning Mistress Natalia as you wish I'm yours and Mistress Dana's willing obedient slave", said Daniel getting on all fours.

Mistress Natalia walked Daniel like a dog out of the cage and over to the metal rack. She helped him up taking off his lead and helped him on to the rack, fastening his wrists and ankles to the rack and putting a ball-gag in his mouth. She got a set of nipple clamps and put them on his nipples before getting a long leather whip raising it high in the air and bringing it down hard on Daniels naked body. He twitched. She continued to whip him harder still then she unfastened his restraints and helped him down before getting him to lay on the floor. She and Mistress Dana took turns to walk over his chest and over his cock and balls. Pressing down on them hard and kicking him. Then they unzipped their catsuits between their legs, taking the gag out of Daniels mouth and took turns squatting over him and pissing over his face. Then Mistress Natalia sat on Daniels face.

"Lick me clean slave", said Mistress Natalia.

He obediently licked Mistress Natalia's piss soaked pussy clean. Then she got off, only to be replaced by Mistress Dana. He did the same for her.

"Now slave time for yet more pain. You won't be able to

see what we're doing and you will be restrained so you can't stop us", said Mistress Dana putting a blindfold on Daniel.

She pulled his arms above his head and cuffed his wrists together. Then she cuffed his ankles together. Before getting two candles out of a small cupboard and a lighter. She passed one to Mistress Natalia then she lit them both and the two of them stood over Daniel. Letting the hot wax drip on to his naked body. He screamed from the pain. Mistress Dana put the gag back in Daniels mouth.

"You will learn to take your punishments slave. Natalia pass me my cane", said Mistress Dana smiling at Mistress Natalia as she got a wooden cane and passed it to her.

She raised it high in the air. Bringing it down hard on Daniels naked body several times leaving red marks on his body. She stood back and looked at her handwork. Smiling to herself as she looked at the red marks on his pale skin knowing he deserved every one of them.

"We will leave you now for a while to consider your actions. I expect better when we return", said Mistress Dana taking Mistress Natalia's hand. The two women left Daniel naked and restrained on the floor. After what seemed like an eternity his mistresses returned.

"I hope you ready to behave slave. We expect better from you. We will clean you up and bathe your wounds then we will take you into our new playroom. You will experience pain, CB torture, domination, humiliation. Everything a slave deserves", said Mistress Natalia unfastening Daniels restraints and removing the gag from his mouth.

She helped him up and put his lead on walking him out of the dungeon. Mistress Dana followed them and they went into the bathroom.

Mistress Natalia ran a hot bath then took Daniels collar and lead off and helped him into the bath. They washed Daniels body clean then helped him out of the bath and gently dried him before putting cream on his wounds.

Then they took him into the playroom. They walked him over to a leather chair with restraints on it and strapped him down. They got several metal clips placing them on his balls before getting an electro wand and took turns to use it on his cock first then his nipples.

Daniel bit his lip taking the pain to please his mistresses. They continued to torture him until they decided he'd had enough.

"Well done slave, you are learning well. Keep that cock hard for us. We may need it later. Our lovers not available today so our slave will have to pleasure his mistresses as a thank you for what we've done for you. What do you say?" said Mistress Dana trailing her latex covered hand over Daniels cock it twitched beneath her fingers.

"Thank you Mistress Dana. Thank you Mistress Natalia", said Daniel.

"Good slave. I've got an idea. Dana, get me the cock ring we bought for Daniel when he first came to live here", said Mistress Natalia smiling.

Mistress Dana went out of the playroom returning a few

minutes later with a leather cock ring. She fastened it around the base of his cock.

"There that will keep you hard. Come here Natalia, let's tease our slave. I'm so horny", said Mistress Dana pulling Mistress Natalia close and kissing her passionately while unzipping her catsuit.

She responded to Mistress Dana's kiss, unzipping her catsuit. They slowly took off each others catsuits. Daniels eyes were fixated on his mistresses naked bodies. He watched as Mistress Natalia pushed Dana on to a latex covered bed and got on top of her, grinding her pussy against Mistress Dana's while she sucked licked and gently bit her nipples. She got a strap-on off the top of a cupboard and put it on Mistress Dana before sliding herself down on to the dildo, taking it all in her wet pussy, bouncing up and down. The two women moaned with pleasure, kissing passionately as they brought each other to climax over and over again. Mistress Natalia got off Mistress Dana and took off the strap-on. She walked over to Daniel and unfastened his restraints before removing the clips off his balls.

"Time to pleasure your mistresses slave", said Mistress Natalia putting Daniel a collar and lead on and walking him out of the playroom. Mistress Dana followed them and they went into the bedroom.

"On the bed slave. Dana cuff his wrists and ankles to the bedposts. This will be pleasurable for all of us", said Mistress Natalia.

Daniel obediently got on the bed laying down. Mistress

Dana spread his legs and arms out wide. Cuffing his wrists and ankles to the bedposts. She joined Daniel on the bed straddling him, pushing his cock in her wet pussy. Leaning forward so her breasts were in his face as she bounced up and down on his cock. Mistress Natalia squatted over his face. He licked her pussy hard and deep while Mistress Dana rode his cock faster and harder. The two women took turns riding his cock and squatting over his face. He was in seventh heaven. All his fantasies about his mistresses were coming true. He pleasured his mistresses for the rest of that day. They both milked his fat cock dry before letting him rest while they went off to have fun together. Daniel was enjoying his training the pain and pleasure was intense he couldn't get enough of it. Over the next few months Mistress Natalia and Mistress Dana trained Daniel in the art of submission and complete subservience. Making him into the perfect slave. He would do anything they asked of him. No matter how humiliating or how painful it was.

They decided to show off their new slave at the next subs and domes meeting held at the stately home of their good friend Mistress Dominique. They packed a small suitcase and took a limo over to Mistress Dominique's home making sure they got there early so that she could inspect their slave herself before the other guests arrived. She had 15 years experience as a fem-Dom So she knew what to expect from slaves both male and female. When they arrived at Mistress Dominique's they got out of the limo, helping Daniel out between them his arms cuffed behind his back. He was naked except for his collar lead and cock ring. Mistress Natalia got Daniel to kneel on all fours and walked him like a dog up the drive to the front door. She rang the doorbell. A few minutes later Mistress Dominique opened the door dressed in a shiny black skin-tight latex ankle length dress, elbow length gloves and black stilettos. Her long black hair was in a high ponytail and her full lips were emphasised by her glossy red lipstick.

"Hello again Mistress Natalia and Mistress Dana and you must be Daniel", said Mistress Dominique smiling at Daniel.

"Hello Mistress Dominique. We thought we would get here early so that you can inspect our new slave for yourself before the other guests arrive. He's very well trained and good at giving us pleasure when required to. He takes his punishments without so much as a whimper. He's the perfect slave", said Mistress Natalia smiling.

"I will be the judge of that. Come on in you ladies, go into the lounge. Master Lee is waiting in there for you. My husband would like to have a private meeting with you both. He's got a proposition for you. He will discuss it with you after he's pleasured you both. You know how he likes to mix business with pleasure", said Mistress Dominique smiling.

"As you wish Mistress Dominique slave. Do as Mistress Dominique instructs you, we will check on you later", said Mistress Dana handing Daniels lead to Mistress Dominique.

"Yes Mistress Dana I will be on my best behaviour", said Daniel looking straight as his mistresses as they walked into Mistress Dominique's home going their separate ways. Mistress Natalia and Mistress Dana went into the lounge while Mistress Dominique and Daniel went down into the basement which had been turned into a dungeon. She walked him over to a metal rack helping him into it and fastening the leather cuffs around his wrists and ankles. She got a long leather whip off a hook on the wall, raising it high in the air before bringing it down hard on his naked body giving him 80 strokes of the whip, each one harder than the last leaving red welts on his body. He took each one without so much as a whimper – his cock rock hard.

"Good slave, I see you enjoyed that. Let's see how good you are at pleasuring your mistress", said Mistress Dominique unfastening the cuffs holding Daniel on the metal rack and helping him down then walked him out of the dungeon and upstairs to her bedroom. She took off his lead and made him stand in the corner off the room while she took off her latex dress before laying on the bed.

"Come here and fuck me slave. Make me cum over and over again. If you do well I'll give that cock of yours a good suck. I'll have you filling my throat with your cum while you lick my pussy clean", said Mistress Dominique licking her full lips suggestively.

Daniel joined Mistress Dominique on the bed, getting on top of her and sliding his cock in her wet pussy, putting her legs over his shoulders and fucking her hard and deep. She moaned with pleasure.

"Oh god yes slave, fuck me harder", said Mistress Dominique breathlessly.

Daniel obliged fucking Mistress Dominique harder, faster, deeper. Making her scream with pleasure. Her juices squirting over his cock and balls. He continued to fuck her harder and faster bringing her to climax over and over again.

She began grinding her pussy against his cock making it go deeper inside her until his balls slapped against her ass as he pounded her pussy. Her legs shaking as he brought her to a shuddering climax. Her juices covering his cock and balls and soaking the sheet.

"Good slave, now pull out so I can give you your reward for pleasing your mistress", said Mistress Dominique. Daniel gently pulled out of Mistress Dominique's pussy and laid on the bed next to her she sat over his face.

"Lick my pussy slave while I suck your cock", said Mistress Dominique grinding her pussy against Daniels mouth.

He obediently began to lick Mistress Dominique's pussy. Running his tongue over every inch of her pussy before pushing his tongue deep inside, licking her hard and deep. She leaned forward taking his cock in her mouth, sucking it hard and deep. Running her tongue up and down his shaft. He felt his cock swell. His balls filling with cum. He was ready to explode.

"Oh god yes, slave. That's a good boy. Lick me harder make me cum in your mouth while I deep-throat your cock. I can tell you need to cum", said Mistress Dominique momentarily removing her mouth from Daniel's cock. He obediently licked her pussy harder and faster. Her legs shaking as he brought her to a shuddering climax. Her juices filling his mouth. He licked her clean while she deep-throated his cock, wanking him into her mouth. His body arched as he climaxed filling her throat with his cum, emptying his loaded balls. His cum dripping down her chin. She swallowed every last drop sucking him clean before removing her mouth from his cock, scooping the remainder of his cum from her chin.

"You have done well slave go and clean yourself up then we will go and see how your mistresses are getting on. I hope we will be able to come to an arrangement. I'm impressed with your performance in the bedroom", said Mistress Dominique getting off the bed and walking towards the bedroom door.

Daniel got off the bed and went into the en-suite bathroom cleaning himself up then he waited for Mistress Dominique to put on a latex bather stockings and thigh high boots on. They went downstairs and into the living room where Mistress Natalia and Mistress Dana were sat on the sofa either side of Master Lee big smiles on their faces.

"I hope our slave served you well Mistress Dominique. He has had a lot of training", said Mistress Natalia.

"He served me very well thank you Mistress Natalia. Has my husband explained my proposition? I'm hoping you agree to it. We will discuss things further later tonight. The other guests will be arriving shortly", said Mistress Dominique.

"We accept your proposition. We look forward to working with you. As for our slave, we will let you use him whenever you need", said Mistress Dana.

"I was hoping you would let me keep him. He will help with the training of my slaves. They're not doing so well recently especially my latest slave, Mercy. She is not yet submissive enough", said Mistress Dominique.

"Slave, do you wish to become Mistress Dominique's slave?" said Mistress Natalia.

"Yes Mistress Natalia I do. It will be an honour to serve such an experienced mistress", said Daniel.

From that day on Daniel served his new mistress in every way he could. He helped to train Mercy showing her what it meant to be a slave. Mistress Dominique was pleased with Daniels hard work. He obeyed her every command. No matter how humiliating it was or how painful.

He would do anything to please his mistress. He worshipped the very ground she walked on. She was his dream mistress.

School For Slaves

Mistress Jo ran a successful school for slaves. Today she had some new students arriving. She hoped they would be on their best behaviour. She expected the very best from her students. She smoothed out the creases in her shiny black skin-tight latex catsuit and pulled on her matching elbow length latex gloves and her thigh high boots. Brushing her long blonde hair and putting it in a high ponytail before getting her cigarettes and her lighter then headed downstairs and into her office to wait for the students to arrive. She lit a cigarette while she waited. A while later there was a knock on the office door.

"Who is it?" said Mistress Jo.

"It's Amelle Mistress Jo. Your students have arrived. There at the main entrance waiting for you", said Amelle Mistress Jo's assistant and former slave.

"I'll be right out Amelle thank you for informing me", said Mistress Jo stubbing out her cigarette and walking out of her office.

"You're welcome Mistress and may I say you look beautiful as always. Latex really suits you", said Amelle.

"Why thank you Amelle you always were my favourite. Come with me I need to show my slaves what I expect from them", said Mistress Jo.

"Yes mistress", said Amelle following Mistress Jo to the

main entrance. Where ten new slaves were waiting five males and five females. Mistress Jo walked up to each of them in turn. Looking them up and down then she stood still smiling.

"Right as you will all be aware. I'm Mistress Jo I run this school. I expect nothing less than perfect slaves do. I will train you all in the art of subservience. Amelle show these slaves what to do when mistress tells you to assume the position", said Mistress Jo. Amelle got on her knees arms behind her back head bowed.

"Good girl Amelle now let me try out a little task with one of you. Hmmm which one of you shall I choose?" said Mistress Jo looking along the line.

"You will do. Come with me", said Mistress Jo talking to a tall slim blonde haired girl.

"Yes mistress as you wish. I am your willing slave. My name is Lucy", said Lucy following Mistress Jo down to the dungeon. She took her over to a metal rack fastening her into it and laying her flat. She got a cat 'O' nine tails whip and gave Lucy ten of the best Lucy screamed at the pain.

"You need to learn to take the pain slave. You will learn to gain pleasure but I tell you when you can cum", said Mistress Jo running her hand over Lucy's small pert breasts.

"Oh mistress I will do my best for you. You're so beautiful and those tits are magnificent. I wish mine were as big as those. What I'd give to caress them and bury my face in them. If I had one day to live I'd spend it being smothered by those juicy tits", said Lucy.

"If you do well with your training Lucy maybe one day you will get the chance to be smothered by them", said Mistress Jo smiling at Lucy as she unfastened the restraints holding Lucy on the rack and helping her down.

"Thank you mistress I will be your willing slave", said Lucy.

"Yes you will Lucy now let's get back to the others. I need to get you all collared. Before your lessons begin", said Mistress Jo taking Lucy's arm and leading her out of the dungeon and back to the other slaves.

"Now slaves follow me and I'll get you all collared before your lessons begin", said Mistress Jo walking down the corridor to a large room she opened the door and walked in her ten new slaves followed her in.

"Stand in line slaves ready to be collared", said Mistress Jo smiling.

The ten slaves stood in line for their mistress. Heads bowed arms behind their backs. Mistress Jo walked over to a small cupboard and took out ten identical collars. She put one round each of her slave's necks then she stood and looked at them smiling to herself.

"Now slaves follow me. It's time for your first lesson at my school for slaves, you will learn the art of subservience and complete submission. I expect the very best from each of you", said Mistress Jo walking out of the room.

Her ten slaves followed her along the corridor to a small room with several hooks on the wall along with a rack with various whips, leather paddles, canes and riding crops on it. She walked in followed by her slaves and got each of them to stand with their legs and arms spread wide. She cuffed their wrists with the leather cuffs attached to the metal hooks. Then she walked out of the room and went to find Amelle. She soon found her knelt on the floor in front of Marcus, Mistress Jo's right hand man. She was too busy sucking his long fat pierced cock to notice her mistress. Marcus smiled as he noticed Mistress Jo.

"How are your slaves getting on Mistress Jo?" said Marcus.

"It's going well Marcus. I wanted to borrow Amelle to show my slaves what a good slave is like", said Mistress Jo.

"Very well Mistress Jo she's yours. Amelle go with your mistress. We will continue later", said Marcus.

Amelle obediently removed her mouth from Marcus's cock and got up. Following Mistress Jo to the classroom. Where her mistresses slaves were cuffed – waiting for their lesson to begin.

"Now Amelle bend over for your Mistress", said Mistress Jo getting a cat 'O' nine tails whip off the rack.

Amelle obediently bent over for her mistress. She raised the whip high in the air bringing it down hard on Amelle's bare ass and giving her 60 strokes. Amelle took each one without so much as a murmur.

Mistress Jo's slaves watched their mistress as she whipped

Amelle.

"Well done as always Amelle. What do you say to your mistress?" said Mistress Jo.

"Thank you mistress. I live to please you", said Amelle.

"Good girl Amelle, now kiss my boots as a sign of your respect. Then I want you to choose a slave to go first in today's lesson", said Mistress Jo turning Amelle to face her.

She knelt in front of Mistress Jo and kissed her boots. She got up and walked over to the slaves – looking each one up and down before choosing a sexy tall dark haired male slave.

"This one Mistress should go first. I think he will need a lot of training", said Amelle looking directly at her mistress as she unfastened the slave.

"Come here slave and show your mistress how good a slave you can be", said Mistress Jo smiling to herself. The male slave whose name was Ben walked over to Mistress Jo and knelt at her feet.

"My name is Ben I am your willing servant Mistress Jo. I will do anything to please you", said Ben, his head bowed.

"Good slave bend over for me so I can give you 60 strokes of the whip. And I don't want to hear a peep out of you", said Mistress Jo.

Ben got up and bent over for his mistress. She gave him 60 strokes of the whip, each one harder than the last. He took them all without a sound. His cock getting harder as his mistress whipped him. Mistress Jo turned Ben to face her.

"Don't you ever get hard without my permission slave", said Mistress Jo squeezing Ben's cock with her hand.

"S.. sorry mistress... I can't help myself. Pain gets me hard and you're so beautiful. Being your slave is an honour", said Ben stuttering nervously.

"Come with me slave seen as you have been good. I will put that cock of yours to good use. It's big and fat just how I like cocks to be. I rarely fuck my slaves but for you I will make an exception. Amelle take over with my slaves while I have a little extra curricular fun with my slave Ben. I'll see you later", said Mistress Jo smiling at Amelle.

"Yes mistress I look forward to it. I will teach your slaves to be obedient like I am for my mistress and for Marcus when he's not busy with his many female sex slaves", said Amelle.

"Very good Amelle", said Mistress Jo walking out of the classroom and upstairs to her master bedroom.

Ben followed his mistress into her bedroom. She pushed him on the bed. Cuffing his wrists and ankles to the bedposts before getting on top of him. She unzipped her catsuit between her legs and lifted herself up a little. Pushing Ben's cock in her wet pussy. She began to ride him. Bouncing up and down on his hard fat cock hard and fast.

"Oh mistress please may I see your tits. Smother me with

them if you want. I'm yours to do with as you see fit", said Ben breathlessly.

Mistress Jo unzipped her catsuit down over her large firm breasts. Leaning over and pushing them in Ben's face as she bounced up and down faster and harder, moaning with pleasure. Her legs shaking as she reached a shuddering climax. Her juices squirting everywhere.

"You may cum now slave. Fill your mistresses pussy with spunk", said Mistress Jo unfastening Ben's wrists.

He grabbed her hips pounding her pussy until he reached his own climax filling Mistress Jo's pussy with his hot sticky cum. He gently pulled out and let Mistress Jo get off him. She zipped herself up then unfastened Ben's ankles.

"Let's get back to class slave I'm pleased with your performance. I will see how you get on with your training along with the other nine slaves", said Mistress Jo walking out of her master bedroom Ben followed her.

"Thank you mistress I live to please you", said Ben following his mistress back downstairs to the classroom where Amelle was busy using a cane on one of the female slaves while a male slave licked her boots.

"I see your getting on well with my slaves Amelle. I'll take over now go and continue with Marcus. I'll come and find you later", said Mistress Jo taking the cane off Amelle and helping the male slave to his feet.

"Have these slaves not behaved appropriately?" said Mistress Jo.

"No mistress, I gave them both a good thrashing with the whip but they enjoyed it a little too much so I thought the cane would be better. They need to learn to obey their mistress. I think they should be restrained as well. It's too easy for them to try and pleasure themselves", said Amelle.

"Get the gauntlets I use on you along with the spare set. They're in the small cupboard in my office. Bring them to me then go to Marcus, you know how frustrated he gets", said Mistress Jo.

"Yes mistress", said Amelle walking out of the classroom and into Mistress Jo's office.

She got the gauntlets which had metal chains holding them together. Making the slave unable to move his or her arms and wrists. She took them to Mistress Jo then went to find Marcus. Mistress Jo put the gauntlets on the two female slaves Rebecca and Louise before caning them severely. The male slave stood and watched.

"Kneel slave and lick my boots clean while I punish these two slut slaves, you please your mistress. Well what is your name?" said Mistress Jo.

"My names Liam mistress. I will be your willing slave for as long as you wish. I'm willing to learn", said Liam running his tongue over Mistress Jo boots while continued to cane Rebecca and Louise leaving red welts on their bare ass then she cuffed them.

"I hope you have learned your lessons", said Mistress Jo.

"Yes mistress", said Rebecca and Louise in unison.

"Right slaves, which of you hasn't been caned or whipped yet?" said Mistress Jo looking at the slaves. She unfastened Lucy, Leilani, Kayla, Joey, Darren and Kyle standing them in a line.

"Bend over slaves ready to be punished", said Mistress Jo. The six slaves obediently bent over for their mistress. She caned them all severely. They took the pain in silence.

"Well done slaves now I have business to attend to. Lucy you will come with me. The rest of you stay here on your knees. I will cuff each of you so you can't pleasure yourselves while I'm away as for Rebecca and Louise I will deal with you later. I think Marcus will help me in my dungeon", said Mistress Jo cuffing Leilani, Kayla, Ben, Joey, Darren, Liam and Kyle before walking out of the classroom with Lucy.

She took her into the lounge. Where Amelle was knelt on the floor. Sucking Marcus's cock while he whipped her bare ass. Mistress Jo unzipped her catsuit taking out her breasts. Then she pulled Lucy against her pushing her face into her breasts.

"Suck on them slave", said Mistress Jo breathlessly as she rubbed her pussy through her latex. Lucy obediently began to suck on her mistresses nipples like a hungry baby. Burying her face in her breasts.

"Mmmmm, yes caress them slave. Maybe I'll let you try Marcus's big cock once he's finished with Amelle", said Mistress Jo.

"Please mistress anything but that. I can't handle a big

cock. I'm only young and tight. He'll hurt me", said Lucy.

"You will take it slave. We'll open it up with dildos, he loves a tight pussy round his cock", said Mistress Jo a sly grin on her face. Lucy caressed her mistress's breasts gently while continuing to suck on her nipples.

"Use your strap-on on her Mistress Jo. Get her ready for my cock", said Marcus gently removing his cock from Amelle's mouth. Mistress Jo smiled.

"Amelle bring me my strap-on. I need to prepare my slave for Marcus's cock", said Mistress Jo smiling as she unzipped her catsuit between her legs.

Amelle got Mistress Jo's strap-on out of a small cupboard. Taking it over to her mistress she helped her put it on then sat on the sofa next to Marcus.

"Bend over for me Lucy spread those legs", said Mistress Jo gently pushing Lucy's face away from her breasts.

She obediently turned round and bent over, spreading her legs for her mistress. Mistress Jo gently pushed the dildo in Lucy's pussy, grabbing her hips and fucking her hard and deep. Lucy moaned with pleasure, grinding her pussy against the dildo. Mistress Jo fucked her harder, grabbing a cane and caning her bare ass as she fucked her harder still.

"Cum for your mistress slave. Marcus come here I think you should take over. Lucy needs to learn how to obey and be a good slave, cuff her wrists and gag her. I want both her holes breaking in. I'll look after Amelle. She's been so good she deserves a little treat", said Mistress Jo gently pulling the dildo out of Lucy's pussy and walking over to Amelle sitting next to her.

Amelle knelt up on the settee bending over and sucking the dildo clean while Mistress Jo proceeded to spank her ass and finger her wet pussy. Marcus pulled Lucy's arms behind her back and cuffed her wrists before putting a ball gag in her mouth then he rammed his cock in her pussy, fucking her hard and deep while caning her bare ass leaving red welts on her pulsing skin. He stopped for a while, pulling her hair roughly as he fucked her harder and faster. Mistress Jo brought Amelle to a shuddering climax then she left her with Marcus and went back to her slaves, unfastening Rebecca and Louise and taking them to the dungeon. She put them in metal racks, cuffing their wrists and ankles. Then she got a long bullwhip from a rack. Raising it high in the air before bringing it down hard on their hot naked bodies. Giving them 60 brutal strokes. Each one harder than the last. The two girls screamed from the intense pain.

"You will learn to take the pain and it is time for it to increase", said Mistress Jo walking over to a small cupboard.

She opened it and took out two sets of nipple clamps and two sets of clitoris clips. She put the nipple clamps on Rebecca and Louise's nipples then gently parted their pussy lips and put the clitoris clips on their clitorises before getting a riding crop and spanking their breasts and pussies several times, making the nipple clamps and clitoris clips to move about causing the two female slaves extreme pain. They screamed louder.

"Right slaves I will need to gag you both then I will get my right hand man Marcus to assist me. I'll get him to bring my box of tricks", said Mistress Jo putting a ball gag in Rebecca and Louise's mouths then she walked out of the dungeon and into the living room where Marcus was sat on the sofa while Amelle and Lucy knelt on the floor heads bowed.

"Marcus I need assistance with two of my female slaves come with me and fetch my box of tricks. They need a strict master like yourself, they don't seem to be responding to my training", said Mistress Jo.

"Of course Mistress Jo they will learn once I've finished with them. I will give them an incentive to help them become better slaves as Amelle knows if she is good she gets my cock. She soon learned to be submissive mind you she learned her lesson pretty quickly", said Marcus getting up off the sofa and getting a large box from the corner of the room he carried it while following Mistress Jo out of the living room and into the dungeon.

"Right slaves it's time for you to become good slaves. Do well for me and Mistress Jo and you will get to experience this", said Marcus putting the box down and holding his cock towards Rebecca and Louise their eyes lit up. Mistress Jo took out two large electro dildos pushing one in Rebecca and Louise's pussies. Turning them on. Then she handed Marcus a cat 'O' nine tails whip.

"Give them 10 of the best. I'll take out there gags, see how good they are at holding back", said Mistress Jo taking the gags out of Rebecca and Louise's mouths. Then she stood and watched as Marcus gave each of them 10 of the best.

The two girls took each one in silence. Trying to hold back as the electro dildos vibrated inside them.

"Good slaves your learning. Now let's put them on maximum. I want to see you both coming over and over again until you can't take any more", said Marcus putting dildos on maximum.

For the rest of that day Mistress Jo and Marcus trained Rebecca and Louise in the art of subservience along with the other eight slaves, they all soon learned how to be good. By the end of term all ten slaves were fully submissive. They would do anything Mistress Jo and Marcus commanded of them. Mistress Jo took her ten slaves to various subs and domes meeting. Showing them off to her S+M friends. They were all impressed with their behaviour. Mistress Jo auctioned off a few of her slaves to Mistresses and Masters from various parts of the UK. Keeping Lucy, Rebecca, Louise, Ben and Liam for her own use and made Amelle her assistant. She would help her mistress train new slaves that came to the school as well as keeping a check on the regulars. Making sure they didn't forget their training in between servicing.

Marcus of course, he had been training Lucy alongside Mistress Jo and had taken her as his latest sex slave, enjoying the sight of her struggling to take his cock in her mouth while he whipped her bare sweet ass. He would fuck her mouth hard and deep, filling her throat with his cum before making her suck him clean then he'd fuck her pussy and ass. She was able to take every last inch of his cock now. He made her beg for it though, teasing her with it until she begged him to fuck her harder and deeper using obscene language turning him on immensely. She became his favourite little slut slave. She worshipped her master and couldn't get enough of his cock. He loved to make her wait for it loved seeing her squirm. Sometimes he would make her watch while he fucked Mistress Jo or Amelle – sometimes both of them. She would be restrained so that she couldn't pleasure herself while she watched as her Mistress and Amelle got to have Marcus's cock. Her pussy getting wet and tingling. She was unable to do anything though. Mistress Jo had lots of fun with the rest of her slaves. She continued their training making sure they didn't forget how to behave. She would reward them all for good behavior allowing them to fuck her and pleasure her. Sometimes she would take Liam, Ben, Rebecca, and Louise up to her bedroom. She would take turns with Liam and Ben enjoying their cocks before pleasuring the two girls while they pleasured her as well as each other. As the months passed Mistress Jo's school became more and more popular, she would have Masters and Mistresses, sending their slaves to her for training paying her thousands of pounds which she used to kit out her dungeon.

As well as buying new outfits for herself and for Marcus, Amelle, Lucy and the rest of her slaves, she advertised for fem-doms and masters to work at the school with her as she struggled to cope with the endless amount of slaves that came to her school. She set up interviews with four fem-doms and four masters, making a list of questions for them and a serious of tasks involving some of her slaves, getting them to behave inappropriately so she could test the fem-doms and the masters to see how they would cope with slaves who were difficult to control all of them past the test. One in particular Mistress Taja a 6" tall Russian Fem- Dom. With long jet-black hair, large pert breasts, and piercing blue eyes. Attracted Mistress Jo's attention. She was very strict with the slaves and had a way of making them putty in her hands. She was a beauty she made them drool over her in her skin-tight latex outfits and impossibly high heels. Her full lips showed off by glossy red lipstick, she would drive them wild teasing them with glimpses of her cleavage and her smooth pierced pussy. Mistress Jo got Mistress Taja to come and meet her in the lounge later in the day wanting to speak to her alone. Even though she knew that Marcus had his eye on her too. She wanted to have her to herself for now, wanting a little private fun with her.

"You wanted to speak to me Mistress Jo. I hope I will be a suitable assistant to you", said Mistress Taja, her Russian accent making every word sound so sexy.

"I am very impressed with your work so far Mistress Taja. I wanted to have you to myself a while and thank you for helping me out. The school is so popular I simply can't train this many slaves by myself. I have Marcus and Amelle but I still need fellow Fem-Doms and Masters so that they can each train new slaves as well as the ones who have been here a while", said Mistress Jo moving closer to Mistress Taja, licking her full lips as she slowly unzipped her catsuit.

"I'm glad I have pleased you Mistress Jo, it's an honour to work with such a beautiful Fem-Dom like yourself as well as a hot female assistant who I believe is a former slave and, your right hand man Marcus with that cock. I could get used to having that as well as getting pleasure from yourself, Amelle – and the other female slaves. When they've earned it off course", said Mistress Taja kissing Mistress Jo passionately.

She responded to her kiss. They slowly undressed each other. Then Mistress Taja gently pushed Mistress Jo back on the sofa. She leaned over her running her tongue down her neck towards her breasts, moving her head down licking, sucking and gently biting her nipples while sliding her hand between her legs and fingering her wet pussy, making her moan with pleasure, grinding her pussy against Mistress Taja's fingers. Both women were too lost in the pleasure to notice Marcus walk into the lounge. His hard cock sticking out through the front of his trousers. He walked over to the settee watching as the two women pleasured each other. Stroking his cock as he watched them until he couldn't take any more and walked over.

"Which of you two beautiful dominant woman wants my big cock first?" said Marcus.

"I will, let Mistress Taja have you first Marcus while she gives my pussy a good licking. You know how much I love to be licked out by a woman, give her a good fuck for me, fill her with your spunk so I can taste it when I lick her pussy", said Mistress Jo.

Marcus knelt behind Mistress Taja sliding his cock in her wet pussy, grabbing her hips and fucking her hard and deep while she licked Mistress Jo's pussy hard and deep. The two women moaned with pleasure as they both reached climax over and over again. Marcus fucked Mistress Taja faster, harder, deeper quickly bringing her to a shuddering climax. Her juices squirting over his cock and balls. She tongue fucked Mistress Jo bringing her to a shuddering climax. Her juices filling her mouth. She licked her clean while Marcus fucked her harder until he reached his own climax, filling her with his hot sticky cum. He gently pulled out and let Mistress Taja and Mistress Jo swap places so he fucked Mistress Jo while she licked Mistress Taja's cum soaked pussy running her tongue over every inch of it before pushing her tongue inside, licking her hard and deep while Marcus pounded her pussy bringing her to a shuddering climax before pulling out and beckoning Lucy over to him.

She had been knelt in the doorway watching as Marcus fucked Mistress Jo and Mistress Taja. She crawled over to Marcus and knelt at his feet. Her mouth wide open while he wanked over her hungry mouth. His body arching as he climaxed filling her mouth with his hot sticky cum. She swallowed every last drop and sucked him clean before waiting for Marcus, Mistress Jo and Mistress Taja to get dressed.

She followed them to the dungeon where the other slaves were being trained by Amelle, Mistress Zara, Mistress Adele, Mistress Zoe, Master Leon, Master Daniel and Master Omar. All of them were learning how to be good slaves. Mistress Jo had extended her dungeon to accommodate her many slaves. She had 20 in total now and many more were due to arrive over the next few months. She planned to find herself a bigger building or several buildings. She wanted to expand her school for slaves, taking in more slaves and employing more Fem-Doms and Masters.

She decided to go to London the coming weekend and explore the S+M scene down there. Hoping to get some contacts and maybe find more fem domes and masters. They would have to be up to her standards strict but not too strict. She loved to inflict pain but also loved to give pleasure and receive it. Any Fem-Dom or Master she employed would have to do the same. She would go to the various S+M clubs and take a few business cards with her so that any potential fem-doms and masters could contact her and arrange an interview.

That weekend Mistress Jo headed down to the London leaving Mistress Taja in charge. She spent the weekend going into the various S+M clubs and handing out business cards to a select few potential Fem-Doms and masters. She had lots of calls when she returned. She interviewed them along with Amelle and employed the best ones expanding her work force as well as her school enabling her to take on more slaves.

Before long her school had 25 disciplined slaves.

Spoiled Brat To Submissive Slut

Roxanna Meadows had always been spoilt. As a child she got everything she wanted. She was never satisfied she was a spoiled brat. Now at 18 she was still the same. Although the gifts tended to be bigger. Her parents had given her a Porshe for her birthday as well as a gold master card. Her new boyfriend Jonty spoiled her rotten. He'd bought her designer dresses, diamond rings, the lot. He'd invited her to his London penthouse for the weekend promising her a wild time. Roxanna put on her designer jeans and a low cut designer top showing off her ample cleavage and womanly curves. She finished off the outfit with thigh high boots before getting her suitcase and handbag and leaving her parents house locking the door behind her as fortunately for Roxanna her parents were away on business.

They never liked Jonty they said he was a bad influence on Roxanna. He liked her to wear what they referred to as sluttish clothes and always liked to have his wicked way with Roxanna, not caring if her parents caught them out. Roxanna didn't care Jonty was amazing in bed and treated her like a princess. Well most of the time when he wasn't calling her a slut and a whore which drove her wild. She got into her car putting her suitcase on the back-seat. then set off towards Jonty's penthouse. She couldn't wait to see him again. Her pussy throbbed with anticipation. She wanted his cock so badly, loved the way it filled her pussy and reached deep in her ass. He always made her cum so much. A while later Roxanne pulled up outside Jonty's penthouse flat. She parked up and got out, getting her suitcase off the back-seat and locking up the car. She walked up to the front door and pressed the buzzer to Jonty's penthouse flat. A few minutes later he answered.

"Hi baby come up", said Jonty pressing the button to open the door. Roxanna walked into the building and upstairs to Jonty's, smiling as she saw him stood in the doorway in his black satin dressing gown his hard cock poking through the opening.

"Hi sexy, I've missed you and this", said Roxanne playfully squeezing Jonty's cock.

"Hi baby missed you too, come on in. You look sexy as hell. Let's get you into my bedroom. I want to have some fun with you", said Jonty taking Roxanna's hand and leading her inside. She put her case down and followed Jonty into his bedroom eager to have fun with her lover.

"I hope you're ready for some kinky fun my sexy little slut", said Jonty taking off his dressing gown.

"You know I love it kinky. I want you to spank my bare ass", said Roxanna sitting on the bed and taking off her boots and jeans before bending over and slowly removing her thong. Jonty sat on the bed.

"Over my knee you sexy little slut. You will soon learn. From now on you will be my submissive slut. I will have you begging for more. When I've finished with you", said Jonty a wicked grin on his face. Roxanna bent over Jonty's knee he spanked her bare ass hard.

"Oh yes Jonty spank me harder. I'm a bad slut. I've been masturbating over your big hard cock", said Roxanna spreading her legs wide for Jonty he slid his hand between her legs.

"Your soaking you dirty little slut. I think it's time for me to train you. Come with me were going to my dungeon", said Jonty getting off the bed.

Roxanna followed Jonty out of his bedroom and into his dungeon. He helped her take off her bra and top. Then he cuffed her wrists with leather cuffs attached to chains. Which in turn were attached to a hook in the wall.

"Mmmm, this is kinky gorgeous. I want you to fuck me while I'm helpless like this", said Roxanna licking her lips suggestively at Jonty.

"I will decide when to fuck you slut your mine now. You will learn to obey your master. you will go from being a spoiled brat to being my submissive slut", said Jonty getting a cat 'O' nine tails whip he teased Roxanna trailing it over her body before raising it high in the air bringing it down hard on her naked body making her scream from the pain.

"Please stop I'll do anything you want master", said Roxanna.

"You will learn to take the pain Roxanna", said Jonty getting a ball gag out of a drawer and putting it over Roxanna's mouth.

He got a pair of nipple clamps, a clitoris clip and an electro vibe. He put the nipple clamps over Roxanna's nipples. Then he gently parted her pussy lips and put the clitoris clip on her clitoris before spreading her legs wide and cuffing her ankles. He pushed the vibe in her wet pussy, switching it on to maximum. The electro pulses making Roxanna's body shake causing the nipple clamps and the clitoris clip to move around. Jonty stood and watched stroking his hard cock while Roxanna struggled against her restraints. He took the gag out of her mouth.

"Please make it stop. I can't take any more. I need your cock master", said Roxanna.

"You will beg for it slave", said Jonty unfastening Roxanna and taking the nipple clamps and clitoris clip off then he removed the vibe from her pussy.

"On your knees and beg for your master cock", said Jonty. Roxanna knelt in front of Jonty.

"Please fuck me master. I'm so horny. I'm your submissive slut. I need to be punished for teasing you", said Roxanna spreading her legs wide and parting her pussy lips.

"On all fours slut ready for your cock", he said smiling.

Roxanna obediently got on all fours for Jonty. He knelt behind her spreading her legs and ramming his cock in her wet pussy. Fucking her hard and deep. She moaned with pleasure grinding her pussy against his cock. He pulled her hair roughly. As he fucked her harder and deeper. Making her scream with pleasure.

"Yes that's it slave take your master cock", said Jonty pushing his cock deeper inside Roxanna's pussy his balls slapped against her ass as he pounded her pussy.

"Yes master fuck me good and hard. I'm your submissive slut", said Roxanna.

He fucked her harder still. Her legs shook as she reached a shuddering climax. Her juices squirting over Jonty's cock and balls. He continued fucking her until he climaxed coming deep in her wet pussy. He pulled out and turned her to face him.

"Suck my cock clean my submissive slut", said Jonty holding his cock towards Roxanna's mouth.

She obediently took his dirty cock in her mouth and sucked it clean.

"Good slave your master is pleased with you. Now for some more training in the art of subservience", said Jonty removing his cock from Roxanna's mouth.

He helped her up taking her over to a gynaecology chair. He sat her in it fastening the straps over her legs and ankles before strapping her arms down. He used a metal instrument designed to spread her pussy lips before getting a large dildo and pushing it in her wet pussy. Turning it on to maximum.

"Keep it in place my submissive slut. You will experience the delights of pain and pleasure now", said Jonty getting a clitoris clip nipple clamps and a cat 'O' nine tails whip.

He put the nipple clamps over Roxanna's erect nipples. Then he put the clitoris clip over her clitoris before raising the whip high in the air. Bringing it down hard on Roxanna's bare breasts and pussy She screamed with the pain.

"Take the pain my submissive slut", said Jonty.

"Please master I can't take any more of this. I'll do anything and I mean anything", said Roxanna licking her lip suggestively.

"You will be my submissive slut Roxanna if it takes me forever to train you. You're a spoiled brat who needs to be trained. You will do as I say for once when I say jump you say how high. I'll gag you for now. I'm hoping that soon I won't have to that mouth of yours will be put to better use", said Jonty getting a ball-gag out of a drawer and putting it over Roxanna's mouth.

He continued to whip her harder still, her naked body jerked, her juices gushing out of her pussy causing the dildo to slide out. Jonty pushed it back in and got a butt plug using it to hold the dildo in place forcing her to climax over and over again. He stopped whipping her and admired his handy work before walking towards the door.

"I will leave you to consider what you've done my submissive slut. Mistress Vixen will be with you shortly. she's dominant and won't take any of your nonsense. I'm sure you will enjoy your time with her. She's beautiful and she loves to dominate both male and female slaves. She will love those tits of yours and that pussy. I know she'll have you coming for her", said Jonty as he walked out of the dungeon.

Roxanna felt nervous she wasn't used to being told what to do and the pain was getting a little too much for her despite her pussy getting extremely excited. But she always had been sensitive down there. A while later a tall woman with long red hair walked into the dungeon dressed in a shiny black latex catsuit, shiny black latex elbow length gloves, and thigh high boots.

"I'm Mistress Vixen you must be Roxanna Jonty's submissive slut. He's told me all about you. This will be fun", said Mistress Vixen walking over to Roxanna and removing the gag from her mouth.

"Hello Mistress Vixen I hope you don't cause me as much pain as Jonty. I'm willing to please you in any way. I've had experience with females as well as males", said Roxanna licking her lips suggestively.

"You will please me Roxanna. As for the pain – it depends how good you are", said Mistress Vixen unzipping her catsuit between her legs and squatting over Roxanna's face.

"Lick my pussy slut make your mistress cum", said Mistress Vixen spreading her pussy lips for Roxanna.

She pushed her tongue in Mistress Vixen's pussy, licking her softly and slowly then gradually faster and harder. Mistress Vixen pushed Roxanna's face against her pussy, moaning with pleasure. Her legs shaking as Roxanna expertly brought her to a shuddering climax. Her juices filling her mouth. She licked her mistresses pussy clean.

"Well done submissive slut. Now let's see how you get on with the rest of my training", said Mistress Vixen removing the butt plug and dildo from Roxanna's pussy then she got an electro dildo from a small cupboard.

"Right I want you to control yourself you will not cum. until I say you can. while I'm giving you pleasure you will also get a little pain. I'll introduce you to mistress cane and my favourite the riding crop. You will learn to submit", said Mistress Vixen pushing the electro dildo deep inside Roxanna's pussy switching it on to the lowest setting.

She got a wooden cane and a leather riding crop. She started to fuck Roxanna with the dildo making her moan with pleasure while alternating between the cane and the riding crop using them on her breasts and pussy. Roxanna screamed at first. Then she began to enjoy the sensation. Her pussy tingled and a warm feeling spread through her whole body.

"Oh god mistress fuck me harder. Treat me like the submissive slut I am. I wish my master was here. I could suck his big hard cock. While you fuck my pussy", said Roxanna licking her full lips suggestively at Mistress Vixen.

"He will be with us soon. Now concentrate on your training", said Mistress Vixen fucking Roxanna harder she switched the dildo on to maximum making her scream with pleasure.

"Yes that's a good submissive slut. Enjoy the pleasure I'm bringing you", said Mistress Vixen leaning over and running her tongue over Roxanna's swollen clitoris making her body tremble.

"Oh god let me cum mistress I need to so badly. I'll do anything for you and my master", said Roxanna her eyes lighting up as she saw Jonty walking into the dungeon his hard cock sticking out beneath his satin dressing gown. He walked over to her pushing the full length of his cock in her mouth. She eagerly sucked it hard and deep while Mistress Vixen brought her to a shuddering climax with the dildo.

"Good submissive slut make your master cum. I want to fill that mouth of yours with my spunk before I give you a good fucking. But not before I've given that ass of yours a caning", said Jonty fucking Roxanna's mouth hard and deep.

She continued to suck her master's cock. His body arched as he reached climax. Filling her throat with his hot sticky cum. She swallowed every last drop. Sucking him clean while Mistress Vixen removed the electro dildo from her pussy and replaced it with her tongue. Licking her clean. She took the metal instrument off her pussy and unfastened the straps holding her down. Jonty slowly removed his cock from Roxanna's mouth and helped her off the chair. Taking her over to a specially designed horse like the ones she'd used in gymnastics except this one had leather cuffs attached to it. He helped her on it cuffing her wrists and ankles before he got the cane off Mistress Vixen and raised it high in the air, bringing it down hard on her bare ass over and over again – leaving red welts on her pale skin. Then he spread her ass cheeks and rammed his cock in her tight hole. Fucking her hard and deep. She moaned with pleasure.

"Yes that's it my submissive slut. Take your masters cock in your tight ass. You're learning well", said Jonty roughly pulling Roxanna's hair as he fucked her harder still. Making her scream with pleasure.

"Oh god yes master fill my ass with your spunk. I'm your submissive slut. Yours to do with as you see fit", said Roxanna breathlessly.

Jonty fucked Roxanna harder still. Pushing his cock fully inside her tight hole. His balls slapping against her wet pussy. He groaned as he climaxed. Filling her tight hole with his hot sticky cum. He pulled out then unfastens Roxanna's cuffs and helped her down, taking her over to a metal rack. He put her on it spreading her legs wide and putting her arms above her head before cuffing her wrists and ankles. He pushed a dildo in her pussy and one in her ass putting a leather strap between her legs and fastening it to hold them in place.

"You will stay here tonight. I'll be down in the morning for your training. Your learning well but you're not fully submissive yet. You soon will be though", said Jonty.

"Please master take me to your bed. I'm willing to please both you and Mistress Vixen in any way you want me to. I want you both so badly. You know how horny I can get and how much I please you in bed. You've taught me so well", said Roxanna.

"Silence submissive slut, you are my slave", said Jonty putting a gag over Roxanna's mouth then walked out of the dungeon followed by Mistress Vixen. They both smiled.

Roxanna quickly realised that from now on Jonty and Mistress Vixen were in control. She had to obey their every command. She decided that she would be on her best behaviour. The next morning Jonty came down to the dungeon. He unfastened Roxanna and helped her down off the rack.

"On all fours submissive slut", said Jonty.

Roxanna obediently got on all fours. Jonty put a collar and lead on her walking her like a dog out of the dungeon and into the living room. Where Mistress Vixen was sat on the settee.

"Were taking you out slave. This will be a test to see how submissive you can be", said Mistress Vixen getting up of the settee.

She helped Roxanna up and put on a latex Basque, matching stockings, and boots. Then she wrapped a long black coat round her shoulders. Jonty walked Roxanna outside to a waiting limo. He helped her in, getting her to kneel on the floor of the black limousine. He cuffed her wrists taking the lead off the collar and putting it in his jeans pocket.

"Where are we going master? I will obey you and Mistress Vixen. I will be a good submissive slut from now on", said Roxanna looking directly at Jonty as she spoke.

"Yes you will be slave. Were taking you on a trip to see some friends of mine Lord and Lady Divine. They're into the whole S+M scene. I promised to take my latest slave to see them, you must be on your very best behaviour. You will be expected to be submissive. You will only speak when spoken to or told to is that clear?" said Jonty.

"Yes master it's crystal clear", said Roxanna.

A while later the limo pulled up outside Lord and Lady Divines mansion. Jonty unfastened Roxanna's wrists and helped her out of the limo. Taking her arm and walking her up the drive to the mansion, he pressed the doorbell. A few minutes later the door opened – A tall woman with long blonde hair. Dressed in a shiny black latex catsuit, gloves, and thigh high boots smiled at them.

"Hello Jonty. Hello Mistress Vixen. It's so nice to see you again and this must be Roxanna. Come in both of you. Harley's in the lounge with our new slave Alexandria", said Lady Porsha Divine.

Jonty took Roxanna inside and they followed Porsha into the living room. Where Lord Harvey Divine was sat on the sofa smoking a cigar while his and Lady Porsha's slave Alexandria was busy sucking her masters long fat cock. Taking it all in her mouth. Jonty made Roxanna kneel on the floor in front of the settee. He sat next to Harvey and unzipped his jeans. Taking out his cock, pushing Roxanna's head towards his cock. She eagerly sucked his cock deep and hard. Lady Porsha walked over to Roxanna.

"I think you need some pain slut, deep-throat your master's cock. Get on all fours and stick your ass out for me ready for a good caning", said Lady Porsha getting a wooden cane from a hook on the wall. She flexed it as she watched Roxanna obediently get on all fours, sticking her ass out as she deep-throated her master's cock.

Lady Porsha took the leather coat from around Roxanna's shoulders. Before getting a cane off a hook on the wall. She raised it high in the air. Bringing it down hard on Roxanna's bare ass over and over again leaving red welts on her pale skin. She took each stroke without so much as a whimper.

"Good slave spread those legs for me submissive slut. You have earned a little treat", said Lady Porsha kneeling behind Roxanna. She obediently spread her legs wide for Lady Porsha. While continuing to suck her masters cock.

He groaned and began to fuck her mouth. Holding her head in place. His body arched upwards as he reached climax. Filling her throat with his cum till it dripped down her chin. She swallowed every last drop, sucking him clean before gently removing her mouth from his cock and scooping the remainder from her chin. Licking her fingers clean while Lady Porsha gently parted her pussy lips. Pushing her tongue inside her pussy. Licking her hard and deep while rubbing her clitoris. She moaned with pleasure. Her juices running into Lady Porsha's mouth. Grinding her pussy against her tongue wanting it deeper. Lady Porsha obliged pushing her tongue deeper inside. She began to tongue fuck her pussy hard and deep while rubbing her clitoris harder and faster, her legs shaking as Lady Porsha brought her to a shuddering climax. Her juices filling her mouth. She licked her clean then stood up and walked over to the settee. Sitting next to her husband, watching as Adriana sucked her master's cock clean. Then she made her crawl over to her and unzipped her catsuit between her legs. Adrianna obediently began to lick her mistress's pussy.

"You have done well so far Roxanna. I'm pleased with you. Lady Porsha may I use your dungeon for a while please?" said Jonty putting his cock away and zipping himself up.

"Of course Jonty you can use it for as long as you like, as long as I can borrow Mistress Vixen for a while. I need her help with Adriana, she's not quite up to scratch yet", said lady Porsha smiling at Mistress Vixen who was stood admiring the range of whips canes and riding crops on the wall.

"She's yours Lady Porsha. I want to have a little alone time with my submissive slut. She deserves some time with me. She's done well", said Jonty getting up of the settee.

He clipped Roxanna's lead on to her collar and helped her up then walked her out of the living room and downstairs to the dungeon. He walked her over to a hook in the wall which had a small metal chain attached to it. Which in turn had leather cuffs attached to it. He put her arms above her head and cuffed her wrists getting a spreader bar and fastening it to her ankles before getting an electro dildo and a riding crop. He pushed the dildo in her wet pussy before pulling her latex Basque down over her breasts. He began to fuck her with the dildo while using the riding crop on her breasts. She moaned with pleasure.

"Yes that's it submissive slut. Enjoy the pain and pleasure. Let me see how many times you can cum. I want to see you gushing lose control for me", said Jonty turning the dildo to maximum.

The electro pulses causing Roxanna's whole body to tingle. She screamed with pleasure. Her juices gushing out of her pussy as it brought her to climax over and over again. She had never experienced such intense pleasure it drove her wild. Jonty gently removed the dildo and the spreader bar unzipping his jeans and taking them off before ramming his cock in her soaking wet pussy. He wrapped her legs around his waist and fucked her hard and deep. Making her scream with pleasure.

"Oh god yes Jonty fuck me harder. Treat me like the submissive slut I am. I love your cock in my wet pussy. Love you filling me with your spunk till it drips down my thighs", said Roxanna breathlessly.

"You really are a submissive slut. Right let's get you in a more suitable position so I can fuck you like the slut you are", said Jonty removing Roxanna's legs from round his waist and gently pulling out of her pussy.

He unfastened her wrists and got her to kneel on the floor. He got her on all fours and rammed his cock back in her pussy making her scream with pleasure. He roughly pulled her hair as he fucked her hard and deep.

"Yes that's a good submissive slut. Take your master's cock. I'm going to fuck you so fucking hard and deep. You'll be squirting everywhere over and over again. Then I'll pump your pussy full of spunk before fucking that tight ass of yours and your mouth. Then finally covering your tits and pussy with spunk, my submissive slut. You've earned this. I know how much you love my spunk", said Jonty.

"Oh fuck yes master! I'm your little spunk loving submissive slut. I want filling with spunk in every whole and your spunk on my tits and pussy. Feels so good it's so warm and sticky, mm mm", said Roxanna turning her head and licking her full lips suggestively with a wicked glint in her eyes.

Jonty pushed his cock fully inside Roxanna's pussy. His balls slapping against her ass as he fucked her harder and deeper. Making her squirt everywhere over and over again. He continued fucking her, groaning as he reached his own climax pumping her pussy full of hot sticky cum until it dripped down her thighs. He gently pulled out and parted her ass cheeks before ramming his cock in her tight hole. Fucking her hard and deep. She screamed with pleasure. Pushing her ass back against her master's cock. Taking every inch of it in her tight hole until his balls slapped against her pussy as he fucked her harder still, pulling her hair roughly as he pounded her ass faster and harder until he climaxed filling her tight hole with his hot sticky cum. He gently pulled out of her tight hole and rolled her on to her back. Standing over her and wanking his cock hard and fast till he covered her tits and pussy with his cum. He watched while she scooped his cum off her tits and pussy sucking her fingers clean before helping her up.

"Let's go and rejoin the others my submissive slut. We can have more fun later if you keep up the good behaviour. I'm very pleased with your efforts so far. You're learning well your almost fully submissive already although your training will continue. We will be staying here tonight so that you can show my friends just how good a submissive slut you can be. Adriana could learn a few tricks off you. She's a brat but she will soon learn to be submissive like you", said Jonty walking out of the dungeon.

Roxanna followed him and they went back into the living

room. Where Mistress Vixen was busy caning Adrianna while she licked her boots clean. Lady Porsha and Lord Harvey watched their slave slowly becoming a little more submissive.

"Have you too had fun?" said Lord Harvey smiling.

"Yes thank you Lord Harvey. My submissive slut loves a little treat. She can't get enough of her master's cock. She has to earn it though these days. she's had to get used to not getting everything she wants. She loves it though now. The pain and pleasure drives her wild", said Jonty sitting down on a chair and beckoning Roxanna over to him.

She walked over to him and knelt at his feet. Roxanna was on her best behaviour for the rest of that day. She experienced pain and pleasure from her master, Mistress Vixen and Lord and Lady Divine. She had quickly gone from being a spoiled brat to being a submissive slut. She was her master's obedient slave. They spent the night at Lord and Lady Divine making use of their dungeon on several occasions before going back to Jonty's penthouse flat the next day where her training continued.

Over the next few months Roxanna was trained in the art of subservience. She moved into her master's penthouse flat. Becoming his live in slave. She loved every minute of it. Loved to please her master as well as Mistress Vixen. She was now fully submissive. If her master or Mistress Vixen said jump she'd say how high. She would do anything they commanded without question. She was so glad that Jonty had made her his submissive slut. She loved him being in control. The sex was even better and the pleasure. She gained from the pain inflicted on her was so intense. She couldn't get enough of it. Her whole body tingled she found herself gushing and squirting. The more pain the more pleasure she would get.

She loved being a Slave – Nothing came close to it.

Slave To The Boss

As Luke made his way to work he thought about his dream about his boss Dominique. She had come into work dressed like a dominatrix. In a shiny black skin-tight latex catsuit, latex gloves, and thigh high boots. She had a cat 'O' nine tails whip in her hand and her long dark brown hair was in a high ponytail. She'd got Luke to come into her office and ordered him to lick her boots clean. He'd done as he was told, running his tongue over every inch of her boots while she whipped him.

She'd made him strip naked and had cuffed him to a chair. Putting a chastity cage over his cock then she'd sat on the edge of her desk and unzipped her catsuit between her legs before opening a drawer and getting a large fat dildo. Then she'd laid back on her desk and began to fuck herself with the dildo while he watched helpless to do anything.

He'd woken up pre-cum dripping from the tip of his cock. He'd fantasised about Dominique dominating him on several occasions. A while later Luke pulled up outside the office building he worked in. He parked his car, trying to think of something else to stop his cock getting harder but it was no use as he walked into the building. He saw her looking as hot as ever. She smiled at him.

"Morning Luke I need a word with you. When we get upstairs. Come to my office straight away", said Dominique a sly grin on her face as she got into the lift.

"Morning Dominique I will do", said Luke making his way

to the lift.

He got in and went to the 2nd floor first to get a coffee. Then he got back into the lift and went up to the 10th floor. Heading straight to Dominique's office. He knocked on the door.

"Come in", said Dominique he walked in and shut the door behind him walking over to Dominique's desk.

"Sit down Luke I'll make things more private for us", said Dominique getting off her chair and walking over to the door locking it then she walked over to her desk sitting on the edge of it her skirt riding up over her thighs as she crossed her legs.

"Now Luke, I've noticed the way you look at me and how turned on you get. I'm flattered but you work for me. However I have a thing about dominating men. I bet you'd love me to dominate you wouldn't you?" said Dominique.

"Yes I would Dominique. I'll obey your every command", said Luke unable to keep his eyes of Dominique as she teased him with glimpses of her tiny red lace thong.

"On your knees slave and kiss my feet as a sign of your respect. Later we'll go back to mine. From now on, you're my slave. I love to go to S+M clubs when I'm not working at the office. I've always had a dominant side. My name reflects that. It's not my proper name but I don't like to use my real name. Dominique suits me better although you will call me mistress", said Dominique.

"Yes mistress as you wish", said Luke as he got on his

knees and took Dominique's shoes off kissing her feet looking up at her as he did she smiled at him.

"Good slave now get to work I'll deal with you later", said Dominique.

"Yes mistress I look forward to it", said Luke getting up of the floor and walking out of Dominique's office.

He headed to his own office and switched on his computer, getting into his work while trying to get the images of Dominique out of his head as best he could. Later that day Dominique knocked on Luke's office door.

"Come in mistress", said Luke she walked in smiling.

"Let's go slave you can change at mine. I'm taking you to an S+M club in town to show you off to my fellow S+M lovers. I'm sure you will enjoy yourself", said Dominique.

"Yes mistress", said Luke closing down his computer before following Dominique out of his office.

They got in the lift and went down to the ground floor making their way out of the building. Luke got into his car while Dominique got in hers. He followed her back to her house.

When they got to Dominique's they parked up and got out. Luke followed his new mistress up the drive to her front door. She unlocked it and they walked in.

"Come upstairs and you can get changed into something more suitable then you can help me into my latex catsuit", said Dominique before walking upstairs.

Luke obediently followed Dominique upstairs. His cock hard beneath his trousers. She walked into her bedroom and opened her wardrobe door taking out her shiny black skin-tight latex catsuit, a pair of black thigh high latex boots, black latex elbow length gloves, a pair of black latex shorts and a collar and lead. She put them on the bed smiling.

"Put these on slave then I'll put your collar and lead on", said Dominique.

Luke obediently got undressed and changed into the skin-tight latex shorts then let Dominique attach his collar and lead.

"That's better slave. Now kneel on the floor while I get undressed. Then you can oil me up and help me into my catsuit and put my boots on for me", said Dominique.

"Yes mistress", said Luke kneeling on the floor while Dominique took of her work clothes then she laid on the bed naked.

"Come here and oil me up slave", said Dominique getting a bottle of baby oil of the bedside cabinet and holding it towards Luke.

He got up off the floor and joined Dominique on the bed, taking the bottle of baby oil off her. He poured a little on to his hands and began to oil up Dominique's naked body.

"Good slave, now help me into my catsuit. Make sure there are no creases", said Dominique.

Luke obediently began to help his mistress into her latex

suit – smoothing out the material to remove the creases. The latex clinging to her every curve like a second skin.

"Good slave, now put my boots on for me and zip them up then I'll call us a taxi", said Dominique smiling.

Luke helped his mistress into her boots. Zipping them up for her. She smiled at him as she pulled on her elbow length latex gloves then she reached over the bed and got her mobile phone, dialling the number for a taxi.

"The taxi's on its way slave. Let's go downstairs and wait for it to arrive", said Dominique getting of the bed along with Luke she took hold of his lead and they walked out of the bedroom and downstairs into the living room.

A while later the taxi arrived Luke and Dominique walked out of her house and got into the taxi. The driver made his way to the S+M club in the centre of town. When they got there the taxi driver parked up and Dominique paid the taxi fare then they headed inside. Dominique showed the doorman her VIP pass and he let them in. Luke looked at all the people in the club. Dressed in various fetish outfits and S+M gear as he followed his mistress over to the centre of the club where several slaves male and female were being whipped, caned, and spanked by their masters and mistresses. She walked him over to them and made him spread his arms and legs. She cuffed his wrists and ankles then she got a cat 'O' nine tails whip – raising it high in the air and bringing it down hard on Luke's bare chest. Each stroke harder than the one before. He took each one in silence – wanting to please his mistress.

"Well done slave. Let me unfasten you. It's time I showed

you off. My friends will be eager to meet my new slave",
said Dominique unfastened Luke and getting him to kneel
on all fours then she walked him like a dog over to her
friends who she'd met on the S+M scene.

"Everyone, this is my new slave Luke. He works at the
same company as me. I'm his boss so he's now slave to the
boss. He's done well so far although I intend to keep up
his training", said Dominique.

"Nice to see you again Dominique. He's a lucky guy being
a slave to such a beautiful mistress. Come here", said
Master John licking his lips suggestively at Dominique.

They had been lovers on and off for several months. He
had helped her find suitable slaves and got her
membership for the S+M club of which he was part
owner. Dominique walked over to Master John making
Luke kneel on the floor while she straddled Master John,
unzipping her catsuit freeing her large firm breasts. She
pushed them in his face. He sucked on her tits, reaching
between her legs and unzipping her catsuit between her
legs. Then he unzipped his leather trousers and took out
his hard cock. Sliding it in her pussy. She bounced on his
cock hard and fast. Moaning with pleasure. Luke watched
unable to do anything. One of the two females Mistress
Cynthia, beckoned Luke over with a sly smile on her face.
He crawled over to her and knelt. She unzipped her rubber
catsuit between her legs revealing a smooth shaven pussy.

"Lick it slave! You can pleasure me while Master John
pleasures your mistress", said Mistress Cynthia.

Luke obediently began to lick Mistress Cynthia's pussy

softly and slowly at first then gradually harder and faster. Making her moan with pleasure. She wrapped her legs around Luke's shoulders, pulling his face against her pussy. He began to tongue fuck her hard and deep while his mistress bounced up and down on Master John's cock harder and faster. Her legs shaking as he brought her to a shuddering climax. She got off him and knelt down, sucking his solid cock until he filled her throat with his cum. She swallowed every last drop. Sucking him clean while Luke tongue fucked Mistress Cynthia's pussy harder and faster quickly bringing her to a shuddering climax. Her juices filling her mouth. He licked her clean making sure her got every last drop.

"Good slave, you're a fast learner. What do you say?" said Mistress Cynthia.

"Thank you Mistress Cynthia for allowing me to pleasure you", said Luke.

"Good slave, stay on your knees until your mistress is done", said Mistress Cynthia smiling down at him as she gently pushed his face away from her pussy. A while later Luke's mistress sat on the sofa in front of him.

"Come here slave! Your mistress needs an ashtray and a footrest. Kneel on all fours and hold out your hand for me to flick my ash", said Dominique while lighting a cigarette.

She took a drag, blowing the smoke out in rings. Luke knelt on all fours for his mistress holding out his hand. She flicked her ash in his hand every so often then put the cigarette out in a large metal ashtray. She put her feet up on Luke's back and getting comfortable she beckoned a female slave over that she knew to belong to Mistress Cynthia.

"Estelle get me and my slave a drink of champagne. Put his in a dog bowl", said Dominique smiling at the young dark haired girl.

"Yes mistress, I'll see to your request right away", said Estelle walking towards the bar.

A while later Estelle returned with a glass of champagne for Dominique and a dog bowl filled with champagne for Luke. She put it on the floor in front of Luke and passed the glass of champagne to Dominique.

"Thank you Estelle that will be all", said Dominique taking a sip of her champagne.

Luke lapped at his champagne enjoying the taste of it. Suddenly he felt a hand between his legs. He looked down and saw Mistress Cynthia rubbing his cock through his latex shorts. He moaned softly at her touch. She unzipped his shorts taking out his cock. Wanking him fast and hard. Until he climaxed. His cum squirting everywhere. She let go of his cock and beckoned Estelle over.

"How may I serve you mistress?" said Estelle.

"Lick up the mess this slave had made. Then suck and lick his cock clean", said Mistress Cynthia.

Estelle obediently knelt on the floor. Licking up every drop of Luke's cum. Then she took his cock in her mouth sucking and licking his cock clean. Mistress Cynthia and Dominique watched Estelle smiling.

"Good girl Estelle. Come here slave and pleasure me and Dominique", said Mistress Cynthia licking her lips suggestively.

Estelle crawled over to her mistress and began to lick her wet pussy while at the same time finger fucking Dominique's pussy, swapped over every so often. Luke watched as Estelle pleasured both his mistress and Mistress Cynthia. His cock hard, pre-cum dripping from the tip of his cock.

"You deserve a treat slave. You've been so good. Take off your shorts and lay on your back", said Dominique removing her feet from Luke's back.

He obediently took off his shorts and laid on his back for his mistress. She walked over to him followed by Mistress Cynthia. She sat over his face while Mistress Cynthia straddled him, pushing his cock in her wet pussy. She began to ride him softly and slowly. Luke began to lick his mistress's pussy softly and slowly while Mistress Cynthia bounced up and down on his cock faster and harder. Moaning with pleasure. Dominique began grinding her pussy against Luke's tongue. He licked her deeper and harder, making her moan with pleasure.

"Oh god yes slave! Tongue fuck me! Make me cum.", said Dominique breathlessly.

Luke obediently began to tongue fuck his mistress's pussy while Mistress Cynthia bounced up and down on his cock harder and faster. Moaning with pleasure. Her juices running down her thighs. She grabbed Luke's hands and placed them on her hips.

"Fuck me slave! Show me how good you can be", said Mistress Cynthia.

Luke held Mistress Cynthia's hips and began to pound her pussy while tongue fucking his mistress harder and faster. Her legs shaking as he brought her to a shuddering climax. Her juices filling his mouth. He licked her clean, running his tongue over every inch of her pussy. She got off and walked over to the sofa, sitting and watching while Luke fucked Mistress Cynthia. And quickly bringing her to a shuddering climax. Juices squirting over his cock and balls.

"You may cum slave. Fill my pussy with your hot sticky cum", said Mistress Cynthia.

Luke continued to fuck Mistress Cynthia until he reached climax. Filling her with his hot sticky cum until it dripped down her thighs. She got off him and knelt in front of him. Sucking and licking his cock clean before beckoning Estelle over.

"Lick my cum soaked pussy clean slave", said Mistress Cynthia. Estelle obediently licked her mistresses cum soaked pussy clean while Luke watched his cock still hard.

"Put on your shorts and follow me slave", said Dominique zipping up her catsuit and getting off the settee.

Luke obediently got up following his mistress to the back of the club and into a small room. She walked over to a king-size metal bed. Beckoning Luke over.

"Get on the bed for me slave. It's time for some one-on-one pleasure", said Dominique.

Luke got on the bed and laid down. Dominique joined him on the bed. Cuffing his wrists and ankles to the bedposts. She unzipped her catsuit and took off her boots. Straddling Luke, pushing his cock in her wet pussy. She began to ride him slowly at first then gradually faster and harder, leaning over and pushing her tits in his face. He sucked and licked her nipples making his mistress moan with pleasure. She bounced up and down on his cock harder and faster, her legs shaking as she reached a shuddering climax, her juices squirting out over Luke's cock and balls. She lifted herself up letting Luke's cock slide out of her pussy. Then she moved down his body until her tits rested against his cock. She began to tit wank Luke's cock.

"Cum for your mistress. Cover my tits with your hot sticky cum", said Dominique licking her lips suggestively as she used her tits to wank Luke's cock fast and hard.

He groaned with pleasure. His body arched as he climaxed covering Dominique's tits with his hot sticky cum. She lifted each one in turn. Licking them clean before moving further down the bed and kneeling between his legs, taking his cock in her mouth. Sucking and licking him clean. She unfastened him.

"You've done so well slave. You will sleep in my bed tonight but you are not to touch unless I say you can is that clear? I know you love my body but I decide when or if you are allowed to pleasure me, you have to earn it", said Dominique zipping up her catsuit and putting her boots back on.

"Crystal clear mistress. Thank you for allowing me to

pleasure you and for pleasuring me mistress", said Luke putting his cock away and zipping up his shorts before getting off the bed and following his mistress out of the room and back to her friends.

"Were going now. We will see you again soon", said Dominique.

"Bye Dominique I'll see you very soon I hope", said Master John licking his lips as he looked at Dominique.

"Come over tomorrow Master John. You know I can't get enough of you", said Dominique giving Master John a passionate kiss before gently pulling away.

"Bye Dominique. I look forward to seeing you both again soon", said Mistress Cynthia giving Dominique a kiss on each cheek before letting her go. Dominique took hold of Luke's lead and they walked out of the club and getting into a waiting taxi.

"You've done me proud tonight slave. I'm so pleased with you", said Dominique.

"Thank you mistress I live to please you", said Luke.

A while later the taxi pulled up outside Dominique's house. They got out and walked towards the front door. Dominique opened the door and walked in. She took hold of Luke's lead and walked him upstairs to her bedroom. She made him kneel on the floor next to her bed while she took off her catsuit and boots before getting into bed.

"Come join me slave no touching for now. We will just get some sleep. You have a long day ahead of you tomorrow. I will train you some more in my personal dungeon. Once I've done with my lover", said Dominique a sly grin on her face. Luke obediently joined his mistress in bed.

"I won't touch until you give me permission. I want to be the best slave I can be. I will do as you ask of me at all times and take my punishments in silence mistress", said Luke laying down next to his mistress unable to stop himself getting hard as he looked at his beautiful mistress laid next to him naked.

He wanted to touch her again so bad. Wanted to pleasure her but he knew better than to touch her without permission. Dominique smiled as she noticed how hard Luke was beneath his shorts.

"You find me very attractive don't you slave?" said Dominique running her hands over her tits, teasing her nipples with the tips of her fingers making them hard and erect.

"Oh yes mistress I find you very attractive. I always have", said Luke unable to keep his eyes of his mistress as she ran one hand down her flat stomach to her shaven pussy.

She gently parted her pussy lips and rubbed her clitoris moaning softly then she spread her legs wide bending them at the knee before leaning over the bed and getting a large dildo out of a drawer of her bedside cabinet. She slid it inch by inch into her waiting wet pussy and teasing Luke. The dildo was shaped like a real cock. She started to slide it in and out of her pussy, softly and slowly at first then gradually harder and faster. Moaning with pleasure. Her juices running down her thighs.

"Mmmmm, feels so good being filled by a big cock slave. Oh god I'm going to cum! Watch me as I bring myself to climax. I can see your enjoying this. Take off your shorts and let me see how good you are at controlling yourself", said Dominique breathlessly as she fucked herself harder and faster with the pussy toy.

Luke obediently took off his shorts and watched his mistress as she fucked herself with the dildo. Her legs shaking as she brought herself to a shuddering climax. Her juices squirting everywhere. She let the dildo slide out of her soaking wet pussy, pushing her fingers in her wet hole before pressing them against Luke's lips. He obediently opened his mouth, licking and sucking his mistresses wet fingers clean, enjoying the taste of her juices. His cock rock hard. He longed to bury his face in her wet pussy once again and lick her dry but he knew he couldn't do that without permission. His cock swelled aching to be touched.

"Good slave your learning well. Now let's sleep you need your energy for your training", said Dominique resting her head on her pillow and closing her eyes.

Luke slowly drifted off to sleep dreaming of his mistress. He wondered if she would be making him watch her lover giving her a good hard fuck like she had at the club. The next morning Luke woke to find himself alone in the bed. He got out of bed and went to find his mistress. He heard moaning noises coming from downstairs. He followed the noises to the living room. The door was slightly open. He peeked inside and saw his mistress on all fours while Master John fucked her pussy hard and deep from behind.

He couldn't help but get turned on. He knew he shouldn't touch but his cock ached. He began to stroke his cock softly and slowly at first, then gradually harder until he squirted his cum over his stomach. Dominique suddenly noticed Luke.

She got Master John to stop fucking her and walked out of the living room and towards Luke. She dragged him into the room making him stand facing the wall. She helped him out of his shorts then got a cat 'O' nine tails whip. Raising it high in the air and bringing it down hard on his bare ass. Over and over again, leaving red welts on his pale skin.

"You should know better than to touch your cock without my permission slave! You will watch me being fucked by a real man but you will be restrained and I will put a chastity cage over that cock so that you can't pleasure yourself. You will have it on for a week as punishment. What do you say slave", said Dominique turning Luke to face her.

"Thank you mistress. I deserve to be punished. I misbehaved", said Luke, his head bowed in shame.

Dominique got Luke to kneel on all fours. She walked him over to a leather chair with leather straps attached to it and sat him in the chair, strapping him down then got a chastity cage from a small cupboard, putting it over his cock and locking it with a key before putting the key in her pocket. She walked over to Master John.

"Let's continue what we were doing. I want my slave to watch as you fuck me good and hard. He's helpless. Let's make him squirm", said Dominique licking her lips.

"Mmmmm, good idea Dominique. I'll give you a good hard fuck and have you screaming with pleasure as I bring you to climax over and over again. But first I want those lips round my big hard cock", said Master John.

Dominique knelt in front of Master John. Taking his cock in her mouth. Sucking it deep and hard while rubbing her pussy. She got on all fours. Making sure that Luke got a good view of her pussy as she rubbed it hard and fast while deep-throating Master John's cock. Luke watched his mistress sucking Master John's cock. Getting turned on but unable to do anything other than watch. His cock ached to be sucked by those full lips. He thought about how good they felt around his cock. Pre-cum leaked from the tip of his cock. He was helpless to stop his balls swelling. They filled with cum as his mistress brought Master John to climax. His cum filling her throat and dripping down over her chin. She swallowed every last drop sucking him dry before scooping up the remainder of his cum from her chin and licking her sticky fingers clean.

Master John turned Dominique so that Luke could watch him fucking his mistress. He slid his cock in her wet pussy. Grabbing her hips and fucking her hard and deep. She moaned with pleasure. Grinding her pussy against his cock. He pushed it fully into her pussy fucking her harder and deeper. His balls slapping against her ass as he pounded her pussy. She screamed with pleasure. Her legs shaking as she reached a shuddering climax. Her juices squirting everywhere. He continued fucking her. Bringing her to climax over and over again before finally filling her with his hot sticky cum. He pulled out of her pussy and got her to suck him clean before ramming his cock in her tight asshole. Fucking her hard and deep while he fist fucked her soaking wet pussy. She screamed with pleasure, taking every inch of his cock in her tight ass. He groaned as he reached climax, filling her tight hole with his cum until it dripped out down her thighs. He pulled out and put his cock away – zipping himself up while Dominique got up off the floor and zipped up her catsuit before unfastening the straps holding Luke in the chair. She helped him down and made him kneel on the floor. Head bowed – hands behind his back. She cuffed his wrists.

"Master John I need to train my slave some more. We will continue our fun another time", said Dominique pulling Master John close and kissing him passionately before gently pulling away from him.

"Of course Dominique. I have some slaves to train myself anyway. I'll be in touch", said Master John walking out of the living room leaving Dominique alone with her slave.

"Right slave, let's get started with your training", said Dominique walking Luke out of the living room and down to the basement which she'd had converted into a dungeon.

She walked him over to a metal cage cuffing his wrists and ankles. She got a leather bullwhip raising it high in the air bringing it down hard on his naked body. Giving him 80 strokes of the whip before putting nipple clamps on his nipples and attaching a metal chain. She straddled him and pulled on the metal chain making the nipple clamps pull on his nipples. He took the pain in silence.

"You're learning well slave. I will leave you alone for a

while. I've got business to attend to", said Dominique getting off Luke and walking out of the dungeon leaving Luke cuffed to the metal cage.

He knew she would leave him there for as long as she wanted. His cock was rock hard beneath the chastity cage. Wanting to be touched by his mistress. He had fantasied about her so many times but the reality was so much better. His mistress left him cuffed for the rest of the afternoon. The next day Luke and his mistress went into work. Dominique took Luke into her office with her and locked the door behind them. She made him strip naked and put his collar and lead on then she put his arms behind his back and cuffed them. She made him stay on his knees all day while she continued with her work. From that day on Luke obeyed his mistresses every command at work and at her home.

He was truly a slave to the boss. He worshipped the very ground she walked on.